BAD
THINGS
feel
BEST

OTHER TITLES BY IVY SMOAK

The Hunted Series

Temptation
Addiction
Eruption
Devotion
Seduction
The Light to My Darkness
A Whirlwind of Color
This Is Love
Obsessed

Men of Manhattan

City of Sin
Third Chances
Missing Pieces

Empire High

Untouchable
Elite
Betrayal
Matchmaker
Runaway
Homecoming
Exposed

The Society

The Society #StalkerProblems
The Society #ThisIsWar

Single Girl Rules

Single Girl Rules #BFF
Single Girl Rules #BananaParty
Single Girl Rules #ThreeHeadedMonster
Single Girl Rules #GoddessContest

Scarlett

Scarlett and the Kiss Thief

Sweet Cravings

Playing a Player
Those Summer Nights
Going for Gold

Made of Steel Series

Made of Steel
Forged in Flames
Carved in Ice
Hidden in Smoke

Secrets of Suburbia

The Truth in My Lies
Sweet Like a Psycho
Crazy in Love

Fantasy Novels

Sea of Stars
The Ruin of House Hornbolt

BAD THINGS *feel* BEST

IVY SMOAK

Montlake

Text copyright © 2023 by Ivy Smoak

Published by Montlake, Seattle

www.apub.com

Amazon, the Amazon logo, and Montlake are trademarks of Amazon.com, Inc., or its affiliates.

ISBN-13: 9781662513077 (paperback)
ISBN-13: 9781662513084 (digital)

Cover design by Caroline Teagle Johnson
Cover images: ©Dusica Paripovic / ArcAngel; ©Pornsawan Baipakdee / Getty; ©WhataWin / Getty; ©Mensent Photography / Getty

Printed in the United States of America

To Ryan. My OG bad boy.

IVY SMOAK WEEKLY NEWSLETTER

Want a behind-the-scenes look at my journey as an author? The ups, the downs, the movie deals . . . I'll share it all!

And as a special thank-you for joining, you'll get an exclusive copy of my short story "Mr. Remington." You can subscribe to my newsletter at https://www.ivysmoak.com/btfb-amz.

CHAPTER 1

Sunday—August 28

I pulled to a stop in front of the wrought-iron gates. Athena Quinn hadn't mentioned a gate in the email. I looked over at the security booth. A man in a tan security uniform sat there playing on his phone. I had a feeling that he knew I had pulled up but had chosen to completely ignore me.

There was no way I was going to let myself be late for my first day because of a negligent security guard and an unexpected gate. I rolled down the window of my beat-up Honda, and the salty air hit me. Everything around me was lush and green. It was strange that I could smell the ocean from so far away. Or maybe the beach wasn't that far away at all. Who knew what was behind this gate?

I waved my hand to get the security guard's attention.

He ignored me.

I lightly tapped on my horn.

The man finally looked up. He opened the little sliding glass window and stuck his head out. "Turn around and take the first two lefts and you'll find your way back to Route 278." He went to close the window like that was the end of the discussion.

"Wait! I'm not lost." *I hope.*

He just stared at me.

1

"I'm here to see Athena Quinn."

He continued to stare at me.

"Athena Quinn. The romance novelist."

"Oh, I heard you." He shook his head and grabbed a clipboard. "Do you have an appointment?"

"Yes. Well, no, not exactly. But I'm her new assistant. I'm moving in today. She's definitely expecting me."

"What's your name?"

"Hazel Fox."

He checked off something on his clipboard. "Well, Miss Fox, you're in for quite the surprise if you think you're going to see her."

I frowned. What did that mean? Before I could ask him, the window slammed shut, and the gate in front of me swept open. For a second I sat there and stared. Trees lined a long gravel road. The Spanish moss draping from the trees blew in the breeze. It was like I was entering some beautiful old southern plantation.

My tires spit back gravel as I slowly made my way down the long drive. If I looked hard enough, I could spot mansions nestled among the lush greenery. Mansion after mansion after mansion. Before accepting the position, I'd read about the little island off the coast of South Carolina. All of its restaurants and shops were required to blend into the scenery. The mansions had taken on the same aesthetic. Tans, grays, and browns. Each one was more magnificent than the last. They somehow blended into the trees while still standing out.

I passed one mansion with a huge turret on the side and smiled. I'd dreamed of living in a house like that one day. Maybe if I learned enough on this job, I'd be buying one of these properties in a few years. Hell, if Athena Quinn could have a megahit, then I certainly could too. Her books weren't even very good.

I kept driving. I'd tried to google the address, but the whole area was blurred out on the map for privacy. Everyone in this neighborhood must have been filthy rich. Including my new boss.

At the very end of the lane was Athena Quinn's estate. I put my car into park in her circular driveway and stared out at the mansion. Unlike the rest of the buildings I'd seen on the island, this one did *not* blend into the scenery. It was stark white. And something about the way the Spanish moss moved in the evening breeze here was haunting. The house looked older than the others I'd passed. As if it had been sitting there just like that for centuries. I half expected a woman in an old southern dress to burst out the front door to say hello.

But no one came outside to greet me at all. Which was fine. Maybe welcoming guests would be part of my new job. Although, from the way the security guard had greeted me, it didn't seem like Athena Quinn had many visitors. Really . . . what had he meant when he said I was in for a surprise if I thought I was going to see her?

Maybe she was just a horrible person. A woman as old-fashioned and sinister as the house she lived in. I climbed out of my car and slammed the door, the sound echoing around me. I froze when I heard waves crashing in the distance. I turned in a circle. Seriously . . . where was the beach hidden? You'd think the owners of these places would want the beach more visible. At least there were a few palm trees interspersed between the old trees dripping with Spanish moss. That gave it a beachier vibe. *Nope. No. Not even a little.* Beach houses weren't this creepy looking.

My high heels slid in the gravel, and I almost fell over. I looked at the expanse of gravel between me and the front door. *Crap.* I had flats packed in my suitcase, but I knew they were at the very bottom. I'd have to sift through all my clothes to pull them out. And I would make a really weird first impression if Athena Quinn came out and saw me rummaging through my things. I looked back toward the house just in time to see the curtains in one of the windows move.

Shit, is she already watching me? My phone alarm started going off, warning me that I was about to be late. Well, late if I wanted to be early. And showing up early on the first day was a must. I quickly silenced the alarm. I didn't have time to change my shoes or do anything else weird in my new employer's driveway.

I took a deep breath and lifted my chin. I could make it to the door without falling over. *Easy.* After a few steps of worrying my heels were about to snap off, I ended up doing a weird tiptoe thing. Hopefully Athena Quinn wasn't actually watching me through the front windows. Because this was not a great first impression.

I smoothed down my skirt and adjusted my blazer. *You've got this.* I shimmied my shoulders, trying to rid myself of the nervous energy coursing through my veins. And then I grabbed the big brass knocker on the front door and let it fall with one loud thud. *Oops.* I'd meant to do two crisp knocks, not one loud thud. I was about to reach for the heavy knocker again when the door flew open.

I had been surprised by the beautiful gravel drive up to this house. I had been surprised by the house itself. But I was most surprised by the man who opened the door and stared at me expectantly.

He was devastatingly handsome. His dark brown eyes were piercing, and even though his skin was pale, I could tell he spent his days outside. His hair was as dark as his eyes, and it was windswept from the ocean air. It was mussed up and pushed to the side. He was in need of a haircut, but he made it work. He *really* made it work. I hadn't even said one word to him, and I could already envision sinking my fingers into his hair.

He looked older than me but not by much. Five years, maybe? Ten at the most. Maybe it was his slacks and button-up shirt that made him look older. But no . . . the rolled-up sleeves and lack of shoes balanced that out and made him seem casual. Beachy. Like the palm trees and the smell of salt in the air, he seemed like he belonged at a beach instead of in this mansion. And even though he was staring at me like the security guard had outside the gate, I immediately felt at ease around him.

"You're early, Miss Fox," he said in a proper southern accent.

The way he said my name had me blushing, and I wasn't even sure why. "Oh, please, call me Hazel."

"Athena Quinn prefers using our last names. It's more efficient."

4

"It's the same number of syllables," I said with a laugh.

He lowered his eyebrows.

I swallowed hard, no longer feeling at ease. *Okay, apparently he agrees with Athena Quinn.* I made a mental note to listen respectfully to . . . Wait, who was this person? "I'm sorry, and you are . . . ?"

"Mr. Remington." He put his hand out for me.

I quickly shook his outstretched hand. I couldn't help it when my eyes dropped to his strong forearms. There was something about a man rolling up his sleeves that did things to me. *Oh my God, stop staring at his arms.* I snapped my eyes back to his face. "Nice to meet you. What's your first name?"

"We just discussed this. Athena Quinn prefers last names."

I smiled. "But certainly we can call each other by our first names."

"That won't be necessary." He peered around me at my beat-up car. "Did you not bring any of your belongings?"

"I did. They're in my car."

He lowered his eyebrows again and nodded. "How many trunks did you bring?"

"How many what?"

"No bother. I'll fetch your things for you later. Please follow me." His eyes raked down my body.

And for just a second, before he opened his mouth, I thought that maybe he found me attractive too.

"But you'll have to remove your shoes," he said. "Athena Quinn doesn't allow shoes in her house." He turned and started walking through the foyer.

Oh, so . . . not checking me out then. I quickly kicked off my shoes and hurried after him. I was actually happy to abandon them, but I was a little disappointed that he was barefoot only because it was a house rule. Whatever idea I had of him being a laid-back beach person flew out the window.

The marble was hard and cold on my bare feet. I'd have to remember to wear socks around this house.

Mr. Remington passed by a few closed doors without saying a word. When he'd asked me to follow him, I'd kind of assumed that he'd give me a tour. And I certainly needed one if I was going to be able to find my way around this giant mansion.

"What's in those rooms?" I asked.

"All locked doors are off-limits."

"Okay, but . . . what's in them?"

He sighed and stopped so abruptly that I almost bumped into him. He turned around and stared down at me. "Those are Athena Quinn's personal rooms."

"What kind of personal rooms?"

"Rooms you're not allowed in."

Right, I got that. "I'm sorry, but what is it you do for Athena Quinn again? Are you her butler?"

"I'm her personal assistant."

Wait, what? I'm her personal assistant. "Oh. So I'm replacing you?"

He looked very offended. "No. Why would you say that?"

"Because . . . I was hired to be her new personal assistant."

"No. I needed help. You're my assistant."

My face fell. "I thought I was hired to be Athena Quinn's assistant?" That was the whole reason I'd accepted this job. I never would have taken it if I'd known I was going to be the assistant to her personal assistant. What kind of job was that? I wanted to be a famous author one day. And to get there, I needed to learn from someone who'd succeeded. I didn't care to learn what assistants did from Mr. Remington.

"You'll be assisting me to assist her. So yes, in a way, you are her assistant too." He turned and started walking again. "That's the drawing room," he said and pointed to an open door to the right. The room was filled with an uncomfortable-looking love seat and equally uncomfortable-looking chairs. Posters of Athena Quinn's bestsellers hung on the walls. But the author herself was nowhere to be seen.

"And the parlor." Mr. Remington pointed to the left of the foyer to a room that looked almost exactly like the drawing room.

"I'm sorry—what's the difference?" I asked. "Between the drawing room and the parlor?"

He lowered his eyebrows again. No one had the right to look that handsome when scowling. I realized that since Mr. Remington had opened the ornate front door, I hadn't once seen him smile. Maybe that was fitting. A scowl was the only thing that marred the perfection of his features. And I had an easier time looking at him if I stared at his frown instead of focusing on how gorgeous he was.

"A parlor is a sitting room," he said. "And a drawing room is where guests are received."

I peered into the other room. "But they have the same kind of furniture. Doesn't that make them both sitting rooms?"

"Goodness no, they're very different."

"So where will I be meeting Athe . . . Ms. Quinn?"

"She prefers people use her whole name. It's only the help that goes by last names."

The help? Was that me?

"And Athena Quinn is quite busy. Shall we continue the tour?"

Did that mean I wouldn't be meeting her at all? *No. Of course not.* He must have just meant she was busy today. And even though I was the assistant to her assistant, I'd surely still get to talk to her occasionally. There was no reason to panic. But I could feel my heart racing and my head spinning. *I should have taken that marketing job . . .*

What if coming here had been a terrible mistake?

Mr. Remington pointed into another room. "The day kitchen is through there. As is the formal dining room. Feel free to help yourself to some food."

I was too busy worrying about not meeting Athena to bother asking about what a day kitchen was. And I was too nervous to think about food right now.

"And this is—" Mr. Remington was cut off by a buzzing sound in his front pocket. He pulled his phone out. "If you'll excuse me, I need to take this. Make yourself comfortable in the drawing room. I'll be back in one moment. Just don't . . . touch anything." He hurried off before I could ask him which sitting room that was again.

Don't touch anything? He was acting like I was a petulant child. I looked to the left and then the right. And then I looked at the two doors that led to Athena Quinn's personal rooms.

All I wanted to do was go open one of the doors I wasn't supposed to. But I was pretty sure that trying to get Mr. Remington to tell me his first name was already offensive enough for my first day on the job. Not to mention that I hadn't known what he was referring to when he asked me about my trunks. I certainly didn't know the difference between a parlor and a drawing room. And I guessed I'd also offended him when I said I'd be taking over his job. Yeah, this was not off to a great start.

God, it had taken me *months* to find a job this close to a famous author. And if I was going to be only the assistant to the assistant, then why did I have to answer all those ridiculous questions on the application? And in the countless follow-up emails?

I was about to go into the sitting room on the left, but then I paused. I looked back at one of the closed doors again. Mr. Remington didn't seem like he was a fan of mine. At this point, I'd be lucky if he ever let me interact with Athena Quinn. Especially when I came off like I was vying for his job. Which I wasn't. The job listing had been very misleading.

But if I knew one thing about Athena Quinn, it was that she wrote bold female leads. If I was going to get close to her, I'd have to be bold too. It was best if I took this opportunity into my own hands. And if I was lucky, she'd be behind one of those locked doors. I'd talk to her and tell her how excited I was to be one of her assistants. I'd compliment her work and get a rapport going. Soon she'd be the mentor I'd always dreamed of. And I'd be one step closer to having my novel published.

I walked to the closest locked door. I made sure Mr. Remington hadn't reentered the foyer and then wrapped my hand around the knob. There were two things I knew for sure about Mr. Remington. One—he was too handsome for his own good. And two—he was a liar. The door wasn't even locked.

CHAPTER 2

Sunday—August 28

Athena Quinn's large wooden desk matched the wooden panels along the walls. And the floor-to-ceiling wooden bookshelves. The whole room was dark except for a single desk lamp highlighting a typewriter on the center of the desk. Her empty chair was facing away from the desk, like she'd been staring at the wooden paneling instead of working on her next manuscript.

Writer's block. I knew all about that. Maybe that could be the first thing we bonded over. I could crack a joke about it. Make her like me and pull me under her wing. But that would have been a lot easier if she were here. The chair didn't turn at the sound of me opening the door. It must have been empty. I'd chosen the wrong "locked" room. Athena Quinn was not behind door number one.

I looked over at the drawn curtains. I would have stepped inside, but something about the darkness in the room kept me frozen in place. I'd been hoping to be asked in once I opened the door. Stepping into the dark room uninvited seemed like more of an invasion. And I wanted Athena Quinn to like me more than her rude assistant did. Snooping would not leave a great first impression.

There was a squeaking noise, and I looked over at the chair. It started to swivel back toward me. *She is here!* I saw the top of her head behind the high backrest before the door slammed in my face.

"This is not the drawing room." Mr. Remington stared down at me, his fist tight on the doorknob, the look on his face one of pure fury.

He looked so angry that I almost expected there to be heat radiating off him. But it was like his cold feelings toward me had seeped into his skin. I started shivering as a chill ran down my back. Or maybe I was shaking because he was far too close to me. So close that I could smell his expensive cologne. It swirled around me, making me feel light headed. It was intoxicating.

I licked my lips so I wouldn't do something weird, like lick his skin. For some reason, I found it easier to stare at his Adam's apple than into his angry eyes. "I'm . . . I'm sorry, Mr. Remington." God, he already hated me. This was the icing on the cake. I was probably seconds away from being fired. I hadn't stepped into the room, but I knew how it looked. Like I was snooping around where I shouldn't be, when he had explicitly told me to wait in the drawing room and not touch anything.

His Adam's apple rose and then fell. "Let me show you to your room. Certainly you're tired from the long drive."

I'm not fired? I finally managed to make eye contact with him.

He shook his head, his disappointment evident. "And surely you'd like to . . . freshen up," he said, his gaze trailing down my body.

Excuse me?

He turned on his heel and started walking away.

I looked once more at the closed door and then quickly followed him. We went past the two sitting rooms and the kitchen, and then started to climb the large staircase.

I ran my hand along the thick banister. With old houses like this, my imagination always ran wild. How many other people had touched this very banister? How many lives had been lived here? The image of a girl in an old-fashioned southern dress flashed through my mind again. Darting down the stairs, lightly touching the same place my hand had just fallen. I shivered.

"This way," Mr. Remington said.

The staircase split in two halfway up. And Mr. Remington had taken the right staircase.

"What's to the left?" I asked.

"Athena Quinn's wing," he said without looking at me. "You're forbidden to go down that wing as well. And it's best that you heed my warning this time. You don't want to see Athena Quinn angry, trust me."

I didn't trust him. In the slightest. But something about the way he said it made me believe him. Like he'd experienced Athena Quinn's wrath. Seriously . . . what the hell had I signed up for?

An old step creaked underfoot as I hurried after him. We walked down a dimly lit hallway. Past closed door after closed door, and this time I didn't bother to ask what was hidden behind them. I just wanted to get to my room and far away from Mr. Remington's judgmental glare.

He stopped in front of one of the doors and pulled a large, old-fashioned key out of his pocket. It slid into the door with a satisfying click. He pushed the door open just a crack and handed me the key. The metal was heavier than I expected it to be. I closed my hand around it. At least I'd have some privacy here.

"I'll have your belongings brought up. Have a good rest. Work starts at five a.m. sharp tomorrow."

Five in the morning? That definitely had not been in the job description. What kind of psychopath willingly woke up at 5:00 a.m.? Athena Quinn worked from home. She could literally start her day whenever she pleased. Why on earth had she chosen the break of dawn?

He turned to leave.

"Wait. Where is the bathroom?" I didn't love his earlier insinuation that I needed to freshen up, but I really wanted a shower. I still had hope that I'd meet Athena Quinn tomorrow. And if I did, I wanted to look my best.

"En suite. Good night, Miss Fox."

"Good night, Mr. Remington." I watched him retreat down the hall. When he reached the final door, he pulled out a key that looked similar to the one he'd given me and then disappeared into his room. He didn't glance back at me once.

I sighed. Tomorrow was a new day. Maybe I could still fix this. *Or . . . I could just leave.* I'd be lying if I said I wasn't leaning toward that option. I tried to shake away the thought. Tomorrow would be better than today. It had to be.

I opened the door the rest of the way and stepped into the pitch blackness. My hand searched the wall for a light switch. My fingers finally collided with it, and I hit the lights.

The room matched the rest of the house, with its dark wood accents. But they'd paired the wood in my room with crimson wallpaper. Almost the exact color of blood. It made me shiver.

At least the king-size four-poster bed looked comfortable. I was used to sleeping on the twin bed in my college dorm. And the bed in my New York City apartment hadn't been much better. So this was a major upgrade.

Speaking of New York, my best friend there was exactly who I needed to talk to. She'd be able to cheer me up. I pulled my phone out of my purse and plopped down on the bed. I practically sank into the mattress. I was pretty sure I'd never sat on anything this comfortable in my whole life.

I clicked on Kehlani's name in my phone.

She answered after one ring. "Hazel! How amazing is her house? How amazing is she? Did you get her autograph for me yet?"

Unlike me, Kehlani loved love. She was a huge fan of Athena Quinn. She'd read every one of her releases the day they came out and was always looking forward to the next. "Hey," I said, trying my best to keep my voice even.

"Oh no. What's wrong?"

I felt tears welling in my eyes. I wanted to be back in New York with her. Not in this cold mansion with its colder occupants. "It's nothing like the job listing said. I haven't even met Athena Quinn yet. I'm the assistant to her personal assistant. And her personal assistant is a real tool. He hated me before I even opened my mouth to introduce myself. I'm pretty sure he thinks I'm vying for his job. And he's making me call him *Mr.* Remington. He doesn't even want to be my acquaintance." I heard a floorboard creak. "And I swear this place is haunted. What the hell was I thinking?"

Kehlani laughed. "Girl, your first day isn't even until tomorrow. Surely you'll meet Athena Quinn then. And tell me more about this Mr. Remington."

"He's a douche."

"Is he a handsome douche?"

"No," I lied.

"Well, that's a bummer. I was picturing someone young and sexy with one of those scowls that melts your panties."

"I'm working for Athena Quinn, not living in one of her novels."

"Mhm. Well . . . if you really hate it . . . you can always move back."

As much as I loved Kehlani, I didn't love New York. We'd moved there together after graduating in the spring. I had big dreams of being a successful author. But big dreams in NYC meant really high living costs. Which meant I'd had to waitress during all my free time. Which meant no time to write. NYC wasn't the city of dreams. It was the city where dreamers went to realize that their dreams would never pay enough to support them.

"You know I can't afford it," I said.

"I know, but . . . rumor has it that there's about to be a new opening at my marketing firm."

This was not the first time that Kehlani had told me about an opening at her marketing firm. We'd both majored in marketing in school. But it wasn't my dream to have a marketing job. I just wanted to be able to market my books . . . once I wrote them. "I can't quit this job after not even really officially starting. Besides . . . you said 'rumor has it.' I can't move back on a rumor."

"Oh, but it's a really solid rumor. Apparently a kick-ass new hire is about to get promoted after only three months. Including a significant raise. It's me. In case you didn't get that."

I laughed. "Congrats, Kehlani." I looked down at the only blazer I owned, knowing Kehlani had tons of designer outfits in her closet. Her salary was already amazing. I couldn't fathom how good her raise was to make her sound so happy. "Seriously, that's awesome," I said.

"Thank you. And . . . this could be you in a few months. Come on, get your ass back here. This is where you belong."

She had no idea how tempting her offer was. Sitting there in that cold room all alone . . . I was homesick. Not really for a certain place. Just homesick for Kehlani's smiling face. We'd been living together since freshman year of college. And though I wasn't technically alone in this huge house . . . I sure felt alone.

I heard another floorboard creak. God, this place was really freaking me out. "I'll think about it," I said.

"That's all I can ask. Give this gig a couple days, and I'll call you when the job is officially opening."

"Okay."

"Okay?!"

I laughed. "I didn't say yes to the job. Just that I'll think about it."

"Deal. Now, let's go back to Mr. Remington. How tall is he? When he looks displeased with you, does he look like he wants to spank you?"

"You're ridiculous." I stood up and stretched. A nice hot shower would warm me up and make me feel better.

"Does he have a six-pack?"

"How would I know?" I wandered over to the en suite bathroom. Unlike the bedroom, this didn't seem old. It looked like it was newly renovated with white-and-gray marble. The only thing old-fashioned was the claw-foot tub. It must have been here for a century at least. "I finally found a plus to this job," I said.

"Mr. Remington wants an assistant with benefits?"

I laughed. "No. The bathroom is amazing." I turned the knob on the tub to let it start filling.

"Well, that's good. I swear, no matter how many times I clean the bathroom here, I'll never be able to get rid of all the years of grime."

I was willing to bet this house was even older than the apartments in Manhattan. Maybe that was why they'd gutted the bathroom. I wished they'd gut the rest of it. Or at least change the wallpaper to not be the same hue as blood. "I think I'm going to take a nice long bath." My night had suddenly turned quite relaxing.

"Okay, enjoy yourself. Flirt with Mr. Remington for me."

"I won't."

"Lame."

I laughed. "Congrats again on the promotion!"

"Love you, Hazel."

"Love you back." I hung up the phone and quickly pulled off my clothes. I needed to wash this day away.

I slid into the tub with a sigh. The water instantly warmed my bones. I poured the vanilla bodywash into the tub and let the bubbles surround me. This was just what I needed.

I held my breath and dipped my head under.

Boom.

It was like I could feel the vibration of the water. I came up to the surface, gasping for air. Thunder boomed again, practically shaking the tub. I wiped the water out of my eyes, and everything was pitch black. *Shit.*

CHAPTER 3

Sunday—August 28

I blinked again, hoping the lights would magically turn back on. *Screw me.* I couldn't see a damn thing. I had no idea where the towels were, and my clean clothes hadn't been brought up yet. What had I been thinking?

Part of me just wanted to sit there and pray that the power would come back on. I mean, it had to come back on any minute, right? Surely a huge place like this would have a backup generator or something.

The sound of thunder echoed around the bathroom again.

I gripped the edges of the tub.

And then I heard a creaking noise.

Okay, nope. No. I was not staying in here. This was just me asking to be the first person to die, like in all the horror movies I hated. I climbed out of the tub, leaving a trail of water behind me.

I rummaged around in the dark for a towel and almost slipped on the slick tiled floor. I needed light. *Where did I leave my phone?*

I reached out toward the vanity and somehow managed to hit my shin against the toilet. *Ow.* I winced and stepped backward onto something soft. *Oh, thank God.* I reached down and picked up the thin white shirt I'd been wearing under my blazer and pulled it on. My skirt was right next to it on the ground, and I grabbed that too. *Why the hell did I start taking a bath before I had an outfit to change into?* The wet fabric stuck to my skin, but I didn't really have a choice. It was the only thing I had to wear.

I ran my hands along the vanity in search of my phone. Seriously? Where had I left it? I could have sworn I'd put it down right before I'd climbed into the tub.

Another clap of thunder made me jump.

I tried to take a deep breath to steady my racing heart, but then I heard that damn creaking again.

Screw this. I wasn't going to stand here soaking wet in the bathroom waiting for the lights to turn back on and for someone to bring me my dry things.

I kept my hand on the wall to guide me out of the bathroom and toward my bedroom door. I hit the lights to check that the power was off, and nothing happened. The door creaked when I opened it. I bit the inside of my lip. Was that the same creaking noise I'd been hearing? Had someone been coming into my room?

I didn't wait another second to figure it out. I ran into the hall.

Thunder boomed again, and my bedroom door slammed shut behind me. God, this place really was haunted. There weren't any windows in the hall to provide gusts of wind. What the hell else could have made my door slam like that? I backed up until my arm hit something. I screamed at the top of my lungs, even though I'd only collided with the wall.

I heard another creak behind me and ran down the hall as fast as I could. *Fuck all of this.* I was not staying in this haunted mansion with a man who hated me and a boss who couldn't even be bothered to meet me.

I ran down the stairs, taking them two at a time. My feet hit the freezing-cold marble floor, and I sprinted faster. I reached into my pocket to grab my car keys but realized I wasn't wearing my favorite pair of jeans. I was wearing a stupid pencil skirt, and my keys were in my purse upstairs. Along with my driver's license and the little cash I had.

Damn it. I really did not want to go back up to my room. I had turned around to look back up the stairs when I saw a faint light coming from one of the rooms off the hall. Thunder boomed, and a chill ran down my spine. I knew I should just go back to my room, get my things, and get the hell out of this house. But it was almost like I was drawn to the light. I held my breath as I walked toward it.

Maybe this was where I would meet Athena Quinn. She'd make a pot of tea. We'd laugh about how I thought the house was haunted. And we'd spend the whole night talking about our favorite novels and authors.

I walked past one of the sitting rooms and into the kitchen. A candle flickered on the center island, but there was no one there. I stepped farther into the room. The candlelight cast eerie shadows along the cabinets. Who lit a candle and just left it? Especially when the house was so dark?

I heard a creak behind me, and I turned around, slamming into someone. I would have screamed again if I weren't staring directly at a man's hard pecs. His strong hands steadied me. And there was that delicious scent of his skin.

Mr. Remington.

His smell was intoxicating. Again, I had the oddest impulse to lick him. And I felt something when his hands touched my biceps. Like there was an electricity in the air, but somehow the exact opposite. More like ice freezing my veins.

The fear left me, replaced with something possibly more dangerous. I took a step away from him. I couldn't help but stare at his exposed abs. And the way his waist tapered down to his sweatpants. There was a noticeable bulge that I absolutely shouldn't have been staring at.

"Miss Fox, are you all right?"

I looked up at the scowl on Mr. Remington's perfect face. He certainly hadn't felt the same electricity I had. My heart sank. He was standing in the middle of the kitchen without a shirt, holding a carton of milk. It was the most normal scene in the world, but not with him in it. He'd been so strict and rude earlier, and this made him seem almost human.

His eyes traveled down to my chest.

I followed his gaze. *Oh my God.* My white shirt was completely soaked. You could see everything. Literally everything. I was cold and scared, and my nipples were so hard. I didn't know whether covering myself would draw more attention and make it worse, so I just stood there. Dripping water all over the kitchen floor.

"You're supposed to use the day kitchen," he said.

"What?"

Thunder rolled in the distance, and I forced myself not to flinch.

"The day kitchen is for the help," he said. He pointed to the left. It looked like there was a second kitchen attached to this one.

I shook my head. I remembered he had said something about a day kitchen when I first arrived. But I'd forgotten to ask what on earth he was talking about. "Then why are you in here?"

The corner of his mouth ticked up. Just for a second. If I had blinked, I would have missed it.

"We were out of milk." He poured a dash into a steaming cup on the counter.

I watched in silence as he walked past me and put the milk back in the fridge. The muscles in his back flexed as he closed the door.

I turned away from him, trying to focus on anything but his exposed skin. I cleared my throat. "I was just on my way outside to grab my things. If you'll excuse me." I needed out of this room. I needed to get as far away from him as possible before his cologne drove me wild.

"I dropped off your trunks a moment ago."

Who calls suitcases trunks? It was hard to focus on the strange term, though, because he'd just stopped a few inches away from me. He leaned against the kitchen island and blew on his cup.

I swallowed hard, imagining those lips on me. It was like I could feel his breath on my neck. Blowing gently on my skin before he kissed me.

"In your room," he added when I didn't respond.

I shivered, trying to shake away the image of his lips on my skin. "You left them in my room?"

"Indeed."

"You . . . you didn't knock."

"I did, but no one answered. I figured you were touring the grounds."

Touring the grounds after the sun had set? In the middle of a storm? Was he mad? I stared at him, and I swore his eyes darkened. Maybe he was mad. That would explain a lot, actually.

He lowered his eyebrows when I didn't respond again.

"My door was locked," I said.

He shook his head. "No, it wasn't."

I was almost certain I had locked it. "Well, my car was definitely locked." I hadn't even thought to give him the keys when he said he'd bring my stuff up.

He shook his head again. "No, that wasn't locked either."

I always locked my car. I'd lived in freaking New York City. If I'd ever left my car unlocked, I wouldn't have one. But . . . I had been disarmed when I arrived here. The drive up was beautiful. And the man who answered the door was even more so.

"Have you settled in all right?" he asked and blew on his cup again.

I forced myself to stop staring at his lips. "It's . . . spooky."

"You get used to it."

I had kind of thought he'd tell me it wasn't. Or at least lie and say there was nothing to be afraid of. I swallowed hard.

"It's an old house," he said. "A lot of history in these walls."

History as in . . . *it is haunted*? "Are you trying to scare me?"

"No. I only meant it's an old house and rather drafty. Remember that when you hear creaks in the night."

"I wish it was a cat or something instead."

He ignored me. "And you shouldn't walk around with wet hair." For just a second, his eyes landed on my wet shirt again. "Or wet clothes. You'll catch a cold, Miss Fox."

"I was taking a bath when the power went out. I couldn't see anything."

"The power in the whole neighborhood is out. It'll be back on soon. You should go change. You're literally dripping." His voice dropped an octave when he said "dripping."

I felt myself clench. I knew he was talking about the fact that my clothes were dripping wet. But the way he was staring at me made the comment seem more insinuating. More arrogant. *Oh, fuck you.* I finally folded my arms across my chest. It didn't matter if I drew attention to the fact that my shirt was see-through now. He'd already made it obvious three times that he knew. And apparently he didn't want to see. Which was fine. I didn't want to see his stupid naked torso anymore either.

His Adam's apple rose and fell as we stood there staring at each other. *Or maybe he did want to see . . .*

"The view makes up for it," he said.

"Hmm?"

"The view makes up for the creepiness. And the view from your room is one of the best in the house. I made sure of it." He lifted the candle off the kitchen counter and handed it to me. "Have a good rest of your night, Miss Fox."

My fingers brushed against his, and I swore my heart stopped beating.

His eyes met mine for a second, that look of disapproval even more evident than before.

I pulled my hand back. Stupid Kehlani for talking about him being attractive. I was not attracted to that man. He was awful and rude and . . . I lost my train of thought as I watched him walk out of the room and into the darkness. Fine, he was beautiful.

I waited a few minutes before walking back to my room. The last thing I wanted was to run into him in the dark again. Or run into him again at all. I stopped at the top of the stairs and put the candle out in front of me, staring down the left wing. I could barely see a few feet in front of me. But somewhere over there, Athena Quinn was sleeping. I'd probably meet her tomorrow, and this night would be worth it. It had to be.

I retreated back to my room and closed the door behind me. I found my trunk . . . er, suitcase . . . and changed into a pair of warm pajamas. I was about to climb into bed when I looked back at the closed curtains. I lifted the candle off the nightstand and walked over to the window. I pushed the heavy curtains to the side, and my hand froze on the fabric. It wasn't a window at all.

I opened up the french doors and stepped onto the wet balcony. The ocean air swirled around me, and the flame of my candle went out. It was the perfect view of the ocean.

Thunder boomed again, but it sounded farther away now. The view lit up for a second as a streak of lightning broke. For miles and miles, the ocean stretched out. It was breathtaking.

Mr. Remington had said I had one of the best views in the house. That he'd made sure of it. But why? He didn't want me here. Right?

I leaned forward on the railing and looked toward the right at the houses down the stretch of the beach. Every other house had windows that were glowing with light. He'd said that the whole neighborhood had lost power. I looked behind me at my dark room.

Was it another lie? Was everything he said a lie?

The fresh air swirled around me, tangling my hair. I tried to shove away any thoughts of Mr. Remington and stared back at the sea. I smiled and breathed in the ocean air. But my smile faltered. Just like that, my love of the salt in the air died. Mr. Remington didn't wear cologne. He smelled like the ocean.

And I was pretty sure he knew it. He'd wanted me to step out on the balcony tonight. Right after he stood mere inches away from me. He wanted me to know that he was all around me.

Our house was the only one without power. He'd mentioned how old and creaky the house was. He'd sneaked into my room, even though I was almost certain it was locked. And he'd sneaked up on me in the kitchen.

I pressed my lips into a thin line. I knew exactly what he was up to. He was trying to scare me. He was trying to get me to leave. *Well, too bad, Mr. Remington.* I wasn't going anywhere.

CHAPTER 4

Monday—August 29

I didn't sleep. At all. I wasn't sure if it was because of the constant creaking of floorboards or the fact that I was so nervous to meet Athena Quinn in the morning. But it almost felt like I was back in school with first-day jitters, praying that I'd have classes with my friends.

Although when it came to Mr. Remington and I becoming friends, I already knew there was little hope. Mr. Remington was the worst. Seriously. I'd never met someone I instantly disliked so much. I didn't see the two of us ever getting along.

I thought the smell of the salty air in my room would soothe my nerves. But now it just reminded me of Mr. Remington.

Every time I tried to close my eyes, I saw him. Without a shirt.

I'd been so busy the past few months just making ends meet that I hadn't had time to date. I scrunched my mouth to the side. That was a lie. It was more like the past couple of years. When was the last time I'd been kissed? I stared at the ceiling. It had been junior year. He'd been drunk. And I'd been tipsy. Yeah, that explained a lot. I was lusting over Mr. Remington because it had been far too long since I'd even had time to think of dating. That was definitely it.

My 4:30 a.m. alarm went off. *Thank God.* I sat up and pushed the covers off myself. Maybe Athena Quinn was spooked out by her own house and couldn't sleep, hence the ridiculous 5:00 a.m. work time. But I wasn't annoyed by it today. I just wanted out of this room and to get started. Today was a new day. And it was going to go swimmingly.

It didn't take me long to get ready. I pulled on the same pencil skirt I'd worn yesterday, since it was my only one. But I swapped my wrinkled white top for a clean blue blouse. I was out the door in twenty minutes.

And that was when I realized I had no idea where I was supposed to go. I wandered down the long hallway and stared down the hall on the opposite side of the staircase—Athena Quinn's personal wing. I stood there for a moment. It was wishful thinking that Athena Quinn would emerge at the exact same time as me. But still . . . I smoothed my skirt for what felt like the hundredth time before admitting defeat. The last thing I wanted was to be late on my actual first day.

I walked down the stairs. The kitchen wasn't occupied. Maybe I should wait in the sitting room? Or the drawing room? Or whatever stupid thing Mr. Remington had called it.

I heard a clanging noise and turned around, but there was no one there. The same noise echoed through the hall again. And then I smelled the delicious aroma of bacon. It must have been coming from the kitchen. But when I peered back inside, it was still empty. The noise started again, and I turned toward the door off the side of the kitchen. *Right.* The day kitchen was for the staff. I walked through the kitchen and into the almost identical kitchen adjoining it. The only difference was that it was slightly smaller. And there were more burners on the stove. Also, there were no windows, which was a shame because the views were so amazing.

Mr. Remington was sitting at the head of the table lifting an actual metal cloche off the top of his plate, like the kind you see at Michelin-starred restaurants or something. Not that I would know. I'd never been anywhere fancy enough to see one in person.

There was a cloche covering another plate at the setting beside his. He didn't look up or acknowledge me in any way.

I cleared my throat. "Um . . . good morning?"

"You seem unsure," he said as he unfolded his cloth napkin and draped it over his lap. "Did you not sleep well?"

"I slept fine," I lied. "I could use some coffee, though."

"It'll be out in a moment. Eat your breakfast before it gets cold." He gestured toward the other cloche.

"It's just us?"

"Yes." He finally made eye contact with me as he cut into his omelet. "Is there a problem, Miss Fox?"

"No . . . I . . . um . . ."

"I hope your writing skills are more eloquent than your speaking ones."

"Excuse me?"

He stared at me for a moment, his gaze full of disdain, like it had been when I first stepped into the house. "You'll be writing lots of correspondences for Athena Quinn. She'd prefer it if they weren't littered with *ums*."

"I would never write *um* in a . . . correspondence." He meant email, right?

"Great."

"Fantastic," I said, barely holding back the sarcasm in my voice.

He proceeded to ignore me and cut up his omelet.

He was such a complete dick. I knew he was trying to get under my skin. Convince me to quit. And I wasn't going to let him bother me. I sat down next to him and removed the cloche. There was an omelet on my plate as well. This all seemed rather extravagant for a quick breakfast before work.

I took a bite of the omelet and held back a groan. I looked up to see Mr. Remington staring at me. His eyebrows lowered like I'd done something offensive again. God . . . I hadn't actually groaned out loud, had I?

Luckily, I was saved as a coffee machine in the corner magically came to life with a loud beeping noise. "Did you want a cup too?" I asked as I stood up.

"Sit. Miss Serrano will get it. Miss Serrano!" he said a little louder.

"Miss Serrano?"

"The housekeeper. The chef. She does it all."

"I can get my own coffee . . ."

"Then what would Miss Serrano do?"

"Um . . ." *Damn it.* Why had I said that word again?

Mr. Remington just shook his head and continued to cut up his omelet.

A short woman in a maid uniform came running into the kitchen. Her curly gray hair was piled on top of her head. And her eyes darted around nervously as she grabbed two steaming cups of coffee.

"Thank you, Miss Serrano," I said as she placed one down in front of me. "I'm Hazel. The new assistant . . . to the assistant. And the omelet is delicious."

She stared at me wide eyed and then ran out of the room as quickly as she'd come in.

"She doesn't speak," Mr. Remington said.

"Not at all?"

He stared at me for a moment. "No, so please don't speak to her."

"I don't think that's how that works."

"She prefers if you don't."

"How do you know that's what she prefers if she doesn't speak?"

"Just don't speak to her. Or anyone, for that matter. And last names, Miss Fox. How many times do I have to remind you?"

A lot, apparently. Because it seemed rude to address everyone by "Miss" or "Mr." when they had first names. Almost as rude as not speaking to the housekeeper or anyone else who worked here at all. "Does she speak another language or something?"

Mr. Remington blotted his mouth with his napkin and stood up. "No."

I was pretty sure that Mr. Remington just hadn't taken the time to properly get to know Miss Serrano. And I was happy to listen to him while working, but outside of work? I wanted to get to know the other people here.

He started walking out of the room.

"Wait!" I downed a big sip of coffee and stood up. "Where should I start? Maybe there's a manuscript or . . ."

"No." He laughed. "No," he said more firmly. "You can't do anything until you fill out the paperwork. It'll take you most of the day. Please take the rest to make yourself at home."

I couldn't imagine actually feeling at home here. And why, exactly, was there a day's worth of paperwork to fill out? I'd already answered tons of questions during the interview process.

He turned to go again.

"Where is the paperwork?"

"Miss Serrano will bring it to you when you finish eating." And with that he was gone.

I exhaled slowly. I should have run away last night like I'd wanted to. Nothing was going according to plan. How was I supposed to learn anything if I couldn't even meet Athena? I took another bite of omelet. At least the food was good.

After seeing Mr. Remington a little more casual last night, I'd been hoping he'd be in a better mood today. Maybe he hated wearing shirts or something. I got it. Someone with abs like that shouldn't be wearing a shirt anyway.

God, what is wrong with me? I put my fork down. I was pretty sure I'd lost my mind ever since walking into this haunted house. And why was he harping on me about finishing eating when he'd had only one bite of his omelet? He hadn't even touched his coffee. I finished mine and grabbed his cup too. The last thing I needed was to crash while filling out boring paperwork all day.

Miss Serrano hurried in with at least ten folders piled high in her arms. *You've got to be shitting me right now.*

She plopped them down in front of me and produced a pen from her apron pocket.

"Thank you so much, Miss Serrano. Did you have to fill out all these papers too?"

Her eyes grew rounder each time another word fell out of my mouth.

"I'm so sorry, I didn't even catch your first name?"

The question put her over the edge, and she sprinted out of the room.

Okay, then. Maybe Mr. Remington was right. Maybe she hated being spoken to. Or she was so scared of him that she was scared of me by association. And I mean really terrified. It was like she was worried I was going to bite her head off.

I lifted the flap of the top folder. It was filled with very comprehensive NDAs. Why did Athena need me to sign a nondisclosure agreement if I wasn't even going to be seeing her, let alone seeing any of her work? And why were there so many of them? I closed the folder.

If I was being banished all day with paperwork, I at least wanted to enjoy the outdoors while the weather was still warm. I somehow managed to balance the huge stack of folders and my coffee cup as I made my way back into the main kitchen, where a set of french doors led to a stone patio.

The air was definitely still warm, but the storm from last night hadn't completely rolled away yet. A cloudy day was better anyway. I wouldn't have to worry about getting burned or needing to grab a pair of sunglasses.

I was about to set the folders down on a glass table when I froze. Just around the bushes was the most amazing pool I had ever seen. I held the folders to my chest as I walked down a set of stone steps and over to the infinity pool. It felt as out of place on this estate as my bathroom. Modern and elegant and not at all haunted looking. And that wasn't even the best part. I stopped at the edge of the infinity pool and looked out to where the water disappeared over a small cliff edge. It overlooked the most amazing view of the ocean below. There were steps carved into the stone all the way down to the sand. A long pier stretched over the reed grass. And the ocean was endless.

The view from my room was fantastic. But this? I could swim in this pool all day, looking out at the crashing ocean waves.

Sure, Athena Quinn didn't want to see me. Mr. Remington was an asshole. And Miss Serrano was afraid of me. But . . . pros and cons, right? The question was if any of that was worth the view. I bit the inside of my lip. I mean . . . it just might be. As long as nothing I was about to sign was too bizarre. I dumped the folders on the nearest lounge chair and made myself comfortable.

I pushed the NDA folder to the side and opened the next one.

It was a lengthy agreement about which rooms I was not permitted to enter. I looked back at the old mansion. What on earth was Athena Quinn hiding?

CHAPTER 5

Monday—August 29

I opened up the seventh folder with a yawn.

Mr. Remington hadn't been joking. It felt like my hand was about to fall off from signing so many documents. And I'd abandoned reading them word for word about an hour ago. As far as I was concerned, I'd filled out enough paperwork during the application process. There had even been a personality test. And a writing sample. And a questionnaire about my food preferences. It had seemed like overkill, but now all this too?

I let my chin rest in my palm as I flipped through pages, looking for the line to sign.

When I'd been emailing Athena Quinn back and forth about the job, I'd been so excited. But now I wasn't even sure I'd been writing to her. I was pretty sure I'd been corresponding with Mr. Remington on Athena Quinn's behalf. Which meant . . . Athena Quinn didn't really want me here. She wasn't excited for me to work with her. I'd felt so lucky to get this job, and now I just felt defeated.

"New assistant?" said a deep voice.

I looked up. A man wearing swimming trunks and no shirt stood on the edge of the pool, staring at me. His eyes were as dark brown as his shaggy hair. Or maybe they looked darker because his skin was so pale. My eyes wandered down to his abs. Was everyone who worked here a former model or something? By the time I forced my eyes back to his face, the smirk there made it clear that he'd seen me staring.

"New?" I asked. "Does he go through a bunch of them?"

"I don't think he does it on purpose." The guy wandered over to me and collapsed onto the lounge chair next to mine. He folded his arms behind his head and looked up at the clouds.

"Am I going to get in trouble for talking to you too?"

"Did he tell you not to talk to me?"

"He specifically said not to talk to anyone."

He laughed. "That sounds about right. He has so many rules."

"Mr. Remington? Noooo," I said with a laugh.

"Did he seriously ask you to call him Mr. Remington? What an asshole."

I opened my mouth and closed it again. "I feel like this is some sort of trick and you're going to report everything I say back to him. He already hates me."

"I'm sure *Mr. Remington* doesn't hate you." He said the name in a proper southern accent, mimicking almost exactly how Mr. Remington sounded.

"Trust me, he does. I didn't know the difference between a sitting room and drawing room."

He smiled. "What are you, a peasant?" he asked in the same charming accent.

I laughed. "I'm honestly worried I might be. I forgot to tour the grounds last night when I arrived. And I didn't bring a proper trunk either."

"Ghastly."

I was smiling so much that it actually hurt. It was so nice to have a friendly face around here. The whole house and the rest of the staff seemed so . . . cold.

"Does the new assistant have a name?"

"I'm . . ." I let my voice trail off. I was pretty sure I wasn't supposed to be talking to him. Breaking one rule was bad. So maybe I should just say my last name . . .

"He told you to only tell me your last name, didn't he?"

I nodded.

"Can I tell you a secret?" He sat up. Without waiting for me to respond, he leaned in close to my ear. "I'd prefer being on a first-name basis with you."

I wasn't sure if he was actually flirting with me or if I was still wound up from thinking my twisted thoughts about Mr. Remington all night. But I held my breath until he moved his lips away from my ear.

He smiled. "Unless you'd rather keep it formal, that is."

I shook my head. What was I even doing? I was a first-name kind of person. I put my hand out for him to shake. "I'm Hazel."

Instead of shaking my hand, he pulled it up to his mouth and kissed the back of it. "It's a pleasure to meet you, Hazel." His lips were surprisingly cold, given the warm day. And the whole thing felt really refreshing. *Such an old-fashioned and charming thing to do.* And yet he seemed almost the opposite of Mr. Remington in every other way. He locked eyes with me as he dropped my hand.

Okay, yeah. It wasn't just because I was oddly wound up by Mr. Remington. This guy was definitely flirting with me. "And you are, good sir?" I tried to do a southern accent too, but failed miserably.

"That was pretty bad."

I laughed. "Why are you so good at it?"

"I grew up on the island."

"Wow, I should have put that together."

He smiled. "I get it. I'm very distracting." He gestured to his abs.

I laughed. "You're full of yourself."

"You wound me, Hazel."

I rolled my eyes.

When I looked back at him, he was staring at me in a way that had me blushing.

"You never told me your name," I said.

"Hudson."

Hudson. That was a sexy name. And it suited him.

"What do you do here, Hudson?" I liked the way his name rolled off my tongue.

"In the summer I take care of a bunch of the pools in the area. Including this one. And I do some landscaping too."

I noticed the little net balanced by the pool. Despite the storm last night, there wasn't any debris in the pool. He must have already cleaned it before looking at the bushes or something.

"Did you have to sign all these papers too?" I asked.

He reached around me and lifted up one of the envelopes. He flipped through a few pages, shook his head, and tossed it back onto the lounge chair. "Definitely not."

"Really? I wonder why I have to."

"Probably because I kind of stay outside." He shrugged. "And I'm usually only around in the summer."

"Are you in school?" He looked around my age. Maybe a little younger.

"Off and on. I haven't decided what I want to do this fall yet."

"It's like . . . a couple weeks away," I said with a laugh.

He shrugged. "I've never been a big planner. But I think the storm clouds are going to clear soon. I should probably get to my next house before it gets too hot."

"Of course. I didn't mean to hold you up."

He smiled. "You definitely weren't. I was just procrastinating." He got up and stretched.

"Hey, Hudson?"

"Yeah?"

"Did you lose power last night?"

He shook his head. "All the houses around here have generators because of the hurricanes."

I knew it. "I think Mr. Remington is trying to scare me off. He said our power cut out last night, but I saw the houses down the coast all lit up. I was wandering around in the dark, and I was totally freaked out."

He winced. "Maybe don't leave your room at night."

I stared at him. "Why?"

He cleared his throat. "It's an old house. Just . . . don't do it."

The way he said it made a chill run down my spine.

"Don't look so scared. *Mr. Remington* is all bite and no bark."

"I think you have that backward," I said. "All bark and no bite?"

Hudson shook his head. "Oh, is that how the saying goes? I always thought it was the other way."

"Definitely not."

He laughed. "If you're still around this weekend, there's this end-of-summer party on the beach Friday night. You should come."

Well, I didn't love that "still around" implied that Mr. Remington's assistants didn't usually last that long. "Fingers crossed I survive till then. I mean . . . I've already broken all sorts of rules by even speaking to you. But if I do make it that long, I'd love to come. I absolutely do not want to spend my entire weekend in that creepy mansion."

Hudson smiled. "Don't worry, I won't tell Atlas that you talked to me."

"Atlas?"

Hudson winked and then hurried down the stone steps to the beach.

Was Atlas Mr. Remington's first name?

I smiled. Oh, he was going to be so pissed when I called him by his first name.

CHAPTER 6

Monday—August 29

Atlas Remington. The name rolled around in my head all morning and afternoon as I signed page after page. Why did even his name have to be so sexy? Someone so rude should be named . . . Eggbert and have a hunchback or something.

But no. He was named Atlas Remington. The more I said it in my head, the more pompous it sounded. Who named their kid Atlas?

Hudson, on the other hand? That was a good, solid name. I bit the end of my pen as I pictured him lounging next to me.

Seriously, what the hell was wrong with me? I think it had just been a long time since I'd been bored. And a long time since I'd been . . . never mind.

I signed page after page of documents. And when I finally signed my name on the very last sheet, I started rethinking everything. Would Mr. Remington be pissed that I'd signed them *Hazel Fox* instead of *Miss Fox*? I really had no idea. The only thing I knew for sure was that Hudson was right—Mr. Remington was an asshole.

I closed the last folder and tossed it on top of the stack. I didn't know the extent of what I'd just agreed to. But it wouldn't have surprised me if I'd signed away my first child.

At least now I'd be able to do some actual work tomorrow. Today I was supposed to spend the rest of my time making myself at home. I couldn't imagine actually feeling at home here, though. So I planned to tour the rest of the grounds instead.

But I was exhausted from my lack of sleep the night before. I yawned and leaned back on the lounge chair. The sun was still hiding behind the clouds, and the lull of the waves crashing against the shore made my eyelids heavy. I'd take a quick nap and then make my way down to the beach. I wanted to walk out on the pier. I yawned again.

⚜

Someone clearing their throat made me sit up with a start. I swallowed the lump in my throat when I saw Mr. Remington standing next to my lounge chair with his signature frown.

"I'm sorry," I said. "I must have fallen asleep." I grabbed the stack of folders next to me. God, they were heavy. "But I'm all done." I tapped the top of them to emphasize my point when he didn't say anything. "I signed every line."

He lowered his eyebrows. "All of them?"

I nodded.

"Even the ones in the last folder?"

"Yes?" I hated how my words sometimes came out as questions around him. But the way he was staring at me made me really wonder what was in that last folder. It had just seemed like routine stuff about the job.

"Good," he said and grabbed the huge stack like it weighed nothing. "I see you didn't touch your lunch."

I looked over at a tray that was sitting on the lounge chair next to mine. "Oh, I didn't know. Miss Serrano must not have said anything when she brought it out."

He glared at me. "She doesn't speak, Miss Fox."

Maybe not to you.

36

"You must be famished. Dinner will be served shortly."

"That sounds great. I'll be right in."

"Dinner is a formal affair, Miss Fox. If you don't mind freshening up and putting on something more suitable."

That wasn't the first time he'd basically told me I needed a shower. I'd been sleeping, not working out.

His eyes dropped to my legs.

My skirt had bunched up, and now I was showing way too much thigh to my boss. But I also didn't move to push it lower, because the way his eyes were tracing my thighs made it a little hard to think straight.

"Mr. Remington?" I asked.

His eyes snapped back up to mine.

"I . . . this is the fanciest thing I have."

"Very well. I'll see you at seven p.m. sharp. In the dining room. It's off the kitchen."

I nodded and watched him walk away.

I pulled the hem of my skirt lower when I heard the door close behind him. What the hell was that? Why did everything he say and do unnerve me?

I needed to talk to Kehlani. She'd have some advice on how to handle him. I took one last look at the view before making my way back up to the house. The sun was just starting to set, and I couldn't help but think of Hudson's warning to not leave my room at night. *"Just . . . don't do it."* I shivered. But it was only because the temperature had already started to drop. I wasn't scared of this old house.

So why was I standing out here instead of getting ready? I wrapped my arms around myself and forced my feet to move toward the back door. Stepping inside felt like going back in time. Just like it had the first time I'd walked in. Instead of renovating the bathrooms, they should have torn the whole thing down and started from scratch.

I hurried to my room, locked the door behind me, and grabbed my phone. Kehlani answered in two rings.

"Tell me everything about her," Kehlani said before I even had a chance to say hello. "She's brilliant, right? Have you seen her new manuscript? Because I'm dying to know what happened to . . ."

"I didn't meet her yet," I said as I walked into the bathroom. "And I definitely didn't read what she's writing." *Oh, good God.* I stared at my reflection in the mirror. My hair was windswept but not in a sexy way. No wonder Mr. Remington had told me to freshen up. I grabbed a brush and put Kehlani on speaker.

"What do you mean you didn't meet her yet?" she asked.

"I had to sign a bunch of paperwork first. NDAs and stuff."

"Okay. But it's almost seven o'clock. What else did you do all day?"

"I began my tour of the grounds," I said in my terrible southern accent.

"Is something wrong with your throat?"

I laughed. Hudson would have thought it was funny. "Sorry, I'm working on my southern accent."

"Wow, that was terrible," she said with a laugh. "Is it a big estate? Are there statues? I always imagine rich people have statues of themselves in their gardens."

"That is an oddly specific belief."

"I think it's a thing."

"Well, you might be right, because I didn't get very far on my tour. I stopped at the most amazing infinity pool that overlooks the ocean . . ."

"Wait, you have an ocean view? It's been forever since I had a vacation. I'm so jealous."

"This is hardly a vacation. It's more of a nightmare."

"It can't be all that bad with an ocean view," Kehlani said.

"If you'd met Mr. Remington you'd understand."

"Oh, is he still being all sexy and brooding?"

I laughed. "I never said he was sexy."

"You never said he wasn't."

True.

"Aha! And you just paused."

"I didn't pause," I said.

"Girl, you so paused. Tell me everything."

I tried not to roll my eyes. "I swear, he's not my type."

"And what is your type, exactly? Because I'm pretty sure your type during college was a textbook."

"Hilarious," I said.

"So you want me to believe that you're holed up in this mansion with an ocean view and a hot guy and you're not going to tap that?"

"I one hundred percent am not going to tap that."

"Boo. Lame."

I laughed. "I didn't say I wasn't going to tap *anyone*. I actually met someone else today. He's funny and charming, and he invited me to an end-of-summer party on the beach on Friday."

"There are *two* sexy guys living there? What is your life right now?" she asked, practically screaming.

"I never said Mr. Remington was sexy."

"Your pause earlier said it all. But since you won't give me a full description of him, tell me about the other guy."

"Like I said, he's funny and charming."

"And . . . sexy."

"He's very handsome. You'd like him—he has abs of steel." I abandoned trying to fix my hair and pulled it into a messy bun. "Just like Mr. Remington," I said as I started to reapply my mascara. *Shit.* Had I just said that out loud?

Kehlani didn't respond.

Maybe I hadn't said it . . .

"Hazel, why have you seen your boss and sexy guy number two without their shirts on?"

Crap. "His name is Hudson. And he's the pool boy."

"That does not answer my entire question."

I sighed and walked out of the bathroom. "The power cut out last night while I was taking a bath. And there were all these creepy creaky noises. And I hadn't brought up any of my stuff from the car. And I panicked and left my room . . ."

"Naked?!"

"What? No. Why would I run out of my room butt naked?"

"Were you in only a towel?"

"I threw on my shirt and skirt that I'd worn earlier."

"The same shirt you were wearing when you left the city? The white one?"

"Don't you even say it. I know it's see-through when it's wet."

"I didn't say anything. Please continue."

I laughed. "There isn't much else to tell. I saw candlelight in the kitchen and ran into Mr. Remington. Literally. And he was in sweatpants and no shirt because it was after hours. End of story."

"Oh, I don't think you have that right at all. Hazel, you want to be an author one day, but you can't even see what's right in front of you. I think this story is just beginning."

"Definitely not."

"I can already see it. Love triangle."

"You're ridiculous," I said.

"And you're in a love triangle."

"Neither Hudson nor Mr. Remington is in love with me. And I'm definitely not in love with either of them."

"*Yet.* Hence why I said it was the beginning of the story."

She couldn't have been more wrong. But now I just wanted to mess with her. "Well, I'm sorry to cut you off, but I have a formal dinner with Mr. Remington I need to finish getting ready for."

"A formal dinner? Are the two of you going out?"

"Gotta go!"

"Wait, I need so many more details!"

I laughed. "I'll call you tomorrow and tell you all the sinful things he did to me on the middle of the table."

"I honestly can't even tell if you're messing with me right now."

"I'm definitely messing with you. But I do seriously need to go. I'm going to be late to this very normal dinner."

"Will Athena Quinn be there?"

Oh my God. I was so distracted talking about Hudson and Mr. Remington that I hadn't even thought about that possibility. "Maybe. Okay, I really gotta go. Love you."

"Love you too. Have fun with Mr. Remington."

Fun with Mr. Remington? Those words didn't belong in the same sentence. I tossed my phone on my bed and looked through my suitcase, just in case I could find something more *suitable*. I couldn't figure out why the dress code had never been mentioned in the dozens of emails we'd exchanged during the application process. It almost seemed like intentional sabotage.

I had one sundress. I wouldn't exactly describe it as formal. It was more something I would wear out by the pool. But it was probably better than my work clothes. And I had no idea what *formal* meant to Mr. Remington. If he showed up in a three-piece suit, I wouldn't be at all surprised.

I changed into the dress. It was definitely casual, but it was still pretty. I slid on a pair of high-heeled sandals in hopes that they would make it look a little fancier. *Much better.*

My heart was racing, and I honestly had no idea if it was because I was about to meet my future mentor or because I'd gotten a mental image stuck in a loop in my head of Mr. Remington on top of me in the middle of the dining room table.

CHAPTER 7

Monday—August 29

I walked through the kitchen, my high heels clicking on the floor.

There was an archway with a pair of closed doors that I guessed led to the dining room. I went to open one of the doors, but before I could, both flung backward with a *whoosh*.

Wow. The doors to this room should never have been closed. This had to be the most beautiful room in the house. I stepped inside and turned in a circle. The room was encased by floor-to-ceiling windows. Candles lit the length of a huge dining room table. The flickering light gave the whole space a romantic feel.

And the best part? There were three place settings, which meant . . .

"Miss Fox."

I spun around and caught sight of Mr. Remington standing there. And it was impossible to ignore how devastatingly handsome he was. The sleeves of his dress shirt were still rolled up. But he'd added a vest that matched his suit pants. It wasn't a three-piece suit but only because he was missing the jacket. The gold chain disappearing into his vest pocket made it even more sophisticated. I didn't realize anyone even owned pocket watches anymore. But I thought they should definitely bring them back.

"Hi," I said, breaking the silence. "I hope this is okay?" I gestured toward my dress.

His eyes traveled down my body as he closed the distance between us. He stopped only a foot away from me. I could smell the ocean on his skin.

"Just one thing," he said as his eyes dropped to my lips for a moment. I swallowed hard. "Yes?"

"Take them off." His voice came out even lower.

My eyes locked with his. *Wait, what is he asking me to take off?* I felt myself clench under his gaze. It looked like he was seconds away from devouring every inch of me. "What?"

"No shoes in the house. Remember?"

"Oh." *Oh.* Okay, definitely not what I thought he was talking about. "I'm so sorry. I forgot. I heard *formal* and . . ." For some reason, I felt frozen under his gaze. Had he known where my mind had gone?

"Allow me," he said and dropped to one knee in front of me.

My mind was still in the gutter as he leaned forward. His fingers traced my anklebone as he slowly undid the clasp on one of my heels. A shiver ran up my spine at his touch.

I felt his breath on my thigh as he shifted his hand to my other ankle.

If Kehlani had been here, she would have buried her fingers in his hair and pulled him closer. She probably would have ended up with him on top of her on the dining room table. But I wasn't Kehlani. And Mr. Remington was my boss. I kept my hands by my sides as he undid the other clasp.

"There," he said. He stood up and then grabbed my hand to help me step out of my shoes.

"Thank you," I said.

It was like all the air had been sucked out of the room as we stood still. He kept my hand in his as he stared down at me. And suddenly it didn't feel like my imagination was running wild. I swear, it looked like he actually wanted me on the table.

"Your hands are so cold," I said. It was the first thing that popped into my head to break the silence. And I immediately regretted it because he dropped my hand so quickly. Like his touch had burned me.

He cleared his throat. "Dinner's about to be served." He pulled out my chair for me.

No one had ever pulled a chair out for me before. I wished I could somehow ingrain this moment in my head so that the next time I went on a date, I'd remember that this was what I wanted. A proper gentleman. I sat down and he pushed my seat in. *Wait, the* next *date?* I watched him walk around the table. This wasn't a date. But it felt like it to me. Or maybe my lack of dates had really led me astray here. Or Kehlani had gotten in my head.

"I take it that you enjoyed your day?" he asked.

"Indeed, good sir."

He lowered his eyebrows at my response.

For a second there, I'd forgotten that, unlike Hudson, he didn't have a sense of humor. But he didn't look angry at me, like he had earlier. Or disappointed. He looked . . . hungry. For me.

Yeah, Kehlani had definitely gotten in my head. Mr. Remington hated me. Loathed me, really. He'd been trying to scare me out of this job last night. I dropped his gaze. "So is Athena Quinn joining us for dinner?"

"If she's feeling up to it. Sometimes she takes her meals in her quarters after a long day of writing."

"And what about the days when she does eat in here? What do the two of you talk about during dinner?"

"She mostly brainstorms what's happening next with the characters. Or complains about hate mail."

"Hate mail?"

"One of the things you'll be helping me handle. She wants us to screen her emails before she reads them each morning so she never sees any negativity. Same with the daily mail."

"Does she get a lot of it?"

"Hundreds of nasty messages a week."

"Really?" I mean . . . I wasn't exactly a megafan of her writing. But I'd never send her hate mail. There was no need to be rude.

"Really," he said.

I shook my head. People were ridiculous. "So do you help her brainstorm her stories?"

"I offer feedback, but it's more like she wants to talk it out. You'll see."

"I can't wait to meet her." I looked over at the door, hoping she'd walk in any second. "Are you a fan of her writing?"

"What's not to like?"

I eyed the door again. "Well, I mean . . . she hasn't had a big hit in years."

Mr. Remington snapped open his napkin, laying it carefully across his lap. "She's hit the *New York Times* list on all her latest releases. Half of them hit number one."

"Right, but . . . no one's talking about them. They only bought copies because of name recognition, not because the stories were riveting."

He lowered his eyebrows as he stared at me. "And *you're* an expert? You were a waitress before coming here, correct?"

"Yes. For the record, waitressing is hard work."

"I didn't say it wasn't." His clipped tone was enough proof of how he felt about my former profession, though.

"You have to be able to read people. Just like you do in order to write good characters."

"Writing is an art form, Miss Fox."

"I know that. And I wasn't just a waitress. I've been working on a manuscript during my free time."

"Dabbling at a typewriter hardly counts as being an author."

Everything he said was so pompous. "Well, I was using a laptop, since I'm not a million years old. And I'm not dabbling. I'm taking my time because I hope that my books actually mean something one day."

"Unlike Athena Quinn's books, you mean?"

"I didn't say that . . ."

"The movie based off her first book won an Oscar."

"I know. When I said her books weren't riveting, I was referring to her newer stuff. It's . . ."

"It's what?"

"Trivial."

"You're as bad as the supposed fans sending her daily hate mail."

"I'm not. I was merely saying that her earlier books . . ."

"Maybe hold your tongue instead of insulting the author who's paying your salary, Miss Fox." He said my name with such disdain.

So much for my fantasies of him taking me on the table. I pressed my lips together. I wasn't even trying to insult Athena Quinn. I was just trying to have an honest conversation with Mr. Remington. Athena Quinn's books *had* changed. Her first several books made me laugh and cry. I remembered sobbing all over my paperbacks. But her newer stuff didn't seem to have any heart. I wanted to talk to her about her process. Actually, I just wanted to speak to her. Period.

"I'm sorry," I said.

"Well, I'm not the one you should be apologizing to . . ." His voice trailed off as Miss Serrano rushed into the room. She lifted up the third place setting, and my heart sank. She sneaked a glance at Mr. Remington. Her eyes grew round, and then she ran out of the room.

"But it'll have to wait until another day," he said. "And I no longer have an appetite either. If you'll excuse me." He pushed his chair back and stood up.

"Mr. Remington," I said.

He paused on his way to the doors.

"I love dissecting books. I really meant no offense. Please . . . please don't tell her what I said. My best friend is actually her number one fan. All I hear all day is 'Athena Quinn this' and 'Athena Quinn that.' I hope to one day be half the author she is. And I need this job. I want to learn from the best. I'm so grateful for this opportunity."

"If there's one thing I'm good at, it's keeping secrets, Miss Fox. And your secret is safe with me. Now if you'll excuse me."

I didn't secretly hate Athena Quinn. I was just trying to have a conversation. But he was impossible. "You're really going to make me eat all alone in this huge dining room?"

"I think it's for the best," he said.

How was me being isolated for the best? He didn't want me to speak to anyone. And now I couldn't even speak to him?

For a split second, his eyes traveled to my lips again.

Or maybe I just imagined it. Because the next words out of his mouth definitely contradicted him wanting to kiss me.

"Maybe this will give you some time to ponder if you even want this opportunity. Because trust me when I say I can replace you in a heartbeat."

I blinked, and he was walking out of the room. Hadn't he heard anything I said? How much I wanted to learn from *the best*. I knew he wanted me gone. But I wasn't going to make that decision for him.

I'd thought tonight was going to be fun. I'd wanted to think of a clever way to call him by his first name. But everything had spiraled so out of control. And now I was scared to poke him at all.

Miss Serrano came running in carrying a tray covered with a silver cloche. She looked at Mr. Remington's empty seat and then back at me.

"Apparently I made him lose his appetite," I said.

For the first time since she'd met me, she looked like she relaxed. She put the cloche down in front of me.

"Do you want to join me?" I asked. "I'd love to get to know you."

Instead of responding, she ran out of the room. Literally sprinted.

What the hell was I doing wrong here? The only person who didn't seem to hate me was Hudson. And the end of summer was drawing closer. He'd probably be long gone soon. And then I'd be all alone in this huge house with my only friend hundreds of miles away in New York. I wanted to walk away. Run away like Miss Serrano. But I refused to give Mr. Remington the satisfaction.

I lifted the cloche and stared down at the most beautiful meal. I stabbed a piece of chicken and plopped it into my mouth. But I'd lost my appetite too. I pushed the plate aside.

I was a hypocrite. How could I critique any other literature if I couldn't even finish my own book? I grabbed my shoes and made my way back upstairs. My bare feet padded softly across the plush carpet at the top of the stairs. I looked behind me at the dip in the stairs separating this hall from the left wing. I was desperate to meet Athena Quinn. But tonight I was tiptoeing in the opposite direction of her private quarters.

I made my way past my own room and down the hall to the last door. The room I'd seen Mr. Remington disappear into yesterday.

For some reason, I found myself pressing my ear against the wooden door. I held my breath. I wasn't sure what I was hoping to hear. But I didn't hear a single thing. What was I even doing right now? I'd been on my own for two days and somehow turned into a stalker.

I hurried back toward my room. But I glanced back once more at Mr. Remington's room before inserting my key into my own door. I tossed my shoes on the ground, grabbed my laptop, and stepped out onto the little balcony. The salty air swirled around me as I plopped down into a chair and opened my computer.

My eyes scanned the few paragraphs I had written. Over a month ago. Athena Quinn's words weren't trivial. Mine were. I wasn't even a writer, and I already had writer's block.

I opened up a new document and stared at the blinking cursor. Mr. Remington was wrong about me. I wasn't just dabbling on a typewriter. I'd show him. I pictured the scowl on Mr. Remington's face. The way his fingers traced my ankle. His breath on my thigh.

And I started typing.

For the first time in ages.

Apparently Mr. Remington was my muse. *Screw me.*

I pushed the thought aside. It wasn't about that. I didn't like Mr. Remington. I was writing about him because of what he'd said at dinner. I'd pressed my ear against his door for the same reason.

Mr. Remington said he was good at keeping secrets. Which meant he had secrets to keep. And I was going to uncover every single one of them.

CHAPTER 8

Thursday—September 1

Every day this week had been exactly the same.

Mr. Remington had stopped coming to the formal dinners. But I still saw him every morning. He'd say one curt thing to me at breakfast to pretend to be polite, quickly followed by one rude thing after I asked him a personal question.

Then he'd have Miss Serrano deposit a trash bag full of mail next to me. He hadn't been kidding about Athena Quinn not going through it. And apparently he'd been hoarding it for months, waiting for his new assistant to do the dirty work. On the bright side, he promised that I'd be able to meet Athena Quinn once I finished. Hopefully she'd be in a good mood after reading only the kind words readers had sent her.

I heard Mr. Remington's footsteps and looked up from my breakfast.

"Happy September," I said as he walked into the small kitchen.

"Do you enjoy the fall, Miss Fox?"

"I do. It doesn't get enough credit. People are bitter about the end of summer and too down to realize that the fall is full of possibilities. I've never associated the falling leaves with the death of summer. I've always preferred jumping in them instead. And I'm quite the fan of Halloween."

I could have sworn that the corner of his mouth ticked up for just a moment.

"Mhm" was his only response. He sat down at the table and lifted his cloche. But he didn't pick up his fork. He just stared at the food like he was lost in thought.

"When's your birthday?" It wasn't my most subtle question, but he'd evaded all my others. *How long have you been working for Athena Quinn? Where did you grow up? What's really behind all the closed doors in Athena Quinn's wing? Are sitting and drawing rooms a southern thing or a* you *thing?*

He lowered his eyebrows at me.

"Don't be petulant, Mr. Remington. I'm just trying to get to know you. And horoscopes can reveal quite a bit about someone."

He sighed. "No. They can't."

"Of course they can."

He shook his head.

"I bet I can find out without you even telling me. I can just google your characteristics . . ."

"And what are my characteristics, Miss Fox?"

"You're short tempered. Moody. Passionate." I hadn't meant to say that last thing. It just slipped out because his dark eyes were boring into mine. I swallowed hard as the silence stretched between us.

"Is that all?" he asked.

I took a deep breath. "It's all you've let me see, *Atlas.*"

He lowered his eyebrows.

I tried to hide my smile as I bit into my bagel. I couldn't wait to tell Hudson about this. I'd run into him in the gardens yesterday and mentioned that I was waiting for the perfect moment to call Mr. Remington by his first name. Hudson and I were meeting up for the end-of-summer party on the beach tomorrow night. And I was excited for my first night out of this house.

"I take it you met my nephew?"

I shook my head.

"He stops by to clean the pool every now and then. And he works in the gardens."

Hudson is his nephew? I choked on my bagel.

"Swallow, Miss Fox."

The way he said it made me cough harder. I grabbed my coffee and took a huge sip to dislodge the piece of bagel. "Hudson is your nephew?" I managed to get out.

A yes was all he offered.

"But he . . . but you . . ." My voice trailed off. *What?* But God, now that he said it, they did look similar. The same dark hair and pale skin. "But he doesn't look that much younger than you."

"Well, he is."

"How old are you?" Now that I was staring at Mr. Remington's face, maybe he did look older than I first realized. I'd thought he was maybe five years older than me. Ten, tops. But honestly it was hard to tell. Being older certainly explained why he was sterner.

"Old enough to know that you should heed my warning. I told you not to talk to anyone. I said it several times, Miss Fox."

"Even your own nephew?"

"*Especially* my nephew."

"Why?"

"Because I said so."

I laughed. It was something my mother used to say when I was little. I swallowed hard. If my mother were still alive, she'd probably advise me to tell this guy off. *Because I said so* was not a good enough reason. "Well, I'm sorry to disappoint you, but I'm going out with him tomorrow night. There's this end-of-summer party on the beach, and I can't wait for a night out."

He lowered his eyebrows even further. "You're going out with Hudson? On a date?"

"That's what I just said."

"I don't think that's a good idea, Miss Fox. You shouldn't be wandering around the beach at night."

"Funny. Hudson said the same thing about wandering around this house past dusk."

"Did he?"

"Apparently I'm not safe anywhere at night, so I might as well explore a bit. I haven't seen any of the island but this estate. And it's not like I'm wandering around alone. I'll be with Hudson."

Mr. Remington placed the cloche back over his plate, even though he hadn't touched the food. "Miss Serrano will be in with your work for the day in a moment. If you need me today, I left my number on the counter. I have a few errands I need to run. I'll be back before dinner."

"Errands for Athena Quinn? Could I come?"

"No."

I wasn't sure if he meant no because the errands weren't for Athena Quinn or no because I couldn't come. Probably both.

"And I'd appreciate if you stuck to Athena Quinn's rules." He stood up. "How is dating Hudson outside of work hours any of her business?"

"I'm referring to how you address me, *Miss Fox*." He walked out of the kitchen without another word.

Well, that hadn't gone very well. Did he hate his first name or something? Atlas was a really sexy name. *Stop it.* Nothing about that man was sexy. And his mysterious errands had me even more curious. Despite my morning questioning all week, I still hadn't discovered a single personal thing about him. All I'd done was piss him off even more.

Miss Serrano came in and plopped the trash bag full of mail next to me.

"He's in an extra sour mood today," I said.

She ignored me, as usual.

I finished my meal in silence. I had expected this job to be fast paced, energetic, and exciting. But most of it was solitary. Boring. Unimportant. And it involved a lot of eating alone.

I grabbed Mr. Remington's phone number from the counter. I was about to put it in my pocket, but then I paused. He had a 917 area code. And even though I'd lived in New York City for only a couple of months, I knew that was an NYC area code. Not one from South Carolina. It was my first real dose of information about him.

All I could find on Google when I searched "Atlas Remington" was a bunch of stuff about a firearms manufacturer.

I grabbed the trash bag full of mail as I scoured Google for information about a Mr. Atlas Remington of NYC. But it just brought up a bunch of pictures of the Atlas statue at Rockefeller Center.

I deposited the bag of mail on the lounge chair and sat down. Picture after picture of that statue. I pulled up one of the articles about the statue. Atlas was a demigod. Half-man, half-god. He carried the world on his shoulders as punishment.

Was that what made Mr. Remington so moody? Because he was carrying the weight of the world on his shoulders? Or maybe it was the weight of his secret that he was half-man, half-god.

The sun went behind a cloud, and I looked up at the sky. The sun had been shining all week, ever since the storm had cleared. But the clouds were back again today. It was like they reflected Mr. Remington's mood.

I shook my head. Everyone carried problems on their shoulders. That didn't make Mr. Remington unique or give him an excuse to be cruel. And he certainly wasn't half-god. More like half-devil.

I opened up the trash bag and started rummaging through the mail. So far, about three-fourths of the mail could be considered hate mail. Hopefully this last bag would be a little nicer.

I thought I saw movement out of the corner of my eye and looked back up at the house. A curtain was falling into place on Athena Quinn's wing.

It wasn't the first time I thought she'd been watching me. If she was so curious, why wouldn't she come out and introduce herself?

I picked up another envelope and opened it.

The heroine in your last novel was such an idiot. Any rational person wouldn't have made mistake after mistake. I was glad she died. And why haven't you responded to me on social media? I wrote to you three times. Don't you know that you can't improve your writing without criticism? You need to learn to . . .

I stopped reading. *Another hateful troll.* At least that letter wasn't as mean as the last one. And Athena Quinn's characters weren't idiots. They were real. And that meant their lives were messy and raw. They made mistakes and grew. I thought they were bold and daring. I certainly respected that. I actually related to many of her female protagonists. And I bet Athena Quinn related to them too, or she wouldn't have written them into existence.

This supposed fan was basically calling Athena Quinn an idiot if they were calling her character an idiot. *And me.* I shook away the thought. This wasn't about me. But even I felt a little berated after all these letters. Athena Quinn didn't need unconstructive criticism that attacked her on a personal level.

I tossed the letter into the throwaway pile and looked back up at the house. I kind of got why Athena Quinn didn't leave her estate. If this many people hated me, I'd find it hard to leave too.

But she didn't have to be scared of me. I respected her. I wanted to learn from her. And at this point, I'd give anything to meet her.

I bit the inside of my lip. Mr. Remington was off running errands. And it wasn't like Miss Serrano would dare speak and rat me out. I thought it was about time I explored Athena Quinn's private wing.

CHAPTER 9

Thursday—September 1

I tiptoed up the staircase. When it separated in the middle, I went left instead of right. I looked both ways when I reached the landing. But I knew no one was going to see me. Mr. Remington was out. Miss Serrano was probably busy hiding in a closet or something. And I'd seen the curtain move two windows over from the one at the top of the staircase. Which meant the room behind door number one wasn't occupied.

I slowly reached out to touch the knob, like it might shock me. But it was just normal, cold metal. Cold *unlocked* metal. Because Mr. Remington was a liar. He was right about one thing, though: if Athena Quinn wanted more privacy, she probably should have locked all the doors to her personal quarters.

The door creaked on its hinges, and I cringed. Instead of waiting to see if Athena Quinn would pop out from the room next door, I hurried in and closed the door behind me. I exhaled slowly. That had been close. I didn't want to get fired the first time I met her.

I blinked, but I couldn't make out anything. The curtains were drawn so tightly that the whole room was pitch black. My hand ran along the wall until I found the light switch. The room lit up, revealing . . . well, I wasn't entirely sure. There were just a bunch of large objects covered in white sheets. And they were all perfectly spaced out and arranged in a circle.

I lifted a corner of one of the sheets. *Oh my God.* I pulled the sheet entirely off the sculpture. I wasn't a huge art fan, but this had to be the most beautiful sculpture I had ever seen. It actually felt like my heart was breaking as I stared at it. A woman wrapped in a classic Greek chiton leaned over a book, completely engrossed in the words on the page. And there were tears on her cheeks. I reached out and ran my finger along one of the protruding tears.

This was what I wanted my books to one day convey. This feeling. Of being completely consumed.

I lifted a corner of another sheet. The figure beneath had wings erupting from her back. It was definitely based on a different model. But just like the first, it featured a book. And tears stained the woman's face.

All the sculptures were variations on the same theme: a beautiful woman weeping over a novel. Six sculptures in total. Each as breathtaking as the last. The tearstained faces were haunting.

I let the last sheet fall back into place. Why were these statues here? Shouldn't they have been in a museum? But I guessed that if Athena Quinn never left the house, she kind of had to bring the art to her. It seemed almost sinful to keep all these things for one set of eyes.

My heart felt weird in my chest as I turned the lights off and tiptoed back out of the room. I'd been expecting to find answers. But now I just felt confused. My heart ached for the weeping women, which I suppose was a testament to the artist's skill. I looked toward the closed room I knew Athena Quinn was in. But I couldn't just barge in on her. I walked across the hall and opened another door instead.

I stepped in and closed it behind me, draping the room in darkness. I flicked on the lights and spun around. I was standing in a library, the shelves stretching from floor to ceiling. Two walls were covered in old, leather-bound books, and one wall of shelves was filled completely with Athena Quinn's extensive works. The bright colors on their spines made them stand out from the classically bound books. Her novels didn't look like they even belonged in the same room as the other works.

I walked over to one wall of old books. I glanced at a few of the shelves. *Wait.* I moved to the next bookshelf and examined the contents. I pulled one of the books from the shelf and flipped to the first page.

The library was huge, but there were several editions of each book. And only three authors were featured.

Athena Quinn.

Luca Armani, a famous poet from the nineteenth century.

And Finn Bauer, one of the most acclaimed thriller authors who ever lived.

I looked back down at the page to which I'd opened the book and realized I was currently holding a first edition of one of Luca Armani's books of poetry. I gently replaced it on the shelf and grabbed one of Finn Bauer's. It was a first edition too. I turned in a circle and stared at the immense collection.

There must have been hundreds of thousands of dollars' worth of first editions lining the shelves. But then my eyes landed on Luca Armani's first work. *Oh my God.* Two of them. Both first editions. Scratch the hundreds of thousands. This library had to have cost millions.

I stared down at the Finn Bauer book in my hands. A special-edition copy of one of his books from the '60s. *I should not be touching this right now.* But for some reason I kept staring down at it instead of putting it back on the shelf. I flipped to the first page. It felt like I was holding history in my hands. And I didn't want to let go.

I knew Athena Quinn loved romance. Poetry wasn't a huge leap from there. But I was fascinated that she loved thrillers too. That was what I wanted to write. I finally had my in. Finn Bauer was what we could bond over. And maybe once we connected over our love for thrillers, she'd agree to look at mine. Well, my current work in progress. It would be a completed thriller one day, though. Hopefully with her guidance and mentoring.

The sound of gravel crunching made me jump. *Shit.* I pulled the curtain back to look at the circular drive. Mr. Remington was climbing out of his car. *Shit, shit, shit!*

I shoved the book back on the shelf and ran out of the room. I was able to close the door and run to the correct side of the staircase right before Mr. Remington walked through the front door.

"What were you doing?" Mr. Remington asked when he saw me walking down the stairs.

"Using the bathroom."

He lowered his eyebrows as he watched me come down the stairs.

"The one in your room?" he asked.

"Of course. I actually don't even know where any other bathrooms are."

"Good," he said.

"Good? Honestly, it's not great. What if I have a bathroom emergency and need a closer one?" *Good God, why?* Why had I just said that out loud? I'd been trying to think fast of a way to distract him from the fact that I'd been upstairs snooping. But talking about bathroom emergencies was definitely not the best approach.

"What exactly does a bathroom emergency entail, Miss Fox?"

"You . . . don't want to know." *Stop! What is wrong with me?*

He smiled for a split second.

"You're probably correct." He cleared his throat. "I grabbed a few things for you at the store. I'll set them by your door."

"You got something for me?"

He waved his hand, dismissing my comment. "Just necessities."

We both stared at each other. So, like . . . toilet paper? Because if he hadn't bought me extra yet, he certainly would after this conversation. "Well, thank you, Mr. Remington."

"I won't keep you. I know you have work to do."

"Right! Back to work with me." I took the out and walked past him. Before I entered the kitchen, I looked back over my shoulder. He was staring up at the stairs, like he was mentally retracing my steps. But there was no way he could know what I'd done. I'd put all the sheets back on the sculptures. And I'd put the books back exactly where I'd found them.

I think.

The thought nagged at me for the rest of the day. Had I put everything back exactly how I'd found it?

I tried to dismiss the worry as I read through another letter. This one started out positive and quickly became negative, like some kind of dirty trick. Flattery followed by a sucker punch. I tossed it in the discard pile with the other hateful trolls.

But the good news was that I was almost done going through them, which meant that tomorrow I'd finally meet Athena Quinn. I had gone to grab another letter when I saw a light turn on in the house. In the window right next to the staircase. The room I'd been in with all the beautiful sculptures.

Fuck.

I kept my head down and pretended to stare at another letter. But really I was watching the room. There was just a sliver of light coming from between the curtains. I held my breath, slowly dying inside. I'd put the sheets back. I had. Athena Quinn couldn't possibly know. But the light stayed on.

I'm so getting fired.

Finally, the light turned off. I half expected screaming. Athena Quinn had so many rules. She wanted everything just so. Mr. Remington had spoken of her wrath before.

But . . . everything was eerily quiet. Even the crashing of waves in the distance seemed hushed.

Maybe Athena Quinn hadn't noticed I'd invaded her space. Maybe everything was fine. *Maybe . . .*

I didn't want to get fired before I officially met her. The alarm on my phone went off, and I must have jumped at least a foot. *Jesus.* I quickly turned it off and scanned the last few fan letters. *Trash people.* I tossed the last few in the pile meant to never see the light of day. That left ten letters for Athena Quinn's eyes. Ten kind people in the world.

Out of hundreds. Honestly, that sounded about right. People said the world was cruel for a reason. I shoved the hateful mail back into the trash bag, grabbed the nice letters, and headed inside.

The house was even quieter than it had been outside. Not a single noise to distract me from my heart racing. I had this horrible feeling that I was finally about to meet Athena Quinn. She would come to dinner for the first time just to fire me.

I sighed and put the nice letters on the counter, then dropped the trash bag on the ground by the trash bin.

At least I had plenty of time to get ready for my own firing. I climbed the stairs, and my hand paused at the top of the railing. Just staring at Athena Quinn's wing made me feel sick to my stomach. I should have left it alone. I should have stuck to uncovering Mr. Remington's secrets instead. He hadn't fired me yet, and he loathed me. I wasn't sure what his tipping point would be, but now I was worried I wouldn't get a chance to find out.

I shook my head and turned down the staff wing. There were half a dozen shopping bags sitting outside my door. For a second, I thought they contained more hate mail, but when I peered inside one of the bags, I was even more confused. *What the* . . .

Inside was a white box tied with a beautiful red satin bow. This did not look like toilet paper.

CHAPTER 10

Thursday—September 1

I locked my door behind me and deposited the shopping bags on my bed. I peeked inside another bag. It was filled with a couple of boxes too. All had the same white finish and red satin bow. I stared at them for a moment and then called Kehlani.

"Have you screwed your new boss yet?" she asked instead of greeting me.

"Very funny. That is absolutely not happening. But . . ."

"But *what?* Oh my God, something happened, didn't it? Tell me everything."

"Nothing happened. But he bought me something. *Somethings*, actually."

"What did he buy you?"

"I don't know. He mentioned that he picked me up some necessities, but when I got back to my room, there were tons of shopping bags filled with these fancy boxes with bows."

"What's inside of them?"

"I don't know. I kept all the boxes in their bags. I feel like he probably dropped them off at the wrong room. Or maybe Miss Serrano was confused and dropped them off here instead of at Athena Quinn's door."

61

"Miss Serrano?"

"She's the housekeeper."

"Well, why don't you just ask her?"

"She doesn't speak."

There was an awkward pause. "What do you mean she doesn't speak? Is she mute?"

"I don't know. I have a feeling she's just scared."

"Of Mr. Remington?"

"Or Athena Quinn. Or both." I wasn't scared of Mr. Remington. I just thought he was rude. But I was a little scared of Athena Quinn. Heck, I'd just been worrying she was going to fire me. Or start screaming or something.

"Have you tried talking to her?"

"Athena Quinn? Or Miss Serrano?"

"Well, both. But I was asking about Miss Serrano."

"Of course I have. But she literally runs away from me."

"Your face is quite frightening . . . ," Kehlani said with a laugh.

I couldn't help but laugh too. "My face is fine."

"I know. You're gorgeous. Whatever. Open the boxes."

"I'm not going to open them . . ."

"He told you he'd bought you some things. They're definitely for you. How much stuff is it, exactly?"

"I don't know. Hold on." I balanced my cell phone on my shoulder as I pulled out box after box after box. "There's a ton of boxes." My fingers paused on one of the last boxes. There was an envelope stuck beneath the satin ribbon. "Wait, I think there's a note."

"Open it!"

"But what if it's not for me?"

"But what if it *is* for you? Open it. Open it!" she yelled again.

The envelope wasn't sealed. I wouldn't have opened it otherwise. But it would be easy enough to replace the card if it wasn't for me. I pulled out the plain white card and read the note.

Miss Fox,

In case you'd like something more suitable to wear.

—*Mr. Remington*

More suitable? My jaw actually dropped. *What the actual fuck is this?*
"Well . . . the boxes are for me."

"What did the note say?"

"He is such an asshole."

"Girl, the note did not say that. Tell me what he wrote. I'm slowly dying here."

I shook my head. "And I quote: 'Miss Fox. In case you'd like something more suitable to wear.' Signed 'Mr. Remington.'"

"That's so hot," Kehlani said.

"What? No, it's not, Kehlani. It's rude. The clothes I wear are plenty suitable."

"Eh . . ."

"Don't even with me."

"You have one nice skirt and a sundress."

"I like my clothes."

"Well, apparently Mr. Remington does not."

Ugh. "I don't care what he does and does not like."

"You sound very defensive right now. Kind of like you *do* care what he does and does not like."

"I don't care. Mr. Remington can go fuck himself."

"As opposed to you fucking him?"

"Stop it."

"You stop it," Kehlani said. "He's gotten you so worked up. I'm not even there, and I can feel the chemistry. Would you open one of the boxes already?"

"I don't want any of this crap."

"You don't even know what's in the boxes yet. It would be rude to refuse his presents. They're probably a peace offering."

"Peace offering, my ass."

"Open just one. Pretty please."

"Fine. But I'm going to hate it."

"You're bad at receiving gifts, Hazel."

This had nothing to do with me. It was some kind of sick power play by Mr. Remington. I shook my head and pulled an end of one of the bows. The satin dropped away. I lifted the lid and pushed aside the tissue paper. I picked up the dress and had to hold it up pretty high to keep the hem from dragging on the ground. It was a beautiful burgundy color. "It's a dress." A really pretty dress. One that I couldn't possibly accept.

"Try it on."

"I . . . can't. It's too much." I searched for a price tag, but it had been removed.

"Come on. Pics or it didn't happen."

I laughed. "Fine. Give me one second." I pulled off my blouse and pencil skirt. It was a wrap dress with a low neckline and a long slit up the left side, with slits up the sides of the fluttering short sleeves too. It was somehow sexy and reserved at the same time. It was almost old-fashioned looking. I stared at my reflection in the floor-length mirror. The hem of the skirt just brushed the ground when I was barefoot. It was a perfect fit. I didn't own anything like it. I swallowed hard. And I hated how much I loved it.

"Picture, please," Kehlani said.

I snapped a photo in the mirror and sent it to her.

"Wow. It fits you like a glove. And that color makes the green in your eyes pop."

Yeah. I wore different shades of red a lot because it made my eyes look more green than hazel.

"Mr. Remington has good taste. Specifically tailored to you. He's definitely been observing you."

"He definitely hasn't been observing me. Unless you count when he's scowling."

"Oh, that's the best kind of staring."

I shook my head.

"He's going to drool when you wear that down to dinner tonight."

"No, he won't. One, because he hasn't joined me for dinner since the first night. And two, because I'm not wearing it."

"What do you mean you're not wearing it?"

"There's no price tag, but it came in a beautiful box with an equally beautiful ribbon. And there was tissue paper in it. Tissue paper, Kehlani. It's way out of my price range."

"Which doesn't matter because it was a gift. What's in the other boxes?"

"I'm not . . ."

"Just look. Come on. You know you want to."

"You're a terrible influence on me."

"I know. Do it."

I laughed and opened up another box. And another. There were dresses, skirts, and even some more casual clothes, like jeans and super-soft V-neck sweaters. I wasn't usually a sweater person, but this one was one of the softest materials I'd ever touched. And I knew the weather was going to be growing colder soon. I bit the inside of my lip as I stared at the huge stack of clothes on my bed. It was more clothing than I'd brought with me.

"You have to keep it all," Kehlani said.

"Not happening. I'll put it all back and . . ."

"That would be incredibly rude. Wear the burgundy dress to dinner. Make him drool. It's time to officially kick off this love triangle."

I cringed. "Oh God, I forgot to tell you. Hudson is Mr. Remington's nephew."

Kehlani gasped. "Plot twist!"

"Seriously, stop it."

"That probably takes a threesome off the table . . ."

"Come on. I'm not dating either of them. I'm hanging out with Hudson tomorrow night, but it's casual."

"Mhm," she said with all the sass in the world.

"It's a group thing down on the beach."

"Mhm," she said again.

"He's not even picking me up. And don't you dare say 'mhm' again. It's more of a friendship thing, I think."

"Just like you think Mr. Remington was simply being nice by buying you all these fabulous clothes?"

"I don't think he's being nice. I think he's being controlling."

"Wear the dress, Hazel."

"No."

"You're being ridiculous."

"I'm being reasonable. I'll go shopping this weekend and . . ."

"If you take it off, I'll never speak to you again. Unless you're taking it off so you can go to dinner full nude. Now *that* would make him drool."

I laughed. "I'm not going to dinner naked. And I don't believe you."

"I'm serious. I won't answer a single emergency call. I'll leave you on your own in that big scary house to languish away."

I opened my mouth and then closed it again. "But . . ."

"Please. Do it for me. I'm living vicariously through you right now. You're literally living in a romance novel . . ."

"Stop it. I'll wear the dress. Just cut it out with the romance novel stuff. I have a hateful boss and a new friend."

"You're lying to yourself, but fine. If you wear the dress, I'll stop talking about it."

"You swear?"

"Yeah, I'll stop talking about it. For a day," she said really quickly. "Gotta go, bye! Wear the dress!"

"For a day, what?"

But she'd already hung up.

I tossed my phone on the bed and stared back at my reflection in the mirror. This had to be some kind of game to Mr. Remington. But I really loved this dress. And I'd be lying to myself if I said there wasn't a small piece of me that wanted Mr. Remington to love how this dress looked on me. I shook the thought away. Mr. Remington was my boss. My boss who I was pretty sure hated me.

So why did I keep thinking about how good his fingers had felt as they traced my ankle? Just one small touch had turned me on more than I'd like to admit. And his breath on my thigh? In that moment, I'd wanted it to be more. In my dreams he'd kissed my thigh. Higher and higher.

I sighed. There was no point in thinking about that. A kiss from Mr. Remington wouldn't be sweet. It would be sinful like him. God, why did the thought of it being sinful sound even better than it being sweet?

∽∾

The dining room was empty. I sat down at the long table all by myself.

I'd worn the dress. Not because of Kehlani's threat—she'd never stop speaking to me—but because I thought wearing a fancy dress would make meeting and subsequently getting fired by Athena Quinn at least a little more dignified.

But Athena Quinn wasn't here. Neither was Mr. Remington. And there was only one place setting again this evening. *Mine.*

I lifted up the cloche. Miss Serrano was an amazing cook. I was sure the chicken parmesan with the heaping side of pasta would be delicious. But I wasn't hungry tonight. I was a nervous mess, and my nerves had spread into my stomach. I looked down at the slit in my dress, which had ridden up when I sat down. It almost touched my hip bone. What the hell was I doing?

I needed to get out of this dress. I'd package everything up to be returned and bring it down to breakfast tomorrow for Mr. Remington. If I still had a job. Maybe Athena Quinn would leave me a notice of termination on my door tonight. Or maybe she'd tell Mr. Remington to axe me himself. I stood up to leave.

The floorboards creaked, and I turned to see Mr. Remington standing in the doorway. His hair was more mussed up than usual, like he'd been running his fingers through it. Or maybe he'd just been out walking along the beach. For some reason I looked down at his bare feet.

"Miss Fox," he said.

"Mr. Remington."

"Were you leaving? Aren't you hungry?"

I pressed my lips together. "I don't really like eating alone."

He walked toward me. "Well, I'm here." My heart raced faster with each step closer. He hadn't said a word about my dress. I wasn't expecting a compliment or anything. What if it wasn't for me? What if he didn't know how to tell me I'd made a terrible mistake by putting it on?

He stopped right in front of me.

"Thank you for the clothes, Mr. Remington. But it's too much. If you could return . . ."

"The dress fits you perfectly, Miss Fox."

It felt like my heart was beating in my throat as his eyes trailed down my body. "I'll pay for this dress. But I can't afford the rest."

"They were gifts."

"That's very kind, Mr. Remington, but I can't accept them."

"Do you not like the clothes?"

"No, I love them. But it's too much. I'll go shopping myself this weekend."

"That won't be necessary. If there's anything else you need, just let me know."

I stared at him.

"Please, sit." He pulled my chair out a little farther.

I still wasn't hungry. But I wasn't done with this conversation.

He put his hand out to help me sit down.

I didn't need help. But I was growing a little addicted to the way his cold skin made a shiver run down my spine. I slid my hand into his and pictured him the first time he'd eaten dinner with me. When he knelt in front of me to remove my high heels, his lips only inches away from my thighs. I swallowed hard and tried to ignore the way his touch affected me.

He slowly dropped my hand and slid my chair in.

For just a second, I thought I felt his breath on the side of my neck. I turned to look at him. But he was already rounding the table. My imagination was running wild. I think there was a small piece of me that hoped he'd kneel in front of me again and do what I thought he'd been about to do the other night. Just a really small part. *What is wrong with me?* I tried to shake the thought away. I definitely *did not* want him to do that again.

He sat down across from me and stared into my eyes.

I stared back. He was going to fire me . . . *right?* He was just looking for the right words? But he didn't break the silence.

I cleared my throat. "How did you know my size?"

"I guessed."

"There's no way. This dress fits me perfectly." Kehlani said he'd been looking at me. "Did you sneak into my room or something?"

"Miss Fox, I don't make a habit of sneaking into rooms where I'm not supposed to be."

Holy shit. I pressed my lips together. *He knows. He definitely knows.*

"Why do you look scared?"

"Do I?" My voice gave me away completely. Why was he torturing me? *Just get it over with.*

He nodded. "You look utterly terrified. Am I really that scary?"

I wasn't scared of him. I was scared of Athena Quinn and of getting fired before my job even really began. "I'm not scared of you, Mr. Remington."

"Are you sure about that?"

"Do you want me to be afraid?"

He lowered his eyebrows as he stared at me. "It's good to approach strangers cautiously, don't you agree?"

"We're hardly strangers. We've lived together for several days." I laughed, but it came out forced.

"Acquaintances, then."

"Is it often that an acquaintance buys another acquaintance clothes?"

He put his elbows on the table and leaned forward slightly. "If it's required."

"My clothes were perfectly suitable, Mr. Remington."

"I like this on you better."

I hadn't taken a bite of food, but it felt like my throat was clogged. I coughed and grabbed my water glass.

He stared at me as I drank, like he was studying an odd creature.

"I think it would be best if you returned the rest of the clothes," I said.

"If you don't want them, give them back to me, and I'll throw them in the trash."

What? "I'm not going to let you throw them in the garbage. They're surely worth a small fortune."

"Then I guess you're keeping them."

I opened my mouth and then closed it again. That was a terrible argument. Either I kept them or he trashed them? The clothes were beautiful. They didn't deserve to be in a dumpster full of hate mail.

"You said you needed an audience."

What?

He must have noticed my confused expression because he nodded at my untouched plate. "To eat, Miss Fox."

"That wasn't what I said." He was acting like it was odd for me to want company while I ate. I was almost certain that was a pretty normal thing.

He didn't respond.

"I'll wait until your food comes out," I said.

"That won't be necessary. Please eat."

I eyed the door, hoping Miss Serrano was seconds away from appearing with another plate. But the doorway remained empty. And

Mr. Remington's stare was making my stomach feel strange. Maybe I did need some food.

"Now, Miss Fox."

I cut into my piece of chicken. And I was very aware of how Mr. Remington watched me as I put it in my mouth. His eyes were locked on my lips. Mr. Remington was always intense. But there was something different about the intensity of his gaze tonight.

His gaze traveled down my throat as I swallowed.

"Will you be here for dinner tomorrow night?" he asked, then quickly added, "Miss Serrano will want to know."

It kind of seemed like *he* wanted to know. He couldn't possibly be offended that I wasn't joining him for dinner tomorrow. He'd ditched me the last two days. "I'll probably just grab something small before I head down to the beach."

"Very well. I'll let her know."

"Okay."

"I need to go out of town for the day."

"Tomorrow?"

He stared at me for a moment. "No, I'm leaving tonight. In just a minute."

"Is it some kind of emergency?"

"No" was all he offered.

I smiled at him. "Is it another mysterious errand that's going to end with a ton of clothes showing up outside my room?"

"No, Miss Fox."

I pressed my lips together. I'd forgotten that Mr. Remington had no sense of humor. I wondered if he even knew how to laugh.

"I assume I can trust you to follow the rules in my absence?" he asked.

God, he so knows what I did. "Mhm," I said, my throat making a weird squeaking noise.

His eyes drifted to my neck again, like he was trying to figure out where the noise was coming from.

"Is it a business trip?"

"No. It's more for pleasure."

The way he said *pleasure* made me swallow hard. Was he going on a date with someone? I wasn't sure why, but the thought made my heart sink. And I realized why I'd been feeling so weird around him. It wasn't because I was nervous that I was about to be fired. I had butterflies dancing around in my stomach. *Damn it, Kehlani.* My stomach was betraying me. I did not like my boss. And even if I did, it wouldn't matter. He was seeing someone else. And he was my boss. And he was the freaking worst.

"I hope you have fun on your trip," I said.

"I intend to."

Well, now he was just rubbing it in.

"I should be off." He stood up. "But Miss Fox?"

"Yes?"

"Do be careful tomorrow. Despite what Hudson has told you, the beach at night is much more dangerous than this house. Trust me on this."

I nodded. I didn't trust him. But for some reason, his words had me feeling nervous all over again. I bit the inside of my lip. So he was going on some overnight adventure, and he wanted me to proceed cautiously with Hudson? He was clearly trying to get in my head. But for what reason, I had no idea.

"I bid you farewell, Miss Fox."

"Good night," I said to his back as he left the room.

I wanted to have learned my lesson about snooping. But I hadn't gotten in trouble. And Mr. Remington had just told me he'd be gone for a whole day. He'd given me inspiration for the hero of my novel, but I still hadn't learned a single thing about the man. Without knowing more, I was afraid my inspiration would run dry.

It was about time I took matters into my own hands.

CHAPTER 11

Friday—September 2

I walked up the stairs and went right at the split. Miss Serrano was cooking something in the second kitchen. Athena Quinn was most likely over in her wing of the house, holed up somewhere writing. And I had absolutely nothing better to do. If Mr. Remington didn't want me to explore, he probably should have left me with some work.

I'd tried to talk myself out of it. I'd already almost gotten caught snooping once. For a few minutes last night, I'd thought Mr. Remington had known what I'd done. But he hadn't fired me. Instead, he'd left for the day. He was practically begging me to snoop again.

Maybe it's a trap. It was definitely possible that he suspected I'd been in a room where I wasn't allowed, and this was all an elaborate ploy to catch me red-handed. But whenever I got an idea stuck in my head, I had a hard time shaking it.

When I'd first arrived at the mansion, I'd been dying to know more about Athena Quinn. Desperate for just one conversation. Somewhere in the past few days, though, my thoughts had shifted. I understood Athena Quinn even without meeting her face-to-face. She ostracized herself from the world because the world was hateful to her. So she brought museums to her. Libraries to her. The whole world to her. She never left her estate. Hell, she never even left her private wing. All for good reason.

But Mr. Remington? I didn't understand him at all. And unlike Athena Quinn, there wasn't a shred of information about him online. Not even in the context of being Athena Quinn's assistant.

I looked over my shoulder as I walked past my room. But no one was following me. The only person in this house who didn't like me was on some kind of pleasure trip.

I pulled two bobby pins out of my hair and looked behind me once more before crouching in front of Mr. Remington's door. Last night I'd researched lock picking. And, honestly, it didn't seem that hard.

It didn't take me long to realize it was harder than it looked in the videos, though. Maybe it was because the lock was so different from the one in the videos. It was like the one on my door . . . one made to be unlocked with a huge old key. I jiggled one of the bobby pins in the lock again. *Come on.* I remembered something about adjusting my tension. Or was it torsion?

My phone started ringing, and I dropped both bobby pins. *Shit, shit, shit!*

I grabbed my phone and answered it so the ringtone would stop echoing around the hall. "What?" I whispered without even glancing down to see who was calling. I was more concerned about looking around to make sure no one was about to see me kneeling in front of Mr. Remington's door. God, I was so screwed. I searched the ground for the bobby pins, but I could find only one. *Damn it!*

"Happy almost-weekend to you too," Kehlani said.

I couldn't stay here after the racket I'd caused. I ran back to my room, hoping that no one else would find the unrecovered bobby pin.

"Why are you breathing so hard?" she asked.

I closed my door and locked it behind me. "I was trying to break into Mr. Remington's room when—"

"Excuse me?"

"Like you're not dying to know more about him too."

Kehlani laughed. "I am. But I was under the impression that you weren't. Does that mean dinner went well last night?"

"No, it means that he's gone for the day, and I want to uncover all his secrets."

"I don't believe you," she said. "I think you have feelings for him."

"The only feelings I have regarding Mr. Remington are negative ones. Kehlani, I'm going on a date with his nephew tonight. What else could I possibly do to prove to you that I don't like the man?"

"I don't know. I'm just really caught up on the whole sneaking-into-his-room thing."

"Don't you have better things to do than assess my love life? It's the middle of the day."

She laughed. "It's my lunch break."

I sighed and collapsed on my bed. "Why is every room in this house unlocked except for his?"

"Are you sure it was locked?"

"Yeah, I . . ."

Kehlani laughed. "You didn't check, did you?"

Son of a bitch. "No. I just assumed it would be."

"I have fifteen minutes before I need to get back to work. And I won't be able to concentrate if you don't go back and look to see if it's locked."

"Fine. But only if you admit that I don't have feelings for Mr. Remington."

"Are we talking about your boss or the pool boy? Because I believe they'd both respond to *Mr. Remington.*"

"Ugh, I didn't think of that. But I'm specifically referring to Atlas." I opened my bedroom door and looked both ways.

"Such a sexy name."

"Stop it," I hissed as I sneaked back down the hall toward Mr. Remington's room.

"Have you snapped a picture of him yet? Because I really need to see what we're working with here."

I didn't bother to tell her to cut it out again. I knew she wouldn't listen. I grabbed the doorknob and turned. And it opened without protest. The hinges squeaked as the door flew back.

"It wasn't locked," I said as I hurried into the room and closed the door behind me. The shades were drawn, but I easily found the lights.

"So . . . what are we looking for, exactly?" Kehlani asked.

I didn't reply. I was a little distracted by the fact that there was no bed. "Um . . ."

"What? Did you find something weird?"

"Kind of." I looked around the room like there'd somehow be a bed hiding in one of the corners or tucked up into the wall Murphy-bed style. "There's no bed."

"You must have the wrong room," Kehlani said.

"No, I definitely saw him go into this room after he said good night to me." The last room in the hall to the right.

"That can't be right if there's no bed."

I shook my head, even though she couldn't see. I didn't have the wrong room. This was definitely it. I walked over to a dresser that was similar to the one in my room and opened it. The top drawer was filled with ties. I pushed a few aside, hoping to find something beneath them. But I really didn't know what I was looking for. The second drawer was filled with boxers. I quickly closed it and walked over to the closet. His was double the size of mine. And there were white dress shirts, suits, and even a few tuxedos. There were fancy shoes lining the floor of the closet, even though I'd only ever seen him barefoot. I could easily picture him outside this house, looking sophisticated from head to toe, though.

"It's definitely his room," I said. "I've seen him wear some of this stuff." I ran my fingers down one of the expensive-looking vests.

"Well, there's only one explanation, then. He must sleep somewhere else. Maybe *with* someone else, if you get my drift."

Her words made me feel the same way I had last night—after Mr. Remington told me his trip wasn't business related. And I had no idea why. I didn't like him. I 100 percent did not. "Who would he be sleeping with? It's only me, Miss Serrano, and Athena Quinn in this huge house."

"Process of elimination. Do you think he likes Miss Serrano?"

"No. And even if he did . . . she's terrified of him. I've never seen them act anything but professional together."

"I think you have your answer, then."

I turned away from the closet. "You think he's sleeping with Athena Quinn?"

"It certainly seems that way."

Yeah. It does. Suddenly it made sense how annoyed he'd gotten when I'd criticized her latest novels. Because it wasn't just a working relationship. It was way more than that. He was protective of her.

"You okay?" Kehlani asked.

"Of course I'm okay." He was probably on some romantic getaway with Athena Quinn right now. My stomach churned.

"You don't sound okay."

I laughed. "Kehlani, I'm not into Mr. Remington."

"Right. You're into Little Remington."

"Don't call Hudson that," I said with a laugh.

"I'm so sorry, but I feel like I'm not going to be able to stop now. Unless you can find proof that he doesn't deserve that nickname. Hint, hint."

"I'm not sleeping with Hudson tonight."

"Why not?"

"Because I barely know him," I said.

"Or is it because you're secretly harboring feelings for Big Remington?"

"I'm hanging up now."

She laughed. "No, you're not."

"Only because I need you on the call in case I find something weird."

There was an awkward pause, and Kehlani cleared her throat. "Are you sure there's even really a mystery to uncover here, Hazel?"

"Absolutely."

Another long pause. "You don't think that maybe this has to do with your parents?"

What? "How does this have anything to do with my parents?" But I already knew what she was going to say.

"I know when they passed away, you were convinced there was some murder mystery plot afoot. It's the author in you. But it wasn't true then."

My parents had died in a car accident right before I went to college. It was too much change all at once. I didn't know how to process it. I was grasping at straws and trying to make sense of a senseless tragedy. I'd never felt so alone. I don't know what I would have done if Kehlani hadn't been assigned to be my roommate. She quickly became my only family.

"And . . . maybe it's not true now," she said.

"I'm not crazy."

"I didn't say you were crazy. I'm just worried about you. I know how alone you felt when we first met. And now you're isolated in that big mansion. Mr. Remington barely speaks to you. Miss Serrano doesn't speak at all. It's barely been a week, but I think it might be getting to your head."

"Well, I call you all the time. And I'm hanging out with Hudson tonight. I'm not completely isolated." Not like after my parents died. It was nothing like that. But she did have a point. My imagination went haywire whenever I felt alone. Was that happening now?

"I know. But I'm still worried. Are you sure you don't want to come back home?"

"I promise I'm okay. I just feel it in my bones that there's a story here." But now I was a little less sure. "For the first time in so long, I'm looking forward to writing every day."

"Okay. But maybe the story is simply a romance. Between you and Little Remington."

I laughed. "Yeah, maybe."

"My lunch break is over. But I can't wait to hear about how tonight goes. I'm living vicariously through you right now, you know, so make it good!"

"Bye, Kehlani."

"Love you," she said and hung up.

I sighed and stared at the center of the room, where the bed should have been. Mr. Remington was sleeping with Athena Quinn. I didn't know what I'd been hoping to unearth by sneaking into this room. But it certainly wasn't this.

It was enough information for the novel I was working on. This was a really juicy plot twist. The hot guy sleeping with his female boss? I loved it. And yet . . . I kind of hated it too.

Was that really all there was to discover about Mr. Remington? Was this anything more than just an imaginary plot in my head? I shoved the thought aside. I wasn't crazy. There was something more going on here.

I walked back over to his dresser. I opened drawer after drawer and found nothing at all out of the ordinary. The only thing out of place was the fact that he was so organized. Everything was arranged by color and folded exactly the same. It was a little obsessive. No wonder he and Athena Quinn got along so well. They were both so rigid.

I wandered into the bathroom and immediately froze when I saw what was sitting on the vanity. It wasn't what I'd been looking for. But it was almost better than some dumb Mr. Remington secret being revealed. I lifted up the page labeled "Chapter 1" and thumbed through the rest. It was the first few chapters of Athena Quinn's work in progress. Mr. Remington must have been reading it to provide feedback.

I stared down at the first few lines.

She looked up at the huge house, her doe eyes wide with wonder. Hopes and dreams clung to her so tightly they were almost palpable. But little did she know that this wasn't the experience she'd signed up for. There was something dark and twisted lurking inside. As soon as she entered, she'd be swallowed whole.

If she weren't so naive, she would have run. She would have been able to feel the coolness in the air. She would have seen the signs unfold along the long drive.

Instead, she walked up to the door with her shoulders pulled back. It would have been brave if it weren't so foolish. She lifted the heavy brass knocker and let it fall with a thud. And with that, her fate was sealed. It was already too late to turn back.

A chill ran down my spine, and I looked behind me. It was like I could feel someone watching me. But no one was there.

I shuddered. I needed to get out of this room. I snapped photos of the pages and put them back exactly the way I'd found them.

This wasn't like Athena Quinn's normal work. It felt heavier. More sinister. And it reminded me of when I'd first arrived here at her estate. How I'd stared up at the house, thinking how haunting it looked. Maybe that was why I was so unsettled. Because unlike with her last few novels, I *felt* these words.

I'd thought I'd unearth something from Mr. Remington's past in his room. But instead I was finally getting a look inside Athena Quinn's head. And I couldn't wait to read more.

As I made my way back to my room, I wondered if that was how she felt about this house she was stuck in. This isolated estate, which could certainly be described as dark and twisted. I felt the random chills. I heard the creaking floorboards.

I just hoped I wasn't about to be swallowed whole too.

CHAPTER 12

Friday—September 2

I only had time to look at the first few pages of the manuscript before it was time to get ready for the beach party. But it was good. Really, really good.

I glanced at my computer and sighed. Athena Quinn's new book had vibes similar to those of the story I was trying to write. But her first draft was a million times better than mine. She'd perfectly captured what I'd been trying to convey.

But it was easier for her, right? Because she knew the secrets that were buried in this house. I was grasping for answers, while she had all of them hidden somewhere in her private wing.

I was tempted to just delete my whole first draft. But I didn't want to go backward. If I kept deleting everything I ever wrote, I'd never have anything to show for all the work I was doing. Sure, what I was writing wasn't the next great American classic. But that didn't mean it wasn't a story worthy of being told. Someone out there would connect with it, even if it was just one person. Besides, I couldn't possibly be the only one drooling over Mr. Remington.

I frowned. I didn't mean that. I wasn't drooling over him. He was the worst. And most likely sleeping with my boss.

But the heroine of my story was more foolish than me. She was very much into the brooding Mr. Remington. I'd leave the swooning to a fictional character.

I folded my arms as I stared at all the new clothes hanging in my closet. I certainly wouldn't be wearing to the party any of the clothes he'd given me. There were some items that could be considered casual but not end-of-summer-beach-party casual. Luckily, I had just the thing.

It took me only a few minutes to ditch my work clothes and change into jean shorts and a tank top. The outfit was very much unsuitable, according to Mr. Remington, but according to any normal person in their twenties, it was perfect. I looked in the mirror. Mr. Remington would have been absolutely horrified by my appearance. And for some reason that made me smile. I tried to push my thoughts of Mr. Remington aside. I was about to go on a date with the much nicer Little Remington.

Damn it, don't call him that. I really had to stop letting Kehlani get in my head. The last thing I needed to do was call Hudson that by accident.

I locked my door behind me and made my way down the hallway. I wasn't sure if Athena Quinn was in her private quarters writing her next masterpiece or on some romantic trip with Mr. Remington. Either way, I wasn't going to be thinking about her tonight. I'd earned a night off after the weirdest first week ever.

I walked down the stairs. I connected with the character in Athena Quinn's new novel. But unlike her character, I wasn't trapped inside these walls. And I couldn't wait to get out of the house.

I'd been excited to go down to the beach all week. But the fan mail had kept me super busy every day. And then I hadn't wanted to miss out on the formal dinners, just in case Athena Quinn arrived. The sun had long since set by then. And even though I didn't believe Mr. Remington's warning about the beach being unsafe at night, I still hadn't gone down.

Tonight, though? The beach would be filled with people. Hopefully a few who weren't going off to school soon. I wasn't sure what I'd do once Hudson left. He was the only normal person I'd met since I'd arrived here. He'd said his plans were still up in the air, though. Maybe he'd decide to stay awhile.

I walked outside. The temperature was already dropping. But I was hoping there'd be dancing tonight. And that would warm me up plenty. The pool was lit up, creating this magical glow. For the first time since stepping into this house, I finally felt relaxed. I was almost tempted to do a cannonball into the pool. Life was better when Mr. Remington was absent.

I walked to the edge of the pool and looked down at the steep stone stairs to the beach. They curved naturally to the left, cutting into the cliff. It looked like there were lights embedded into the steps. But I hadn't seen where to turn them on. Luckily, the moon was bright. Its reflection off the ocean was stunning. For a second I just stood there and stared.

Seriously, swimming in this pool at night? That sounded perfect. I could die happy looking at this view. That was the one thing Athena Quinn's character was missing. Right beyond the creepy walls of the old mansion were breathtaking views. She just needed to step outside to see them. She needed to remember to have a bit of fun. Who wanted such a heavy book about despair?

Definitely not me. I felt a little better about my work in progress as I walked down the stone steps. There was laughter in my book. Sex appeal. And a mystery. A real one that I was still trying to piece together. Now *that* was a good story.

I looked down the beach. Hudson hadn't given me his number. But he'd told me to turn right once I hit the sand. Apparently the party would be impossible to miss. I didn't see anything from up here, though. I could barely even make out the pier in the distance.

The little hairs on the back of my neck rose, and I spun around. But when I did, my foot clipped the edge of the step. I fell backward. I turned to the side so I wouldn't fall down the whole cliff, but I landed hard on the uneven steps.

Ow. I lifted the hem of my jean shorts. It didn't look like I'd gotten cut, but that was going to leave one hell of a bruise. I gingerly touched my skin as I looked back up the stairs. It felt like someone was watching me. But the moon had just gone behind a cloud, and I couldn't see more than a few steps in front of me.

Maybe this was a mistake. I was only halfway down, and it was so dark.

I stayed seated as I looked back down the beach again. Why weren't there any lights? Why wasn't there any music drifting through the air? I was tempted to turn back and go for that late-night swim instead of continuing down the death trap stairs. Maybe this was why Mr. Remington said the beach wasn't safe at night. Because it was impossible to see anything. Or maybe he felt like someone was watching him too. The little hairs on the back of my neck rose again.

"Hello?" I called.

But there was no response.

I fumbled with my phone, ready to dial 9-1-1, but then I saw the time. *Oh.* It was only nine fifteen. The party wasn't supposed to start till nine thirty. I had gotten used to arriving to everything early, hoping Athena Quinn would be right around the corner, ready to greet me. It was less appropriate to be early to a party, though. And a nine-thirty start time probably meant a ten-o'clock start time.

I held my phone up, letting the glow from my home screen light up a couple of the stairs behind me. There was no one there. It was all in my head. Living in this house all week had just gotten under my skin.

I yawned. Maybe I was just sleep deprived. I'd woken up at four thirty all week in order to be on time for breakfast by five. There was no way I'd be able to stay up much longer. I hit Kehlani's name on my phone. If anyone could pep me up, it would be her.

She answered in two rings. "Are you deciding what to wear?"

"No, I'm chickening out."

"What? Why?"

"I'm a little tired."

She laughed. "Which is exactly why you deserve a night off. Come on, get your butt to that party."

"I can't. I hurt my butt."

"Excuse me?"

I laughed. "More my hip, really. There are these ridiculously steep stairs down to the beach. I slipped and landed pretty hard." I could feel the bruise already forming.

"Can you stand?"

I stood up. "Yes?"

"Why did you say that like you were asking a question? It's a yes or no."

"I can stand, but it is a little sore."

"You know what's a good pain reliever? Lots of beer."

I laughed. "I feel like if I keep going, I'll never be able to get back up here."

"That's fine. You can sleep at Hudson's place."

"Definitely not. And I'm staring at the beach, and I don't see any party."

"Because it doesn't start until nine thirty. And everyone knows that legit means ten."

I sighed.

"Come on, Hazel. I want to hear all about your fun night with Little Remington."

"Seriously, stop calling him that. I'm worried I'm going to call him that now."

Kehlani laughed. "Well, that would be epic."

"Epically embarrassing."

"Wait," she said. "I have a brilliant solution."

"You want me to seduce Little Remington?" *Seriously, stop calling him that!*

"Well, duh. But I meant about the stairs. Use your phone's flashlight."

That was a really good idea. I felt a little like an idiot for not thinking of it myself. "You're a genius."

"I know."

I turned on my phone's flashlight and pointed it back toward the house. This time, all the steps lit up instead of just a few. And there was definitely no one there. But I still didn't start walking down the steps again. "Mr. Remington said the beach isn't safe at night." And Hudson had said the house wasn't safe after nightfall. Now I was literally right in between both of them, and I didn't know what to do.

"Was that before or after you told him about your hot date?"

I pressed my lips together. "After."

"Told you he's into you."

"He's on a pleasure trip with someone else."

"What the hell did you just say? Pleasure trip? That sounds disgusting."

I laughed. It really did. And I wasn't going to avoid the party just because Mr. Remington had told me not to go. I remembered when he'd stared at me after I asked why I couldn't talk to his nephew and legit said, "Because I said so." Pompous ass. I turned my flashlight the other way and took a step down, then froze. "I forgot shoes."

"What? Aren't you outside?"

"Yeah, but Athena Quinn has this weird rule about shoes in the house. And I've kind of gotten used to walking around barefoot. I should go back, right? To put on shoes like a normal human?"

"Definitely not necessary," Kehlani said. "It's a party on the beach. I'm sure it's the opposite of no shirts, no shoes, no service."

"I still feel like people will be wearing shoes. And shirts, I hope."

"You mean you hope not. Now stop chickening out. You called me for a pep talk. So that's what I'm doing. You're going to go down to that party and wrangle a Little Remington."

I laughed. "That sounds so wrong."

"And oh so right."

I shook my head. But instead of turning around, I started making my way down the steps again. And then I saw a glow in the distance.

"Ah, wait! I think they're setting up now!" A bonfire had definitely just been lit off to the right. And there was finally faint music playing.

"Go knock 'em dead, Hazel. And call me after, all right?"

"I will." I ended the call and made my way safely down the rest of the steps. When I reached the cold sand, I was glad I'd forgotten shoes. It had been ages since I'd been to the beach. And there was no better feeling in the world than the sand between your toes.

The music grew louder the closer I got to the bonfire. Most people were standing around talking, but there were some couples already dancing. A few guys were pulling logs over for people to sit on. And the makeshift bar was packed.

But it wasn't just young college students celebrating the end of summer. There were definitely some guys who looked like they were in their thirties or forties. Some of the women too. But Hudson was nowhere to be seen.

A guy walked up to me and handed me a beer. He looked about the same age as Hudson.

"Thank you."

"You're not a local," he said. "I would have remembered seeing you around."

I smiled. "No, I'm not."

"So you're here on vacation? All by yourself?"

There was something about the way he said "all by yourself" that made me uncomfortable. Or maybe it was the way his eyes dropped to my mouth like he wanted to kiss me, even though we'd exchanged only a few sentences.

I cleared my throat. "No. I actually just started working for Athena Quinn. Well, for her assistant, Mr. Remington, actually."

"Oh, you're Mr. Remington's?" He looked past me like he was no longer interested in speaking with me.

So uninterested that he'd forgotten the end of his sentence. "Mr. Remington's *assistant*, yes. I'm the assistant to the assistant." I laughed at my own joke.

"Huh. Well, nice meeting you." He walked away without really meeting me at all.

That had to be one of the weirdest conversations I'd ever had. I took another sip of my beer, suddenly wishing I'd followed my gut and not come at all. I took another and another, hoping the uneasy feeling in my chest would go away. A chill ran down my spine, and I looked back toward Athena Quinn's estate.

"I heard you work for Mr. Remington," someone said from behind me.

Well, that news had spread fast. I turned to see a guy with a much kinder smile than the last.

"Yeah. I just started earlier this week."

"Hi, I'm Max," he said and put out his hand.

"Hazel." I shook his hand and a chill went up my arm. "Jesus, your hands are freezing. Do you want to move closer to the fire?"

"Nah, I'm good."

I tucked my free hand under my arm. Maybe he wasn't cold, but I certainly was now. I took another sip of my beer.

"And how is it going? Working for Mr. Remington?"

"Eh . . . honestly?"

He nodded.

"It's not off to the best start."

"I bet. After all, you're all alone."

I pressed my lips together. I'd talked to exactly two people, both of whom had commented on the fact that I was all alone. I could hear the warning bells going off in my head. I looked down at my almost empty cup of beer, suddenly worrying it might be spiked.

"Are you all right? Do you maybe want to sit down? You look a little pale."

"I'm fine," I said. I didn't want to go anywhere with him. "And I'm not alone. I'm meeting a friend here."

"Someone invited you to this party and didn't escort you here himself?"

Escort? That was a weird way to put it. I was still getting used to southern phrases. It seemed like everyone I met was a little old-fashioned. "I don't really need to be escorted anywhere. I'm perfectly capable of walking a couple miles by myself."

"You walked here alone? From the estate?" He looked down the long, dark stretch of beach.

I swallowed hard. There was that word again. *Alone.*

"That's a long walk."

"Well, I'm pretty fast." It was the only thing I could think of to say. But now that I thought about it, I *was* pretty fast. Maybe I should just run away from this weird party . . .

"It just so happens that I've always loved the chase, Hazel." His eyes traveled to my lips, just like the last guy's had, even though both conversations had been awkward at best. Actually, I'd probably describe them as downright creepy. There wasn't a chance in hell I was about to kiss him.

"I'm gonna go get another drink," I said.

"Let me . . ."

"No. I think I can *escort* myself to the bar, thank you very much." I walked away from him and was relieved he didn't follow me. My heart was beating fast in my chest. It felt like everyone here was staring at me.

Or maybe my drink really was spiked. I stopped at the bar and looked behind me. It didn't seem like anyone was staring anymore. They were just minding their own business, laughing and having fun.

The unease was definitely in my head. And I was thinking perfectly clearly. My drink hadn't been spiked. Southern people just talked differently. Maybe those guys were trying to be polite and were truly concerned about a woman walking alone at night.

But I wasn't a damsel in distress.

I filled up my own cup instead of taking one of those sitting on top of the bar. And I walked over to the bonfire. I stared at the couples dancing and the people chatting on the logs as I drank my second cup of beer.

Everyone around me was having the time of their lives. But I wrapped my arms tighter around myself. There was a chill in my bones that even the fire couldn't warm.

I'd heard a lot about southern charm and hospitality. I'd seen it in movies. Hell, I'd experienced it with Mr. Remington. At least when he wasn't being condescending. I pictured him dropping to one knee to help me out of my shoes. That was gentlemanly. The conversations I'd had tonight didn't feel the same way.

All alone.

Why was everyone asking me if I was alone?

That wasn't southern hospitality. It was creepy. My heart started beating faster again as I stared into the fire. I downed the rest of my beer and instantly regretted it. The fire seemed to grow higher. And the people laughing grew louder, the sound all around me almost sinister.

All alone. The words echoed through my head. Mr. Remington was right. The beach wasn't safe at night. And I was pretty sure it spun once the sun set. *Or am I spinning?*

"Hazel," a deep voice whispered in my ear.

I was so hyped up that I did the first thing I could think of to do. I threw out my elbow to hit whatever pervert thought it was appropriate to be that freaking close to me.

CHAPTER 13

Friday—September 2

It was like colliding with hard stone. I'd know . . . I'd just experienced it with my ass on the steps.

"Oof," Hudson said and touched his stomach where I'd hit him, although I was pretty sure his abs had hurt me more than I'd hurt him.

I cupped my elbow. "I'm so sorry," I said.

He smiled. "It's fine. Abs of steel."

"You can say that again. I'm so happy to see you." I hugged him before I realized that I'd never hugged him before. I closed my eyes and breathed him in. He smelled like chlorine, and I wondered if he'd come straight here from work.

"Hazel?" he said.

I realized I was awkwardly hugging him for way too long. But for some reason my arms didn't let go. It was so good to see a familiar face after those unsettling conversations. "Yes?"

He laughed.

I looked up at him.

"You're drunk," he said. He cupped my face so I'd focus on him.

"I don't think that sounds right."

He laughed again. "You're definitely plastered."

"Nope." I finally took a step back. "I only had two beers. Your friends are creepy, though. I've been really freaked out. They keep asking me if I'm 'all alone.' What's up with that?"

"They're hitting on you."

"No. That's not what they were doing." *Wait, was it?* I shook my head. "No, they were being weird. You know," I said, trying to drop my voice, "I haven't met many people on this island, but they've all been a little *off.*"

He smiled. "Am I off, Hazel?"

"I don't know. Does lying by omission count as *off*, Mr. Remington?"

He laughed. "Atlas told you we're related, huh?"

"That he did, good sir." I poked him in the middle of the chest. "Why is your body so hard?" My finger trailed down the middle of his abs. "You know, I never would have figured it out. Big Remington is always frowning. And you're always smiling."

"Big Remington?" he asked.

"Yes. And you're Little Remington. Boop." I tapped him on the tip of his nose.

"Did you just boop me?"

Had I? I didn't remember, so I just shrugged. "That doesn't sound like something I'd do, Little Remington."

He laughed. "Little Remington? Really? I don't love that nickname."

"That's what I told Kehlani!"

"Who's Kehlani?"

"My best friend. You'd like her. She's funny. And she knows where I am tonight, in case one of your friends does something shady."

"That doesn't sound funny to me."

I shook my head. "No, she's hilarious." Or was he talking about his shady friends? I stared at him. Wait, what were we talking about again? How many beers had I had?

"We agree to disagree," he said with a laugh. "Either way, it's a very inaccurate nickname for me."

"How so?"

He raised one eyebrow and then looked down suggestively.

"Oh. Ooh. You're talking about your penis!" I realized I had just said *penis* really loudly. Actually, I might have even screamed it. Why was I screaming?

He laughed. "You're wasted."

"You're wasted," I parroted back to him.

He smiled down at me.

"I'm not wasted. And you know what else I'm not? An escort," I whispered.

"What?"

"I think one of your friends thought I was an escort. Or maybe *he* is? Oh my God, I think he wanted to be my escort!" I could feel my eyes growing wide. "He's a prostitute."

Hudson laughed. "You're even more fun than I thought you'd be."

"Thank you? I think? I'd be more fun if I hadn't hurt my butt."

"What?" he said with a laugh. "How did you hurt your butt?"

"I fell down that death trap of a staircase on my way to the beach."

He looked over toward the estate. "Did you not turn the lights on?"

"Nope." I tapped the tip of his nose.

"Would you stop booping me?" he said with a laugh. "And for the record, I think you'll be okay." He placed his hand on my butt. "Your butt feels perfectly fine to me."

"Your hand is on my butt."

He smiled. "Yes, it is."

I shivered. "Your hand is cold. That's the other thing. I keep meeting cold people. With cold hands. Why are you all so cold? And I don't mean your personality. Big Remington is cold in all ways, though. Why didn't you tell me you were related to him?"

"Because he's an ass, and I didn't want you to get the wrong impression of me."

I laughed.

"What's so funny?"

"You called him an ass. But your hand is on my ass, Little Remington."

He shook his head and moved his hand to my waist. "How can I get you to stop calling me that?"

"I don't know how to stop. I didn't mean to say it at all. And now it's stuck in my head and all I can say."

"How about you call me Hudson instead? I don't really go by Mr. Remington. That's reserved for my uncle and my dad."

"Oh no, is your father as stern as Mr. Remington?" I felt my face do an exaggerated frown, but it was like I had no control over it.

He laughed. "That's a very confusing sentence, but yes. They're both very old-fashioned."

"You're a little old-fashioned too, you know."

"Am I? I try really hard not to be."

I shook my head. Why did he have to try hard not to be? "What does that mean?"

"It means I grew up around my father."

Oh. That made sense. Kind of. I stared at him. He had a really nice face. Perfectly symmetrical. Mr. Remington's face was quite symmetrical too. "Do you know what I think?" I squinted at him, examining his perfect face.

"What do you think?"

"I think you have a secret," I whispered.

"Is that so?"

"Yes, it's so. I think there's a reason why everyone I've met here is off. Why you and your uncle and dad are old-fashioned. Why you're cold. You do have a secret, right? You're hiding something?"

He just smiled down at me.

"You can tell me, you know. I won't tell anyone. Your secret will be safe with me." *Kind of.* I'd be writing all about it. But that didn't count. It was fiction. And honestly, I'd probably be the only person who ever read it. I was no Athena Quinn. At least, not yet.

"So let's pretend I do have a big secret. What do you think it is?"

"That you . . . that you're . . ." I sighed. "Old-fashioned."

He laughed. "You already mentioned that. What else am I besides old-fashioned?"

"Cold."

"You already mentioned that too."

Damn it, I did. "You're . . . a pool boy."

He pretended to look offended. "Is that all I am to you?"

I laughed. "You're old-fashioned, cold, and like chlorine. So your secret is that you're a . . . southern gentleman," I said with a sigh. That wasn't a secret. It was just a description.

His eyes searched mine. "But . . ."

I knew there was a but! "But what?" I leaned forward slightly, almost falling into him.

He put his arms on my biceps, steadying me. "I do have a secret, as a matter of fact."

"I knew it!" I booped him on the nose again, and he laughed.

"Do you want to know what it is?" he asked.

"Desperately so."

He leaned forward, dropping his lips to my ear. His breath tickled my neck. "You swear you won't tell a soul?"

My heart started pounding. "I swear it." God, I knew he was hiding something.

"My secret is . . ."

I held my breath.

"That I . . ."

Say it already!

". . . really want to dance."

I laughed and pulled back. "That's not a secret, Hudson."

"Everything is a secret until it's spoken."

"I hate you."

He put his hand to his chest, feigning shock. "You wound me, madame."

"See! Old-fashioned!"

"More French, actually," he said.

I rolled my eyes. "Well, it's your lucky day, monsieur, because I share your secret sentiment." I grabbed his hand. "I really want to dance too." I pulled him toward where the other couples were dancing.

The creepiness of the guys I'd talked to when I first arrived and any desire to uncover secrets all died away when I moved my hips to the beat of the music. I'd never danced in the sand before. There was something freeing about the waves crashing behind us and the fire burning higher in the night. Or maybe I just felt alive with Hudson's hands on my hips.

And even though he was a bit old-fashioned, he definitely wasn't an old-fashioned dancer. I dipped it low and grinded against him. He pulled my waist even closer.

I was vaguely aware of the fact that everyone else on the beach was wearing shoes. And I felt sorry for them. I threw my hands in the air and spun around. Hudson's laughter echoed all around me. I couldn't remember the last time I felt this wild and free.

We danced until sweat was dripping down my back. Until my legs were actually sore from jumping up and down. Until most of the couples had long since departed the beach. Until the music had stopped and we were basically all alone.

I wasn't exactly sure when the party had ended. It was like I had blinked and time sped up. I blamed the couple of beers I'd had to cool off from dancing throughout the night. I looked up at Hudson.

He smiled down at me.

"I think I'm drunk," I whispered.

He laughed. "Oh, yeah, I got that."

"I should probably get back before I do something I'll regret."

"Were you thinking about doing something you'll regret?"

I nodded. "It's so hot."

"It is."

I was pretty sure he thought I meant the chemistry between us. But I meant I was actually really overheated. Not that I didn't feel the chemistry. I did. "And the ocean is calling to me. I've always wanted to go skinny-dipping."

"I'm not stopping you."

"Well, I don't want to go in by myself." I tried to raise an eyebrow at him, but I wasn't sure if my face was working right, so I pulled off my tank top instead and threw it at him.

He caught it with a smile.

"I'll race you," I said.

His eyes wandered to my breasts. "The ocean isn't really my thing, but I have a pool back at my place."

I stared up at him. He'd just asked me back to his place. But I felt like maybe I was about to find something out. His actual secret. And I was much more interested in uncovering the truth. "Afraid of sharks or something?"

"The opposite."

"You love them?"

He shook his head. "No, but I think sharks are probably more scared of me, Hazel."

I laughed, even though he didn't have an ounce of sarcasm in his voice. That was such a macho thing to say. And so very inaccurate. But now that I was thinking of sharks, I wasn't craving a dip in the ocean as much. As soon as the fear of sharks crept in, it was like the rest of it piled on. Those guys kept talking about me being *all alone*. And now I was all alone. With a virtual stranger. I was drunk. Standing in the middle of the beach in my freaking bra. What the heck was I doing?

But I also didn't move to go home. "So no ocean?"

He looked over at the water. It was calling to me, but it definitely wasn't calling to him. "It's much safer to skinny-dip in my pool."

I laughed. "Safer for the sharks, I presume?"

"Exactly."

"You're hilarious. But I'm not a one-night-stand kind of girl." *Despite how it probably looks right now.*

"I didn't say you were."

"Yeah, but you're leaving soon, right? To go back to school?"

"I haven't decided if I am or not," he said.

"When will you decide?"

"Honestly, I was kind of hoping to see how tonight went."

I smiled. That was sweet. Really, really sweet, actually. "So this was some kind of test? How'd I do?"

He laughed. "So far, so good."

I shook my head. "So far? I'm not sleeping with you tonight, Little Remington."

He laughed again. "That's not what I meant. I just meant the sun won't rise for another four hours."

The thought of the sun rising had me yawning. And once I started yawning, it was like I couldn't stop. "I'm sorry. I've been up before five every day this week. And now that the music has stopped, I'm in desperate need of falling asleep in my own bed. Do you think maybe we could put a pin in this amazing date?"

"To be continued?"

I nodded. "I really like the sound of that." I took a step away from him. "See you around, Little Remington." I spun in a circle, the music still going in my head.

He grabbed my hand before I could retreat.

I laughed as he pulled me back toward him. He silenced my laughter with a kiss.

It had been a really long time since I'd been kissed. I didn't remember it being like this. All consuming. I just wanted more. I reached up to wind my hands behind his neck, but he pulled back.

"See you around, Hazel." He winked and walked away from me.

It wasn't until he disappeared into the darkness that I realized he still had my tank top. *Shit.*

CHAPTER 14

Friday—September 2

The flashlight on my phone lit up the stone stairs for me. I hummed to myself, swaying slightly on each step. There really should have been a railing. This truly was a death trap.

I laughed out loud. *Death trap.* As opposed to what other kind of trap? An alive trap?

Hmm. Maybe that was how Athena felt. Like she was stuck in her haunted mansion. Alive and trapped. That was so sad. She needed to come outside and dance in the sand. There was magic in the air out here. I could feel it. Someone needed to show her what it was like to have fun again.

I continued humming in my head. The stone steps seemed steeper going up than they had going down. And the music in my head wasn't as distracting as the actual music on the beach. My hip hurt more with each step up.

They should get an elevator. I'd have to tell Mr. Remington that. Big Remington. I laughed as I finally climbed the last step.

The backyard was dark, but the water in the pool was reflecting the moon and the stars.

I touched my lips as I paused by the edge of the pool. I'd kissed Hudson. Would he kiss me again the next time he came to clean the pool? Definitely. I felt the corners of my mouth curl up when I remembered how he had pulled me back in close. *What a kiss.*

I couldn't wait to tell Kehlani. But I would have to wait until tomorrow.

I looked back out at the ocean and smiled. The long week had been worth it for a night like tonight. I spun in a circle again and then started tiptoeing past the pool. I wasn't exactly sure why I'd started tiptoeing. Maybe it was because the air was so still and quiet up here. I didn't want to break the peace. Not a soul could see me out here, though. Unlike the pool, I didn't light up from the moonlight. I continued tiptoeing anyway.

But the tiptoeing didn't matter. A floodlight turned on, highlighting me in the middle of the patio.

Crap. I ducked behind a bush.

I started laughing again. Why was I hiding? I pushed myself up from my hands and knees and noticed what I was wearing. *Oh, right. No shirt.*

I looked around, like there'd magically be a shirt nearby. But alas, no such luck. I shook my head. No one else would be up at this hour anyway. Mr. Remington probably wasn't even back yet. Athena Quinn refused to grace me with her presence. Besides, she might be with Mr. Remington. And if Miss Serrano saw me, she'd never tell a soul. I laughed at my own joke as I slipped through the back door. The silence was almost deafening in the kitchen. All I could hear was my own feet treading across the floor.

I hummed a tune to break the eerie silence as I made my way over to the fridge. I needed an ice pack for my hip. Eventually the alcohol would stop coursing through my veins, and I'd feel the full effect of that ugly bruise.

I opened the freezer door. The shelves were lined with glass storage containers filled with tomato sauce. Tons of containers. I'd had the sauce the other day with the chicken parmesan Miss Serrano had made. It was good. But it honestly wasn't my favorite meal she'd made or anything. Apparently she prepared the sauce in bulk. I lifted one of the containers. It was still warm, like it had only just been put in the freezer. There was an identical one behind it. Athena Quinn must have had a thing for the tomato sauce. Maybe that was why she never came to dinner. Because she was weird and put tomato sauce on everything. I'd heard of people doing that with ketchup but never with tomato sauce.

I moved a few more of the containers. Was there seriously no ice pack in here? Or frozen peas or something?

"What are you doing, Miss Fox?"

I jumped, and the container fell out of my hands.

Mr. Remington grabbed it midair before the glass had a chance to shatter on the floor. His reflexes were a million times faster than mine. But I blamed the alcohol. I definitely would have caught it if the room weren't spinning.

I looked up at him and swallowed hard. He looked beyond pissed. The angriest I'd ever seen him. But that wasn't why my heart was suddenly racing. He wore only a pair of sweatpants, like the first time I'd run into him. This time his hair was wet, though. His chest even looked a little wet, like he'd gotten caught in a rainstorm.

But it wasn't raining. I shook the thought away. He must have just taken a shower. My mind was having a hard time catching up tonight.

He put the container back in the freezer and slammed the door closed, making the kitchen pitch black.

"You're supposed to use the fridge in the day kitchen." His voice rumbled in the darkness.

"Right." I'd completely forgotten. "Sorry, I just needed . . ." My voice died in my throat. I wasn't sure if he'd stepped closer in the darkness, but I could suddenly smell him. And he didn't smell like his normal expensive cologne. He smelled like the ocean. Like he'd just taken a midnight dip in the salty water. Just like I'd been tempted to do earlier.

I cleared my throat. "Sorry," I said again. "I'll just go to bed . . ." I stepped to the side to move past him and rammed my hurt hip into the kitchen island. I held back a groan, but a small whimper escaped.

He grabbed my wrist before I could walk away. "Are you hurt?"

I shook my head, even though it was too dark for him to see me.

"Answer me."

"Yes." My voice came out weird and small.

His fingers tightened on my wrist, and he pulled me into the other kitchen. He hit the lights, and I winced.

"Sit down," he said and released my wrist.

"Mr. Remington, I don't . . ."

"I said sit. Now." His tone left no room for argument.

But for some reason, I didn't want to listen to him. Why did he always treat me like a petulant child? Instead of sitting in a chair, I leaned against the table and watched him rummage around in the freezer. He finally pulled out a tray of ice cubes and dumped them into a towel. He twisted the towel and walked back over to me.

"Where?" he asked as his eyes scanned my body.

"How did you know I needed ice instead of a Band-Aid?"

"What?" His angry eyes snapped back to my face.

Why did I get so nervous when I looked into his eyes? My heart started racing even faster. "I said I was hurt, but you didn't ask me what was wrong."

He lowered his eyebrows. "You were looking around in the freezer. I figured you needed ice."

Oh. Yeah, that makes sense. And it wasn't like I was covered in blood or anything.

He perched on the edge of the table next to me and pressed the ice against my hip. I'd never told him where I needed it, but he'd found the spot anyway. I stared down at his hand holding the ice to me. This was nice. It had been a really long time since someone had taken care of me.

"What happened?" he asked. His voice was gentler this time but still tense.

"I slipped on the steps."

"And Hudson didn't catch you?"

I laughed.

He frowned.

Was he serious right now? It had all happened so fast that even if Hudson had been with me, he couldn't have helped. "No, Hudson wasn't with me."

"He didn't walk you home?"

"I didn't ask him to . . ."

"You shouldn't have had to ask, Miss Fox."

"Well, it doesn't matter. I slipped on my way there, not my way back."

His nostrils actually flared. "You hurt yourself on the way there, and he didn't think it was suitable to escort you home?"

What was with everyone and that word tonight? "I'm not in need of an escort, Mr. Remington."

He raised an eyebrow at me. "You could have really hurt yourself on those steps. Especially since you've been drinking."

"I . . ." My voice trailed off. It wasn't like I could deny that I'd been drinking. He could probably smell the beer on me. "I'm capable of walking myself home."

"It's not what you're capable of that's the problem. It's that he should have offered. I told you the beach was dangerous at night. What were you thinking?"

Is that what he had meant by *dangerous*? That the steps were dark? I'd thought he meant something more sinister. I'd been so jumpy when I first arrived at the party. Because of him. My imagination was getting away from me. "I was thinking that I wanted to have fun."

"At what cost, Miss Fox? Do you have any idea how fragile you are?"

"Excuse me? I'm not some dainty damsel. I can take care of myself."

He shook his head. "I meant that life is fleeting. One wrong move and it's over. It's just over. There is no do-over. You could have been killed."

I swallowed hard. I hadn't really thought of it that way. "But you did it too, right? Walked on the steps by yourself for a late-night swim?"

He didn't respond. Instead, he ran his fingers through his wet hair and stared straight ahead like I was no longer in the room with him.

"You should really be more careful, Mr. Remington."

He didn't respond.

I stared at his profile. He'd just been on a short vacation. I thought that he'd be relaxed the next time I saw him. He seemed anything but.

"Did you have fun on your trip?"

He finally turned toward me. "Where is your shirt, Miss Fox?"

I could feel my face turning red. "So you don't answer my questions, but you want me to answer yours?"

He let go of the ice and stood up. He didn't say a word to me as he left the kitchen. No "Good night." No "I hope you feel better."

Asshole.

I removed the ice and looked down at the bruise. It was even worse in the light. I pushed the hem of my jean shorts up to get a better look. The bruise covered my hip and spread onto the side of my butt cheek. *Fuck.* I hated that Mr. Remington was right. If I hadn't caught myself, I could have fallen down more stairs. I could have been seriously hurt.

Mr. Remington cleared his throat.

I turned to see him standing in the doorway, a folded shirt in his hands. I pushed the hem of my shorts back down, very aware of the fact that I'd practically just mooned him.

"Put this on," he said and handed me a shirt.

I felt a little bad that I'd just called him an asshole in my head. But only a little bit. I put my arms through his dress shirt and buttoned it up.

I thought he'd turn around or something, but he watched every movement I made. I rolled up the sleeves and looked over at him.

He didn't say a word. He just stared at me.

The silence stretched between us.

"Thank you," I finally said. "To answer your question from earlier, I took my shirt off because I wanted to go for a late swim too. But I chickened out. Unlike you."

He didn't respond.

"Was it scary? I almost did it. But then I thought about the sharks. They feed at night, right?"

He didn't seem at all fazed by anything I said. I wasn't sure what he wanted from me, but I was pretty sure I had my answer right there. He didn't want anything from me. There was a lump in my throat that wouldn't seem to go away. "I should probably get to bed . . ."

"Take your shorts off."

I could practically hear the sound of my heart racing in the quiet kitchen. I'd dreamed of being in a situation like this with him. Usually in the dining room. I'd dreamed about it on repeat. Despite how infuriating I found him, I couldn't deny that I had. And I was also a little drunk. Or a lot drunk. That was probably why I followed his instructions. I unbuttoned and unzipped my shorts, then let them fall to a puddle on the floor.

"Turn around, Miss Fox."

I turned around, my heart crashing against my rib cage.

"Hands on the table."

I put my hands on the table. My back arched of its own accord when his fingers traced up the back of my thigh.

"Does that hurt?" he whispered.

"No." *The opposite.* I felt more alive than I had dancing on that beach.

"What about now?" His fingers inched closer to my bruise.

I shook my head, not trusting my own voice.

His other hand pushed the fabric of the shirt up over my ass. His fingers lightly traced my hip bone. "What about now?"

I shook my head again.

His thumb dipped slightly under the waistband of my thong as his hands splayed across my ass cheek.

"Now, Miss Fox?"

Good God. He had to see how wet I was. How badly I wanted him to pull down my thong. His fingers were even colder from the ice. And I hadn't expected his touch to be so gentle. I should have after the night he helped me remove my high heels. The way his fingers had traced my ankle.

"Miss Fox? How does that feel?"

I stifled a moan. "So good."

His hand immediately fell from my skin. He cleared his throat. "I was just checking to make sure you didn't break anything. It's only a contusion, though."

Wait, what? I turned around and stared into his eyes.

For the first time ever, he didn't look angry. But his eyebrows were still pulled together. "You'll be fine in a few days," he said. "Keep the ice on it for a bit longer. And take an Advil for the pain. That should help your hangover as well."

My hangover. I crossed my arm in front of my chest, wishing I could somehow make myself smaller and disappear. He was looking at my bruise to make sure I wasn't hurt? Not because he was into me? I pressed my lips together. I'd read that whole situation extremely wrong. God, how much had I had to drink?

I felt the heat rising to my cheeks. Angry, embarrassed tears stung the corners of my eyes. Of course he wasn't into me. He'd been on some romantic getaway all day. He didn't even have a bed in his room because he was sleeping with Athena Quinn.

"Right," I quickly said. "Thanks for checking. I'll be more careful next time. I'm sorry if I woke you coming in. It won't happen again." I grabbed my ice and hurried past him.

He didn't try to stop me. And I think that almost stung just as much as the misunderstanding, which was beyond mortifying. I didn't even feel the pain in my hip as my sprint turned into a run. The tears finally fell down my cheeks as I closed my bedroom door behind me.

I collapsed on my bed and closed my eyes, wishing I could make today vanish.

But all I saw in my head was Mr. Remington.

Touching me.

Taking care of me.

My heart felt so weirdly . . . full. And I didn't know why. It was probably just full of embarrassment.

I opened my eyes and stared at the ceiling.

It was like every ounce of me was on high alert around the man. Like everything just felt bigger. More important. And I'd never felt more stupid.

I took a deep breath, and the smell of Mr. Remington's salty skin invaded my senses. It was all around me. I looked down at his shirt. I was so wrapped up in him. And I was so freaking screwed.

CHAPTER 15

Saturday—September 3

My stomach growled, but I ignored it. I stared at the blinking cursor on my computer screen. I was writing a thriller, not a romance. But every time I closed my eyes or stared at my screen . . . all I could think about was the feeling of Mr. Remington's hands on my skin. Apparently the book wanted to be more romance than mystery, which was probably fitting, because I hadn't found out a single concrete thing about him or Athena Quinn in the week I'd been here. I was a terrible detective. And likely a terrible writer.

The wind blew, and I looked out at the ocean. I should have been thinking about Hudson and our kiss. It was a good kiss. A great kiss. *And yet . . .*

My phone buzzed again. Kehlani had been calling me nonstop. I'd texted her and told her I didn't feel well. But apparently that had her only more worried.

I felt more settled now that I'd been writing for a few hours. And I needed her advice. I finally answered her call.

"Hazel! You can't tell me you're ill and then refuse to pick up the phone!"

"I wasn't ready to face the day." My stomach growled again. But there was no way I was leaving my room until I had to on Monday morning. Just the thought of seeing Mr. Remington again was worse than starvation.

"Uh-oh," she said. "Did something happen last night?"

"Yeah. I mean . . . kind of. Sort of."

"Okay . . ."

I didn't respond.

"You're going to make a great author, Hazel. You always leave me hanging on your every word."

"Thanks." I closed my laptop and put it aside. Maybe one day I'd be a great author. When I stopped writing about dream sexual scenarios with my boss.

She laughed. "You're welcome. But would you spit it out already? The suspense is killing me."

"I had a really great time with Hudson. We literally danced the night away." I smiled, remembering the feeling of dancing barefoot in the sand.

"Did you dance right into his bed?"

I laughed. "No. But we kissed."

Kehlani squealed. "On a scale of one to ten, how great was it?"

"Definitely a ten. It was the best kiss I've ever had, hands down." There was no denying that Hudson was a great kisser.

"Well, hot damn."

I laughed.

"But now you're sick? Were you just out too late? Or is he diseased?"

I shook my head. "He's not diseased. I'm just feeling off." I pulled my knees to my chest and cringed at the pain in my hip. I hadn't taken an Advil like Mr. Remington had advised. Just because he'd told me to. I really hated how he was always telling me what to do. I hated even more when he was right. I looked down at the bruise on my hip. God, did it hurt.

"So . . . ," she said.

"So nothing. It was great. I can't wait to go out with him again."

"You're saying all the right things," Kehlani said. "But your voice is all wrong. Why don't you sound excited?"

"I am."

"You're not."

I took a deep breath. "I really am. He's so much fun. And so handsome and charming." I couldn't help but smile at the thought of him.

"But . . ."

I laughed. "There is no but."

"I think there is. It starts with *Mr.* and ends with *Remington.*"

My stomach churned.

"You paused, you paused!" she yelled even louder. "Something happened, didn't it?"

"How could you possibly know that? I'm pretty sure you were a mind reader in another lifetime."

"Maybe so. A fortune teller turned marketer. Kind of a natural turn, if you ask me. It's my job to predict what consumers will connect with. Almost like I'm telling the future."

"Mhm." I knew Kehlani could go on and on about this. She had a thing for past lives. I didn't understand any of it. Maybe that was why she was a hopeless romantic—because she thought she had a million lives to figure it all out.

"But stop distracting me with talk about reincarnation."

"I wasn't," I lied.

"You definitely were. Tell me what happened, and we'll figure out a solution together. Easy peasy."

This was not that easy. "I did something really dumb, Kehlani."

"Okay . . ."

"You know how I fell down those stairs on the way to the beach? Well, I was looking for ice when I got home. In the wrong freezer."

"How many fridges does Athena Quinn have?"

I shrugged. "Two that I know of. But this house is huge, and I'm only allowed in half of it, so who knows?"

Kehlani laughed. "We just got really off topic. I bet she does have at least three refrigerators. But back to what happened last night."

I scrunched my eyes closed tight, like that would somehow make this story more bearable. And then I spit it all out as quickly as possible. "Mr. Remington caught me at the wrong fridge and was all pissed off, just like how he normally is. He was beyond furious that I was touching Athena Quinn's tomato sauce. As if just being near her food was despicable. But then he could see that I was in pain. And he got me ice and put it on my hip. And he gave me his shirt because I didn't have one. And then he told me to take my shorts off and caressed my ass. And I thought it was sexual, and I'm pretty sure I moaned. And then he was so uncomfortable because he was just checking to make sure I hadn't broken anything. And then I ran away."

Kehlani didn't say a word.

"I thanked him for checking. Before I ran away. Not that that helps. Does it help? No, definitely not. It was so bad, Kehlani. Please say something."

"That's a lot to sort through. Wait, why weren't you wearing a shirt?"

"I had contemplated going skinny-dipping earlier in the night. It doesn't matter! I was in front of my boss in only my bra, and he touched my butt, and he's going to sue me, right? For sexual harassment? Damn it! That was probably his plan for getting rid of me the whole time. He's going to complain about me to Athena Quinn . . ."

"Take a breath, Hazel. If anything, it sounds like he was being inappropriate. He's probably more worried that *you'll* report *him*."

"He was being gentlemanly."

Kehlani laughed. "Since when is telling your female coworker to strip and then touching her gentlemanly?"

"He . . . I . . ." *Huh.* "Fair point. But that doesn't mean he won't tell Athena Quinn about it. He may have already. I swear, he's been trying to get me fired since the minute I stepped into this house. From being all formal with last names, to trying to freak me out with that fake power outage, to telling me I'm not allowed to speak to anyone else, and now the butt thing."

"I have two words for you," Kehlani said.

"Sue him?"

"Nope. *Love triangle.*"

I groaned. "Stop it. It's not funny. Mr. Remington doesn't like me. And I kissed his nephew. And God, I have to tell Hudson, right? That I let his uncle touch my ass? What is wrong with me?"

"Love triangle."

"Shut up!"

Kehlani laughed. "Do you like Hudson?"

"Yes."

"Do you like Mr. Remington?"

"No. I actively dislike him."

"Mhm," Kehlani said. "But here's the thing. You have strong feelings toward Mr. Remington. Whether they're good or bad . . . I think the line is pretty fine between both emotions. Were you thinking you'd pretend it didn't happen or apologize and move on?"

"Neither. God, it doesn't even matter. I'm never leaving my room again." As if on cue, my stomach growled.

"That'll make work difficult."

"He doesn't give me any real work to do anyway. He probably won't even notice if I show up on Monday."

"He'll notice if he's pining for you."

I stared out at the ocean view. "He's not. Not even a little bit. He's just . . ." I didn't know how to finish the sentence. Gentlemanly? Conniving? Rude? Hot? *Damn it, not that last one!* "There's something off about him. There's something off about everyone I've met here, honestly."

"You're just not used to southern hospitality."

"That's what I thought too, but . . . I don't know. I can't explain it. I just feel like there's something to uncover. And I don't know how to solve it."

"Well, I can solve one mystery for you. You said Mr. Remington was pissed that you were touching Athena Quinn's tomato sauce, right?"

"Yeah. He caught me red-handed." I laughed, thinking about the fact that I was literally holding a container filled with red sauce in my hands.

"Well, that wasn't why he was upset. He must have been pissed because you were touching *his* tomato sauce."

"No, it was in Athena Quinn's refrigerator. The one we're not allowed in. It was definitely hers."

"Impossible. Athena Quinn is allergic to tomatoes."

"Wait, what?" I leaned forward in my chair. "That's not possible. There was so much of it. Miss Serrano must have been cooking it all day."

"I read it in an article a while back, but yeah, I'm almost positive. She's deathly allergic to tomato sauce."

I opened up my computer and typed "Athena Quinn tomatoes" in the Google search bar. Athena Quinn had always been notoriously private about her life. But there was a Q&A article detailing exactly what Kehlani was saying. "You're right."

"I know my Athena Quinn facts."

"So why was there so much tomato sauce in her fridge if she's allergic?" My heart started beating faster.

"And why did Mr. Remington get so angry that you found it?"

"I don't know." I felt a chill run down my spine and turned around. But the room was empty. I didn't know if it was because of the mystery I was trying to write or because there was some real merit to my thoughts, but ever since I had set foot in this house, I had felt a sinister presence. I couldn't shake it. It almost felt like I was being watched.

"What if . . . he's trying to kill her," Kehlani whispered, as if she could tell we were being watched too.

"What?!" I hissed.

"Think about it. You haven't gotten to meet Athena Quinn. You thought it was her choice, but what if he's not letting her leave her private quarters? How terrible is the allergy? Could he be giving it to her slowly? Slowly killing her?"

"Jesus, I don't know." I heard Kehlani typing on her computer.

"It seems like it depends on how severe the allergy is," she said. "Cooking them sometimes helps. I don't know, Hazel. I have a really bad feeling about this."

"*You* have a bad feeling? Kehlani, I'm the one stuck in this creepy mansion with a possible murderer on the loose!"

"Well, maybe it wasn't tomato sauce. Maybe it was something else."

I shook my head. "What else could it possibly be?"

"Go look."

"I just told you I'm never leaving my room again."

She laughed.

"I'm serious. I didn't want to leave because I was embarrassed. And now I'm worried I'll be offed next." But she had a point. Maybe this whole thing was a misunderstanding. Maybe it wasn't tomato sauce. It wasn't like I'd opened up the container and smelled it.

"I'll stay on the phone with you," Kehlani said. "If anything happens . . . I'll call 9-1-1 right away."

"This is a bad idea." But I'd already stood up. It didn't matter how uncomfortable I was. I couldn't just sit here all weekend and let Mr. Remington get away with murder. "You swear you won't hang up?"

"Promise."

I took a deep breath and opened my bedroom door. I looked both ways before hurrying into the empty hallway. The house was eerily quiet. I padded down the stairs and into the kitchen. I wanted there to be anything but tomato sauce in the freezer. I wanted Mr. Remington to go back to being rude and hoity-toity but not a murderer. I wrapped my hand around the handle of the freezer.

The cool air hit me, and I blinked. I blinked again. "Kehlani?"

"Open one of the containers and give it a good taste."

"I can't do that."

"Why?"

"Because there's nothing in here."

I stared at the barren shelves. The fear that had been pulsing in my veins evaporated, replaced by confusion.

"What?"

"It's completely empty." It had been packed with containers last night. It had been so full that I had to move some around in my search for an ice pack.

"Well, that's great! You must have imagined it . . ."

"I didn't imagine it."

"You were drinking, right?" Kehlani asked.

"Yeah, but . . ." My voice trailed off. Had I imagined it? Kehlani was right—I had been drinking. A lot. That was why I was dumb and moaned when Mr. Remington touched me. I guessed maybe I could have imagined the tomato sauce. "Or . . . Mr. Remington moved it."

Kehlani gasped. "Girl, you need to get out of there. You're living with a murderer!"

"I can't leave. I'm the only one who knows what he's planning, so I'm the only one who can stop it."

"Or you can call the police. What if he's planning on murdering you next?"

I knew I should have been scared. I'd seen the tomato sauce containers. And yet . . . I wasn't. Ever since I'd arrived at this house, it seemed like Mr. Remington had been trying to scare me off. But why would he have hired me if he wanted me to leave? If he was about to kill Athena Quinn any day? It didn't make sense. I pictured the way he'd gently touched my bruise.

"He's not going to hurt me," I said. "If he wanted to, last night would have been the perfect time. Instead, he took care of me."

"Then explain the tomato sauce."

"Maybe he just loves it. And it didn't fit in the staff kitchen's fridge."

"I don't love that logic," Kehlani said.

"Yeah, I don't either. But there's something else going on here. And I feel like I'm finally getting closer to figuring it out."

"I really think you should come back to New York."

"Being here in this house has been the spark of inspiration I've been waiting for. I can't leave."

"But what if I'm right?" Kehlani asked. "It doesn't matter if you've written one page or half a novel if you're not alive to see it through."

"I'll be careful, I promise."

Kehlani sighed. "I really don't like this. What else do you even know about Mr. Remington?"

"Besides his first name? Nothing." I knew absolutely nothing about Atlas Remington. But I was going to figure out what he was hiding. Hopefully before he had a chance to murder anyone. Including me.

CHAPTER 16

Monday—September 5

I stared at the list I'd made about Mr. Remington. But I was no closer to putting all the pieces together.

1. Uses old-fashioned words and phrases.
2. Southern gentleman.
3. No bed in his room.
4. Cold hands.
5. Strict about Athena Quinn's rules.
6. Angry about tomato sauce and then . . . hid it?
7. Won't let me meet our boss.
8. Gentle when he touches me.

I'd tried to google various combinations of those things all weekend, but the search engine was being stupid. Or I was being stupid. All I could figure out was that he probably had bad circulation, which caused his hands to be cold. And maybe he was deficient in vitamins found in tomatoes, so he binge ate them. But I wasn't fond of those results, and I kept coming back to the same two conclusions—Mr. Remington was either having an affair with Athena Quinn or planning on killing her. Maybe both.

But I still couldn't figure out why he wanted me here, then. I bit the inside of my lip. God, I should have listened to Kehlani and skipped town. Just the thought of facing Mr. Remington this morning had my heart racing. And it wasn't just because of the whole murder thing. I was still embarrassed about how I'd reacted on Friday night.

If I didn't go downstairs soon, though, I'd be late for work. I shoved my notebook under my pillow. I was overthinking all of this. Hopefully Hudson would come by to check on the pool today, and I could ask him some questions. His hands were also cold. Maybe it was a hereditary thing. I wished I had gone back to his place so I could have looked for a bed. I shook the thought away. Of course Hudson had a bed. And so did Atlas—he just shared it with Athena Quinn.

I made my way downstairs. I felt like a chicken for camping out in my room all weekend. If Athena Quinn was in danger, I'd just sat there hiding. That made me complicit, right?

I reached the landing, but my hand gripped the railing. *Oh my God.* Was Mr. Remington trying to frame me for the murder? *Shit.* Technically, I was an embittered employee, because Athena Quinn seemed too snooty to meet me. The similarity of our novels probably made me look even more bitter.

I swear my heart stopped beating. Mr. Remington had left his bedroom door unlocked while he was away. Had he somehow known I'd sneak into his room and find the manuscript? If there were cameras or something . . . it might even look like I had read Athena Quinn's pages and *stolen* her book idea. And then killed her to get away with it.

Damn it, and I touched the tomato sauce containers! My fingerprints were all over them.

My heart started racing. That was it, wasn't it? It had to be. Mr. Remington had never wanted me here, but I was a necessary part of his plan. *Fuck.* I took a step back, and two cold hands grabbed my biceps. Speak of the devil. But I bet a devil's hands were hot.

"Miss Fox, are you quite all right?"

"I'm fine," I said, stepping away from him. But by the concerned way he was scanning my face, he knew I was anything but fine. I couldn't let him find out that I suspected what he was up to. Then he'd have no reason to keep me alive. I pressed my lips together because I was pretty sure that my bottom lip was trembling.

"Are you sure? You look a little pale. I didn't see you leave your room at all this weekend. Have you eaten anything?"

No. I was scared to leave my room because you're a murderer! "Yes," I lied. "We must have just missed each other in the kitchen."

"I presume so," he said, his eyes still glued to my face.

I'd never been a good liar. He could see it, right? That I was scared of him? He'd asked me that once. Why it seemed like I was scared of him. I hadn't been at the time. Not really. But it was almost like he was bothered by the fact that I wasn't. Like he was almost warning me to run.

"I believe I need to clear the air with you. About Friday night . . ."

"Nope," I quickly said. "Nothing to clear up. Honestly, I had a little too much to drink and barely remember a thing." *Lies!*

"Regardless, I feel as though I owe you an explanation. I went to medical school for a while before I realized it wasn't a good fit for me. So when I saw you were hurt . . . I was just making sure you hadn't broken anything."

I swallowed hard. "Yeah, I knew that," I quickly said. God, why had I said that?

He raised his left eyebrow. "You knew I went to medical school?"

I cleared my throat. "No, I just meant I knew you were being professional. That makes sense that you went to med school. I could tell by the way you were touching me." *Stop talking!* My fear was quickly turning into severe mortification. I'd been trying to avoid this conversation all weekend, just as much as I'd been trying my best not to get killed.

He nodded. "It just seemed like maybe you thought I was being inappropriate . . ."

"Nope. Not at all. I could tell you were doing doctorly things." I could feel myself starting to sweat. Could he see it? Could he tell I was melting?

"Excellent. I'm glad we cleared that up."

Had we? "Of course. I'm definitely not going to report you to Athena Quinn for sexual harassment or anything. You have nothing to worry about. It wasn't unprofessional. If anything, it was nice." *What the hell am I saying right now?*

He stared at me. "Is that something that crossed your mind, Miss Fox? To report me for sexual harassment?" He didn't look very concerned. If anything, he looked slightly amused by the thought.

"No. Were *you* going to report *me*?"

"For what, exactly, Miss Fox? You said it yourself. I was acting in a way befitting a doctor."

I hadn't used those fancy words. "I meant because I was walking around without a shirt. Being drunk. Holding Athena Quinn's tomato sauce." *Why did I just say that last thing?!*

"Tomato sauce?"

"I didn't say *tomato sauce*."

He lowered his eyebrows. "You most certainly did."

"What?" I laughed, even though it was forced. "Oh, right. When I was looking for an ice pack, I noticed that the freezer was full of containers of tomato sauce. I barely remembered it."

He shook his head. "Well, I don't remember that at all." His eyebrows lowered. "Are you sure it was tomato sauce?"

"I'm pretty sure."

He shook his head again. "Athena Quinn is allergic to tomatoes."

I pretended to look surprised. Why had I mentioned the sauce? "Is she? Well, that's odd, isn't it?"

"Excuse me." He walked past me toward the kitchen.

For a second I debated running out the front door. But I was too curious to see what he was about to do. I ran after him.

Mr. Remington pulled open the freezer door in the main kitchen, revealing the very empty freezer. He looked back at me. "I was distracted Friday night. But I do remember you had something in your hands." He shook his head. "The freezer is completely empty now, though." He gestured with his hands toward the shelves, even though I already knew.

"Weird," I said, trying to keep my tone even.

He nodded. "But I think you're right. I think there was some tomato sauce in the container in your hands. I think the shelves were full of it."

"Maybe I was just drunk," I said. I wasn't sure where he was going with this, but I didn't want it to end with me being stuffed in the freezer.

"No, I remember it too. You don't think . . ." He looked around like we might be overheard. "You don't think that Miss Serrano made a large batch while I was gone the other day? And then moved it once we discovered it?"

Did I have it all wrong? Was it actually Miss Serrano who was up to no good? After all . . . *she* was the chef. "Well . . . why would she do that?"

Mr. Remington closed the freezer door. "Come with me." He grabbed my hand.

I'd been scared of him all weekend. But I wasn't scared in the slightest when he snatched my hand. His fingers were icy, but I still found them comforting. He pulled me toward the dining room, but instead of going in, he opened an adjacent door.

He closed the door behind us, bathing us in darkness. He'd led me to a spot perfect for a murder. I tried to step back but hit a shelf. My eyes slowly adjusted to the dark. We were chest to chest, cramped together in a small pantry. My heart started beating faster. Not because I thought he was about to murder me but because he was close. And I could smell the salt water on his skin again. And I remembered the way his palm felt sliding up the back of my leg.

He stared down at me, not saying a word.

I'd felt this heat between us on Friday night. But he'd basically just told me I'd imagined it. That he was just being professional. How could I be reading this all wrong?

He leaned forward, and for a second I thought he was going to kiss me. Instead, his lips almost brushed against my ear.

"Do you think anyone can hear us in here?" he whispered.

"No." My voice sounded so small. There was something twisted in my head. I suspected him of plotting a murder, and yet all I wanted was for him to bite down on my earlobe. Press my back against the pantry shelves. Devour every inch of me. Really, he was probably wondering if anyone would be able to hear me scream when he slit my throat.

"This has to stay between us," he whispered. "Athena Quinn would crucify me if she knew I'd let it slip."

Crucify. That was an odd choice of word.

"Do you promise not to say anything, Miss Fox?"

It was impossible not to promise him exactly what he wanted when his body was so close to mine. "I promise."

"Miss Serrano has been quite unpleased for some time with Athena Quinn's outbursts."

"Outbursts?"

"When she's struggling with a scene, she gets a little . . . violent."

I swallowed hard. "Violent how?"

"She has a temper. She screams. Throws things. Breaks things."

A chill ran down my spine.

"It's a lot for Miss Serrano to clean up. Maybe Miss Serrano is sick of it. Wants revenge for how poorly she's treated."

"Revenge as in . . . killing Athena Quinn?" I tilted my head so I could try to see his face in the darkness, and the tip of my nose ran across his jawline.

But he didn't flinch. He didn't move. Our lips were only a fraction of an inch apart.

He stared into my eyes. "Is that what you think she's trying to do?"

I couldn't read the expression on his face. Was he being genuine here or trying to throw the blame on someone else? "I don't know, Mr. Remington."

"Regardless, we need to be careful. If Miss Serrano thinks we're onto her . . . who knows what she'll do."

I nodded. "I won't say a word." And I wouldn't. I didn't know who to trust here. Him? Was he framing Miss Serrano? Was he framing me? "Should we go check to make sure Athena Quinn is okay?"

"She's fine. I was just with her this morning."

Well, that cleared up that suspicion. He was with her because they'd been together all night. But it didn't explain why he kept his lips so close to mine. Why it seemed like he loved breathing in my exhales. Or maybe it was just me who was enjoying this.

Neither of us said a word. We just stood there in the dark pantry. My heart was thumping so fast that I was worried he might hear it. I could hear it. Pulsing in my head.

I could've sworn that he drew a fraction of an inch closer.

"Is it better today, Miss Fox?"

"What?"

"Your hip."

I wanted him to touch me again. To run his cold fingers up my thigh. Minutes ago, I was worried he was plotting to kill our boss. But now? Standing in here this close? I couldn't imagine him doing that. All I could picture was him kissing me. "Why? Do you think you might need to examine me again, Dr. Remington?" *Seriously, what the hell am I saying?*

"Dr. Remington," he said slowly. "It's been a lifetime since someone's called me that."

"A lifetime?"

He pulled back. "Figure of speech, Miss Fox. We should get back. We don't want Miss Serrano to catch us in here." He opened the pantry door and gestured for me to leave.

Everything he'd told me was probably a ruse. But I couldn't tell from the way he was staring at me. And it wasn't like I could question Miss Serrano to hear her side. I'd have to take matters into my own hands. If I could find where the tomato sauce had been moved to . . . I could get rid of it before either Miss Serrano or Mr. Remington got away with murder.

Besides, I didn't really have a choice. My fingerprints were on the containers. And I was the only person in this mansion who I knew for sure wasn't a killer.

CHAPTER 17

Monday—September 5

Apparently Athena Quinn had decided she wanted to partake in the Inbox Zero philosophy. And by *she*, I meant that she was making me do it. I stared longingly at the pool from my lounge chair. Even the beautiful end-of-summer day didn't make the silly email task any better. I looked back down at the thousands of emails sitting in Athena Quinn's inbox. She hadn't opened a single email in months. Maybe in a year, even. It was going to take me forever to sort through them all and have her inbox hit zero.

It was busywork. And I couldn't help but think this wasn't a task set by Athena Quinn at all. Mr. Remington was just delaying my meeting with our boss. Because maybe . . . maybe she was already dead. My stomach churned. *Please, God, no.*

I looked back at the house. Mr. Remington had gone upstairs instead of joining me for breakfast. And Miss Serrano would be done cleaning up in the kitchen by now. I honestly didn't know where Miss Serrano spent most of the day. But I'd keep an eye out for her. If Mr. Remington was telling the truth, Miss Serrano was the one to look out for.

But I didn't really believe Mr. Remington. It was easy to trust him when he was staring at me in a confined space. But now that I was outside and away from his alluring scent? That asshole was definitely trying to frame me. And I needed to find that tomato sauce before it was too late.

I jotted my number on a sticky note and stuck it to the top of my laptop for Hudson. I really needed to talk to him about all this, and I hoped he would stop by today. Because I was quickly heading to crazy town, and only Mr. Remington's nephew would be able to talk me off the ledge. Or maybe I shouldn't even mention it to Hudson. *God, what if Hudson's in on it too?*

I stood up and stared at the cliff's edge overlooking the beach. I needed to be careful. Really careful. Or I might wind up at the bottom of that cliff. Even talking to Hudson could be dangerous. Maybe I could casually bring up tomato sauce out of context and gauge his reaction. That would work. But first I needed to get my fingerprints off the evidence.

I looked both ways before sneaking back into the house.

Where could someone hide all that tomato sauce?

It had to be in a refrigerator somewhere. And it wasn't in either of the fridges I'd seen. Maybe they had an old one in the basement? I wasn't even sure this house had a basement. But looking for one seemed like a good place to start.

The kitchen was a bust. So was the entry hall. I hadn't explored the left side of the house at all. I looked around to make sure Miss Serrano wasn't going to pop out of nowhere before I walked down the hall. The cold marble floors on this side of the house felt even colder under my feet. Probably because no one ever wandered down here.

The first few doors were locked.

So was the next one.

And the next.

That was awfully suspicious. So far, every room Mr. Remington had said would be locked wasn't. And all of these were? Had he gone around locking them because he knew what I'd been up to? He'd acted like he knew I was snooping when I'd found Athena Quinn's very specific library and mini art museum. But he hadn't called me out. And he certainly hadn't said a thing about me snooping in his room.

But he wouldn't have, right? Because he wanted me to snoop. He wanted me to find that manuscript. I swallowed hard. Yeah, he was definitely framing me.

I reached the last door and turned the knob, but it didn't budge. *Damn it.* I definitely should have seen that coming, though.

I was about to turn back around when I noticed a tiny piece of wallpaper peeling down the side of the wall. It was just a small imperfection. And if I hadn't noticed it, I wouldn't have seen that all the wallpaper there was slightly . . . off.

I ran my hand down the edge of the peeling wallpaper and felt a small gap. It went from the ceiling to the floor, almost like it was some kind of hidden doorway . . .

I lightly pushed near the gap, not really expecting anything to happen, but hinges creaked as the wall flung backward.

A cloud of dust hit my face, and I coughed, waving my hand in front of me. The dust cleared, and I was staring into a small, empty wooden closet. It looked like some of the floorboards had rotted through. I turned to see if there was anything hidden in the corners. *What the . . . ?* I ducked my head into the closet. But it wasn't a closet at all. I grabbed my phone and hit the flashlight feature. I was staring down a narrow corridor that appeared to run the length of the house. There were doors lining the right wall.

Secret doors. That I definitely wasn't supposed to be seeing. I was pretty sure they were secret entrances into all those locked rooms.

A chill ran down my spine, and I looked behind me. No one was in the hall. If anything led to a basement, this creepy hidden hallway was probably it. I needed to go in and close the door behind me before I was seen. But I'd also watched a few horror movies in which the characters walked into places just like this and were immediately stabbed to death.

They were always alone, though. I clicked on Kehlani's name in my phone, stepped over one of the rotten boards, and closed the door behind me.

"Hey," she said after a few rings. "I have a meeting in a few minutes. Can I call you back?"

"No. I just entered a creepy corridor, and I'm going to die if you hang up." I turned the speaker phone on so I could use my phone as a flashlight.

"Excuse me?"

I held up the light. "You heard me, Kehlani. Don't you dare hang up." Cobwebs crisscrossed the tight space. It didn't seem like anyone used this corridor anymore. Or maybe someone who was shorter than me did. I ran my hand through one of the cobwebs to get it out of my way. I knew one person who was shorter than me in this residence: *Miss Serrano.* I would have felt claustrophobic if anyone had been in there with me. But I was definitely alone. At least for right now.

"Are you trying to give me a heart attack? Get out of the creepy corridor!"

"I can't," I said. "I need to find the tomato sauce containers because my fingerprints are on them. I'm pretty sure either Miss Serrano or Mr. Remington is framing me for the murder."

"Athena Quinn's dead?!"

"No. I mean, I don't know." I wasn't allowed to see her to check. "Maybe." Saying it out loud made my heart start pounding faster. What if I was already out of time? I walked forward, careful to step over the loose-looking boards. There were lots of doors lining the corridor. All most likely leading to the rooms behind locked doors in the hall. I tried to open one, but it was locked from this side too.

"I don't understand what you're still doing in that creepy house."

"I just told you. I need to get my fingerprints off the tomato sauce." I stopped and stared at a small wooden door. It looked like something a safe would be hidden behind. I pulled on the handle and was surprised when it creaked open.

"What was that!?" Kehlani yelled.

I coughed as another blast of dust hit me in the face. "It's . . . a . . ." I let my voice trail off as I stuck my head inside and looked up. There was an old rope going up, up, up. It probably led right to one of Athena Quinn's private rooms. "It's a dumbwaiter," I said and stepped back. I looked back down the cramped hall. "I think I'm in some kind of servants' corridor."

"Hazel, I'm freaking out. What even is a servants' corridor?"

I swept my flashlight across the small space. "It seems like it's a way for them to go unnoticed as they do their tasks." *All the doorways.* There were even a few more dumbwaiters I could see with my light.

"Unnoticed. Well, that's suspicious."

"I know, right?" As creepy as it was, it was also pretty cool. I grabbed another door handle, but of course it was locked.

"Why do you sound so calm right now?" Kehlani asked.

"It doesn't seem like anyone's been in here for a century . . ." My voice died away in my throat.

"What? Did you see something?"

"There are footprints in the dust." One set coming and one set going. I moved my light to the left up a narrow flight of stairs. *This shit went upstairs too?*

"Get out of the haunted mansion!" Kehlani screamed.

"Keep your voice down—you're on speaker."

I moved my light toward the other set of footprints. They led to a door up ahead. I slowly made my way across the wooden floor to the door. I turned the knob, but it resisted.

"What's going on?" Kehlani asked. "Are you still there?"

I turned my light and caught sight of a set of stairs heading down. *Bingo.* I ducked under another cobweb and grabbed the railing. My hand paused.

"Are you still alive?!" Kehlani yelled.

I had the same feeling as when I'd first touched the railing on the staircase upstairs—that so many others had touched this railing before me. It was like I could feel them in the cramped space. Children running in the corridor and laughing. I blinked. I didn't know why I was imagining joy back here. I was almost positive that wasn't the atmosphere of this old manor a hundred years ago. I felt that the first night I was here too. That there was some kind of sinister presence.

"Hazel! Answer me!"

I shook my head. "Sorry. I'm fine. I think I found the basement." The floorboards creaked even more on the narrow stairs.

"My meeting is about to start . . . Give me one second to postpone it before you go in."

"Okay." I heard her talking to someone else on her end. But I couldn't wait another second. I opened the door to the basement and went down. It was just as old and dusty as the corridor. It looked like nobody had been down there in ages. There were tons of things draped in white bedsheets, just like in the room with all the beautiful sculptures.

I picked up an edge of one of the sheets, expecting to see another sculpture. But it was a framed portrait of . . . *What the . . . ?*

The same dark eyes. The same windswept hair. It was Mr. Remington. But also . . . it wasn't Mr. Remington. Because he was wearing clothes I'd seen depicted in schoolbooks of the people who'd come over on the *Mayflower*. And even though his hair was a similar shade, it was a lot longer in the painting.

"I'm back," Kehlani said. "Are you okay?"

"No . . ."

"God, what's wrong? Do I need to call 9-1-1?"

"No," I said with a laugh, even though it was forced. "I'm staring at an old portrait of Mr. Remington."

"Like . . . as a child?"

"No. He looks the same age as he is now, but it looks like it's from the sixteen hundreds or something."

"Well, that doesn't make any sense. Are you high right now or something? That would explain the walking-into-a-creepy-corridor-alone thing. Have you never seen a horror movie?"

"Very funny." I shook my head and lifted the corner of another portrait. Again, it was of Mr. Remington. "There's another one. Maybe from the eighteen hundreds?" He was wearing a vest like the one I'd seen him wear to dinner once, but he definitely hadn't been wearing the top hat at dinner. There was a woman with him in this one. She was wearing a petticoat. And I knew I'd never seen her before, but there was something so oddly familiar about her face.

"Oh, I know what it is!" Kehlani said. "Remember spring break junior year? We went to the beach, and there was that photography place where you could dress up in old-timey clothes and pose?"

"Yeah, I remember."

"He must have gone to one of those."

I touched the side of the portrait and felt the uneven surface of the paint. "It's not some cheap photo. It's painted. It's a real portrait."

"Well, that's extra fancy. But it has to be the dress-up thing. It's just pretend."

"I guess so." Kehlani was right. There was no other explanation. I knew that. And yet . . . the portrait looked old. The frame even looked worn. Mr. Remington didn't seem exactly the same, though. I glanced over at the first portrait. He looked . . . lighter, maybe? A little less stern. He just looked . . . happier. I looked back at the portrait in front of me. The one in which he was wearing a top hat. He was more serious here. Every bit the part of a man from the 1800s. It was the gaze I was used to having fixed on me. In this one, he looked almost exactly the same as he did now.

Which meant Kehlani had to be right.

I lifted up the cover on one more portrait. Mr. Remington was wearing the same top hat in this one. But the woman on his arm was different. I put my flashlight right over her face, but she didn't look familiar like the other woman had. I turned the light back on Mr. Remington. He seemed the same as he had in the other portrait, and the same as he did right now. He may have even been wearing that exact same vest a few days ago. It was just some souvenir from a trip, albeit a very expensive souvenir. I let the cloth fall back in place.

"Kehlani?" I asked.

"Yeah?"

"Regardless of where the portraits are from, why are they here? In Athena Quinn's basement?"

"Well, they're having an affair. And he lives there. Where else is he supposed to keep all his personal possessions?"

I nodded. "Right." I picked up a corner of another sheet. Mr. Remington was in this painting too. And so was another man I didn't know. But based on the familiar scowl and dark eyes, I knew it had to be Mr. Remington's brother. Hudson's father. He looked . . . cruel. Even more serious than Mr. Remington, if that was possible. They were both wearing tuxedos. But they certainly weren't from this decade. "His brother looks like a total dick." The complete opposite of Hudson. No wonder Hudson didn't want me to know he was related to Mr. Remington. He wasn't anything like his uncle or his father.

"In a sexy way?"

I laughed. "No." I kept staring at Hudson's dad. "Well . . . kind of." I had a feeling that if the man smiled, he'd look just like his son.

A floorboard creaked, and I spun around.

"What was that?" Kehlani's voice came loud and clear through the speaker.

I hit the speaker button to turn it off. But I knew she was still on the line to hear whoever was creeping up on me. "Hello?" My voice echoed in the emptiness. "Hello?" I said again.

No response.

My phone started ringing. *Shit!* It fell out of my hand as I tried to stop the noise. It landed facedown on the wooden floor, and the flashlight feature lit up my face in the darkness. I pressed my hands over the light. *Shit, shit, shit!* I must have hit the "End Call" button on Kehlani instead of taking her off speaker. Whoever was there had to have just seen me.

For two seconds I crouched there, staring at the darkness. I couldn't see anything because of the stupid light that had blinded me. But then I heard another creak.

Fuck this. I wasn't going to sit here and wait to be killed next.

I pulled the phone to my ear. "Kehlani, he's going to kill me! Call 9-1-1!"

"Hazel?" said a deep voice through my phone.

I screamed at the top of my lungs. How was Mr. Remington calling me right now? "Murderer!"

"What the fuck, Hazel?! Hazel?!" yelled the voice.

I was about to throw my phone in the direction of the creaking noise when I finally registered who was on the other end. And it wasn't Mr. Remington. "Hudson?"

"Hazel, are you okay? Where are you?"

A sob escaped my throat. "I'm in the basement. There's someone here . . ."

"I'll be right there."

I heard another creak and took a step back. But then there was another creak behind me. I spun around as a little light trickled into the basement. *A door!* I beelined toward it and ran straight into Hudson.

He slammed the door closed behind me. "What the fuck?" he said again.

I threw my arms around him. "He's trying to kill me," I said through sobs as I gripped him tighter. "I saw his tomato sauce and the portraits, and I read the manuscript, and he's trying to frame me for Athena Quinn's murder, and I need your help!"

I was pretty sure I was holding him so tightly that I was hurting him. But he didn't seem to care.

"He who?" Hudson asked.

I cringed but kept clinging to him. I really hadn't meant to say any of that. What if Hudson was in on it?

CHAPTER 18

Hudson was staring at me like I'd completely lost my mind. "He who?" he asked again.

I was going to try to play it cool and get information out of Hudson. But I'd just spilled everything. I only lived with one *he*. And there was only one *he* I could possibly be referring to. I pulled back. "You're going to think I'm way off base, but . . . I think . . ." Was there anything I could say to turn this around? I was pulling a total blank. My mind was scrambled, and my heart was racing too fast. "I think your uncle is planning on killing Athena Quinn. If he hasn't already. And he's framing me." *Okay, so we're doubling down here . . .*

"Are you high right now?"

Why did everyone think I was high? *Shit, Kehlani.* I looked down at my phone. She was calling me back. I pulled my phone to my ear.

"Hazel! Hazel, answer me!" she shrieked.

"I'm okay," I said. "I'm with Hudson."

"Well, don't tell him anything! He might be in on it!"

I felt like she was yelling so loudly that he could hear every word, so I just laughed. "Hudson is not in on it." But the way he was looking at me . . . like he thought I was insane . . . *God, he's probably in on it.* Why was everyone here trying to mess with my head?!

"How do you know?" Kehlani asked.

"Because he's here with me right now," I tried to say as calmly as possible. "He helped me get out."

"Oh. Oooooh," she said. "Put me on speaker."

I hit the speaker button.

"Listen here, Hudson," Kehlani said. "I know your last name, buddy. And I know people who know people, so if you do anything to my girl, I'll have cops swarming your residence in two seconds flat."

Not at all what I thought she was going to say. And not at all true. She didn't know people who knew people. If Hudson was in on it, I was totally fucked.

Hudson laughed. "I don't know what the two of you think you know . . ."

"There was tomato sauce, and then there wasn't!" Kehlani yelled. "And Hazel's fingerprints are on it. And your handsy uncle tried to distract Hazel by touching her butt."

Hudson lowered his eyebrows as he stared at me. "Excuse me?"

Oh crap. I hadn't gotten a chance to tell him about that yet. Hudson actually looked really hurt. And the last thing I needed was for him to be mad at me. He was either in on the framing or the only person on this stupid island who was on my side. "Kehlani, I have to go. I'm fine. I'm safe. I love you. Byyyyye!"

"Don't you dare hang up—"

I hung up the phone. "Hudson . . ."

"Did you hook up with my uncle?"

"What? No. Absolutely not."

"Your friend just said—"

"I just told you that I think he's going to murder my boss!" I looked around to make sure Mr. Remington wasn't anywhere nearby listening in. But it appeared that we were alone in the shaded garden. *All alone . . .*

I swallowed hard. There was a fresh patch of dirt only a few feet away from us. If Hudson was in on the murderous plot, it would be pretty easy for him to whack me over the head and hide my body right there . . . Or was Athena Quinn already under there? *Shit.*

"Hazel, that doesn't really answer my question."

"How are you not freaking out right now?" Really . . . why wasn't he freaking out? And why had I ended my phone call with Kehlani? If Hudson was in on Mr. Remington's plans, she was the only reason I hadn't already been murdered.

"I'm not freaking out because Atlas is my uncle. I know him. And he wouldn't hurt a fly."

Something about the way Hudson said "he wouldn't hurt a fly" made it seem like Mr. Remington indeed wouldn't hurt a *fly*. But he'd hurt anything that wasn't a fly. Like a person. *Like me.* Why had Hudson said it that way?

Hudson lifted his hand and reached toward me.

I cringed.

"Hazel, I'm not going to hurt you." He pulled something out of my hair. "Your hair is covered in cobwebs."

"Get them out!" I started waving frantically at my hair.

He laughed. "I'm trying to, if you'd stop moving."

I stayed still as he pulled out another cobweb and wiped his hand off on his swimming trunks.

"Did you get them all?"

"Yeah."

I tried to take a deep breath. Why would he bother to get cobwebs out of my hair if he was plotting to kill me?

"Back to the hooking-up-with-my-uncle thing . . ."

"I did not hook up with Mr. Remington."

"It's really weird that you call him that," Hudson said.

"It's what he asked me to call him."

Hudson just stared at me. "Are you going to make me ask you a third time?"

"I didn't hook up with your uncle." Maybe a piece of me wanted to. A small piece. I remembered the feeling of his eyes on me. His hands on me. "I told you—I fell on the stairs down to the beach. My hip was a little sore, and he was checking it out because he was almost a doctor or something."

"Hence the touching your butt?"

"Yeah. Nothing happened. He was just being doctorly."

"Okay."

"Okay, then," I said.

"So you don't fancy him?"

Fancy him? Who talks like that? "No," I said as firmly as possible. "He's a bad person."

Hudson laughed. "Trust me, Atlas is not a bad person. And he hasn't murdered Athena Quinn. I just spoke to the recluse on the phone this morning. If it'll make you feel better, I'll check in more often."

"You spoke to Athena Quinn? Just this morning?"

Hudson nodded.

A murderer would say that his victim was still alive . . . but Hudson didn't really look like a murderer. His uncle, though?

"Let's break down the rest of what you were saying. You mentioned tomato sauce?"

I was glad he wasn't beating around the bush. "Yes. The freezer was filled with containers of tomato sauce when I came home Friday night. Atlas was super pissed that I was touching them. But then the next day, they were all gone. And Athena Quinn is allergic to tomatoes. Today he told me that he thinks Miss Serrano is maybe trying to off Athena, but that was definitely a lie. He's setting me up. My fingerprints are on the sauce—"

Hudson laughed, cutting me off. "Hazel, he's just messing with you. It was his sauce."

"Wait, what?"

"Atlas is allergic to garlic. There's this little restaurant a few hours away that makes tomato sauce he actually likes and can eat. A few times a year, he goes and gets a ton of it. He just went this week."

Wait, that was what he'd done on his mysterious getaway? "But he . . . he said . . ."

"He's definitely just messing with you."

"But why? And where did the sauce go?"

"Who knows? Did you piss him off or something?"

I pressed my lips together. It seemed like I was always pissing him off. But a certain instance popped into my head. "The tomato sauce was in Athena Quinn's freezer. I wasn't supposed to be snooping in it. Maybe he was pissed that I saw him break the rules? Because he was using it for his weird tomato sauce storage? I also broke into his room . . ."

Hudson laughed but stopped when he realized I wasn't joking. "Why, exactly, did you break into his room?"

"Because I knew he was hiding something."

"Hiding what, exactly?" His eyes searched mine.

"I . . ." My voice trailed off. I didn't know. That was the whole problem. "I don't know. That's why I was snooping. But his room is where I found Athena's manuscript. Which is suspiciously similar to the book I'm writing. Which really frames me even more . . ."

"There is no framing. It's Atlas's tomato sauce, and he's being a dick. Anyway, aren't you supposed to read Athena's manuscripts? Isn't it your job to look at her work?"

"My job is to check her emails."

"Well, it was your lucky day, then."

I opened my mouth and then closed it again. *Yeah . . . maybe.* "But what about the portraits in the basement?" I pointed over my shoulder.

"What were they of?"

"They were these super-old portraits of Mr. Remington from the sixteen hundreds and eighteen hundreds. I know it doesn't make any sense. But I swear it was him. And I think your dad may have been in one too." I knew that the conclusion Kehlani and I had drawn made sense, but I wanted to know what Hudson thought of it.

"You mean those super-creepy old portraits?"

I nodded. They were indeed creepy.

"I don't know exactly which ones you saw, but I know Atlas has most of the old family portraits from when our ancestors first came over to America."

I just stared at him. Wow, that made a lot more sense than Mr. Remington dressing up in old-timey clothes at a boardwalk shop . . . Why the hell hadn't Kehlani and I thought of that?

"My dad didn't want them. And I certainly don't—they freak me out. There's a few with my great-great-great-grandfather. Or maybe there's one more *great*? Or two? I can never keep track. But I know there's one of my great-great-grandfather wearing a funny top hat."

"Yeah, I saw that one. But I swear he looked identical to Mr. Remington."

Hudson shrugged. "Strong bloodline."

A really, really strong bloodline. Mr. Remington looked practically identical to his ancestors.

We both just stared at each other. I wanted to believe Hudson. I really did. He'd just explained all my worries away without even pausing. It didn't seem like he was making anything up. But I still felt on edge. Maybe he was just the world's best fast thinker.

"Was there anything else you were worried about?" Hudson asked.

Everyone's hands are cold. You say weird things, like "fancy him," and there's no bed in Atlas's room. I shook my head. I thought I'd said enough. Too much, really. But getting it all off my chest made me feel a little better, especially since Hudson hadn't made a single move to throw me in the pile of dirt and bury me alive. "For the record, if your uncle is allergic to garlic and Athena Quinn is allergic to tomatoes, there really shouldn't be any tomato sauce allowed on the premises. Miss Serrano made me chicken parmesan just the other night."

Hudson laughed. "Yeah, it seems like a pretty bad idea."

"I can't believe he's just messing with me."

"I told you—he's all bite and no bark."

"And I told you that you have that phrase all backward." A chill ran down my spine, and I turned back to the house. A curtain swayed in the window on the second story. Had Athena Quinn—or, worse, Mr. Remington—been watching our whole exchange?

"If you're still freaked out, you can stay at my place tonight."

I turned back to him. "Really?"

"Of course. How about you come over for dinner? I'm cooking."

I nodded. "Yeah, that would be great." Athena Quinn hadn't made a single appearance at one of the formal dinners. There was no reason to think she'd show up at tonight's. And I didn't want to be alone with Mr. Remington right now. Or alone, period, in that creepy house.

Hudson looked up at the sky. It looked like the clouds were about to part.

"I gotta go finish up work before it gets too hot out. Let me text you my address." He pulled out his phone.

"Okay." I could definitely add "Hates heat" to my list of suspicious activity regarding the Remingtons.

My phone buzzed at his incoming text. I looked down and saw that Kehlani had tried to call me a dozen times since I'd hung up on her.

"Feel free to come early. Just let yourself in. I never lock the door."

"I might take you up on that, thanks."

He looked back up at the sky. "I gotta go. But, really, you have nothing to worry about, Hazel. Maybe stop snooping, though? It's clearly pissing Atlas off."

I nodded.

He gave me a quick kiss on the cheek and hurried off.

Hudson had given me an explanation for everything. And yet . . . I still felt uneasy. I turned back and looked at the window where I'd seen the curtains move. They were completely still now.

I took a deep breath. It was going to be fine. At least I didn't have to spend tonight in this mansion.

My phone buzzed, signaling another call from Kehlani. I needed to call her back before Athena Quinn's estate was surrounded by cops.

CHAPTER 19

Monday—September 5

I'd pondered whether to spend the night at Hudson's all afternoon. One minute, I was sure it was the right move. And the next minute? I remembered that Hudson was a Remington. Blood protected blood. What if everything he'd said to me was a lie?

I closed the lid of my laptop. Kehlani trusted Hudson more than she trusted Atlas. She'd made that abundantly clear when I called her back. She practically begged me to temporarily move in with him. I wasn't as convinced.

But as I made my way back inside Athena Quinn's house, I was swayed in the opposite direction again. There was something wrong with this house. Something off. Something that always made the little hairs on the back of my neck rise. It was just like Athena Quinn's manuscript said: *"There was something dark and twisted lurking inside. As soon as she entered, she'd be swallowed whole."*

I didn't want to be swallowed whole by the eerie feeling inside this old house. I'd stay with Hudson. For at least one night. I hurried up the stairs, not bothering to look down the forbidden hall to the left. I didn't want to think about secrets and lies anymore. I just wanted to have a drink and laugh and be normal.

This house was messing with my head, the people inside it more so. And I was done thinking about it today.

I closed my bedroom door behind me and walked over to my closet. I wasn't sure if spending the night with Hudson meant a sleepover situation or something more intimate. I still barely knew a thing about him. But he did make me laugh.

I reached out and ran my fingers down one of the few short dresses Mr. Remington had bought me. The fabric was more comfortable than that of any of the clothes I had. If I fell asleep in it, it would almost feel like pajamas. The only luggage I had was my huge suitcase. It would be weird to show up to Hudson's place with that, so something I could just sleep in made sense . . . even if it was a gift from his uncle. I contemplated calling Kehlani for advice. But I already knew she'd just tell me to wear whatever pushed up my breasts the most. And honestly . . . this dress was a good contender for that too.

Screw it. I changed before I could talk myself out of it. I heard a jangling noise as I pulled the dress over my head. I spun around and stared at the balcony. My heart was racing, but it must have just been the wind, pushing the curtains slightly. *I hope.* I walked over to the curtains and lifted both to the side, then studied the wallpaper beneath them. Nothing looked out of the ordinary. I stepped back and ran my fingers along the wallpaper toward the bed, looking for any imperfections. Anything at all that didn't line up perfectly.

But everything seemed in place. I turned and took in the rest of the walls. I couldn't be positive, but it really didn't seem like there were any hidden doors into my room. I breathed a sigh of relief. The weird servants' corridor must not have had an entrance to my room. I'd seen a set of stairs leading up, but maybe they didn't go to this wing. Maybe they only went to Athena's private quarters.

For the first time today, I actually felt a little safer in this house. At least there were no secret doors in my room. No one peeping at me while I slept or doing anything too sinister. I wasn't sure if it was the house or Athena Quinn's manuscript that had me more on edge.

The curtains made another jingling noise as they rustled in the wind. I closed the french doors to the balcony.

Even the nice view and the feeling of being a little safer weren't going to make me stay tonight, though. I'd feel a lot safer under Hudson's roof. Maybe even in his arms.

I hurried into the bathroom and grabbed my toothbrush. But I paused as I put it in my purse. There was a single bobby pin on the vanity. And not just any bobby pin. One that was bent back. The same one I'd used when I was trying to pick the lock to gain entry into Mr. Remington's room. The same one I'd lost because I panicked and ran away.

My heart started racing. Maybe it was just the one that I had found. I pulled open the top drawer of the vanity. The other bent bobby pin was sitting there, untouched. *Shit.*

A chill ran down my spine, and I turned toward the bathroom door. My room was empty. I'd just been out there. I'd just looked for a hidden door and come up empty. So why the hell did it feel like someone was watching me? I tried to shake the thought away. I was alone. But . . . someone had been in my room.

There had to be an innocent explanation. Miss Serrano cleaned the whole house. Maybe she saw it on the ground and knew it wasn't hers or Athena Quinn's, so the logical conclusion . . .

No, the logical conclusion would have been to throw it out because it was all bent up. This felt more like a message. *I know what you did.*

I just wasn't sure who'd left it. Was it Miss Serrano? Or Mr. Remington? Or Athena Quinn herself? Mr. Remington had been in my room before. That first night I was here. He said I'd left it unlocked and he'd dropped off my things. But I'd sworn I locked the door. Did he maybe come and go more often than I realized?

I put the second bobby pin into the drawer and slammed it shut. If he knew I had sneaked into his room, why hadn't he confronted me? Why did he keep playing games with my head? Hudson thought maybe I had pissed him off. But it was impossible to not piss off the man. And

I'd been as well behaved as I possibly could be, given the fact that I was literally standing in a haunted house.

An image popped into my head of Mr. Remington standing above my bed, staring down at me as I dreamed about him. For several nights I'd tossed and turned as I pictured his fingers slowly tracing up my thigh. There was no way he could have known I was thinking about him. And why the hell did I keep dreaming about him, anyway? How many times did I need to tell my brain that I did not like Mr. Remington?

It was definitely time to get out of here. The bobby pin was some kind of twisted message. But I didn't care what the message was. Because as far as I was concerned, I was done sleeping here. Period. I grabbed a pair of wedge heels and walked out of my room, careful to lock my door behind me.

My bare feet padded down the stairs. I ignored the familiar chill as my feet hit the marble floor in the foyer. I was rummaging around in my purse for my car keys, but my fingers didn't collide with them. Where were they? I pulled one of my purse straps off my shoulder so I could get a better look. I always kept my keys in the center pocket. I spun around and almost ran right into Mr. Remington. I froze as his eyes raked down my body.

"You look lovely, Miss Fox. But dinner isn't for another two hours."

My brain was still not listening to me, because I felt my cheeks blush at the compliment. Or maybe it was because it had been a couple of days since I'd seen him dress so casually. The sleeves of his dress shirt were rolled up again, and his hair looked more windswept than usual. I tore my eyes away from him and kept looking for my keys. "I can't make dinner. I have plans."

"What plans?"

"I'm spending the night at Hudson's." I cringed. I would have worded that better if I weren't preoccupied by the fact that I couldn't find my keys. I was seconds away from dumping the contents of my purse onto the floor to find them. Seriously, where were they?

"You don't have an overnight bag."

I looked back up at him. I really wanted to tell him it was because I didn't plan to do much sleeping. But for some reason, the intense way he was staring at me made me keep my mouth shut.

He lowered his eyebrows at me as we both stared at each other in the middle of the foyer. He shoved his hands into his pockets and cleared his throat. "I didn't take you for someone who partakes in dalliances."

"Excuse me?"

"A dalliance is . . ."

"I know what a dalliance is," I snapped. "And just because you used a fancy word doesn't mean you didn't just call me a whore."

"Miss Fox . . ."

"And I never said I was sleeping with him. I said I was sleeping *over*—if I can find my damn keys." I shook my head as I kept searching in my purse. I hated losing things. I hated even more when people made ridiculous assumptions about me. But I probably shouldn't have spoken so sternly to my boss. I stopped rummaging around in my handbag and looked up at him. "I'm sorry. I misplaced my keys, and I hate losing things . . ."

"Your keys aren't in your purse."

I stared at him. "Then where are they?" Had he taken my keys? So I couldn't leave this freaking house?

"I don't know. But you would have found them already if they were there."

Yeah. I guess. I just stared at him. *It really seems like he knows where they are . . .*

"And it's no worry—you don't need to drive to Hudson's estate. He lives three houses down. On the left."

Hudson's estate? I hadn't looked up the address Hudson had texted me. I was going to put it in my phone's GPS once I got in my car. But I had kind of assumed his living situation was more of the condo variety. Or maybe Mr. Remington called everything an estate. "Okay. Thank you." But that still didn't really fix my missing-keys situation. I'd deal with that later, though. Right now, I just needed out of this house. I stepped past him, but he caught my wrist to stop me. His cold touch made me shiver.

"And all I meant when I said 'dalliance' was that the company my nephew keeps rotates on a regular basis."

"So you're warning me about him?" Again, I didn't get it. Was he sincerely worried about me? Was he jealous? Was he a control freak who needed to know where I was at all times? I couldn't read him at all.

"I just think it's best that you don't leave the house at night."

He'd told me that before. That the beach was dangerous when night fell. And he was right . . . I had felt a little uncomfortable at that party on the beach. But I felt uncomfortable now too. With him staring at me like he wanted to devour every inch of me. I shook away the thought. Mr. Remington liked me just as much as I liked him . . . which was not at all.

But he didn't let go of my wrist.

And I didn't move to leave.

"Just . . . make sure you lock your door tonight," he said.

I pressed my lips together as I stared at him. Lock my door? Was he serious? He'd practically just admitted that he'd left the broken bobby pin on my vanity. He knew I had broken into his room. He knew, and he knew that I knew. "You should lock your door too," I said and pulled my wrist out of his grasp.

He lowered his eyebrows at me.

Seriously, why was he warning me one second, then lying to me the next? He was sending me all the most confusing mixed signals. Hudson had said Atlas was messing with me. But it was more focused than that. Mr. Remington was trying to scare me. That was all that I was certain of. I just had no idea why. He wanted me to think Miss Serrano was up to no good. That Hudson was a manwhore who couldn't be trusted. And that Athena Quinn didn't want to meet me.

Mr. Remington didn't want me to trust anyone.

But it was him. It was all his doing. Had it not been for the fact that he seemed to want me scared of him, I would have thought he wanted me to run into his arms for protection. It felt like I was missing a piece to a puzzle. But I wasn't searching for it tonight. I was getting the hell away from him and his mind games.

"Have a pleasant evening," I said. *Or whatever old-fashioned, fancy way you want to put it.* I hurried out the front door and pulled on my shoes. I glanced over my shoulder as I made my way down the gravel drive. The curtains fell back in place behind the closest window.

I knew he was watching. It was beginning to feel like he was always watching. Or . . . like someone was. That window was in Athena Quinn's office. Was she the one watching?

God, I wished I'd listened to Kehlani and gotten the hell out of here when I still could. Before my keys went missing. As I walked farther away from the house, I didn't feel any better. I was stuck here. I was stuck, and I didn't know how to get out.

CHAPTER 20

Monday—September 5

I tried not to stumble as I made my way past my car and down the long gravel drive. At least this time I was wearing wedges and not heels. But if I fell and Mr. Remington happened to be watching . . .

I shook my head. I would not give him that satisfaction. *"I didn't take you for someone who partakes in dalliances."* God, he had a lot of nerve. I wasn't planning on sleeping with Hudson tonight, but even if I was, it was none of Mr. Remington's business.

The more I thought about our conversation, the more pissed off I became. And I completely forgot to pay attention to how many mansions I passed. I looked back at Athena Quinn's white mansion at the top of the hill. And, for some reason, I just kept staring.

I felt like the naive woman Athena Quinn mentioned in her novel. I was too confused to unravel the secrets that were hidden behind those white columns. What was I missing? Every time I uncovered something, it all made less and less sense. I felt like I was missing one key thing. Just one thing that would put all the pieces together. And the longer I stood there staring, the more it felt like Athena Quinn had wanted me to see her manuscript. Like she was warning me about the sinister secrets behind those doors. But the warning was in vain. I couldn't leave now. I was pretty sure Mr. Remington had swiped my car keys. *Asshole.*

Hopefully a night away would clear my head. I counted the houses I'd passed. *Three houses down. On the left.* I turned and stared at Hudson's house. Mr. Remington was right—it was more of an estate than a house. Not at all like Athena Quinn's, though. It was modern and sleek and blended into the island's natural scenery like it was supposed to. I'd seen new houses like it before, but I always pictured them with more windows. Who needed windows in the front when the back was where the view was, though? I guessed that the whole back wall was one huge pane of glass.

This place must have cost a small fortune to rent for the summer. How had Hudson afforded it? He'd told me he was a student. At least, sometimes he was. When he felt like it. Maybe he worked a lot of odd jobs, but still . . . landscaping did not pay this well, did it?

I walked up to the house and lifted the heavy metal knocker. I let it fall with a thud as I looked around at the large trees and bushes surrounding the property. Despite the fact that Hudson did yard work for other people on the island, this yard was a little unruly. It somehow still looked nice, though. And the whole front yard was shaded from everything being overgrown. It was almost cold, even though the summer air was still lingering.

I waited a moment. Hudson had said I could go right in and make myself at home. Did he really leave it unlocked all the time? I knew the neighborhood was gated, but anyone could wander up from the beach and trespass. Maybe his uncle bugged him so much about locking doors that he was just rebelling or something.

I wasn't sure why I did so, but I looked both ways and behind me before I reached down and turned the knob. The door opened, and a blast of air-conditioning hit me. I shivered as I closed the door behind me.

Hudson was no Mr. Remington, so I figured it was okay to keep my shoes on. I walked through the entranceway. The floors were a grayish wood that fit right into the rest of the elegant beachy vibe of the house. There was tasteful art on the whitewashed walls but no pictures of the owners, which I guessed made sense if they rented the place out frequently.

The arch in the entranceway led to a huge great room that was open to the kitchen. And I was right—the back wall was practically one pane of glass stretching across the whole room. But all the blinds were drawn. I walked over to the closest window. There were no cords to move the blinds. They must have been controlled remotely or something. I pulled one back and stared down at the beach below. There was also the pool that Hudson apparently loved more than the ocean itself. The backyard was just as shaded as the front yard. The sun was beginning to set, casting an orange glow across the water. It was breathtaking.

Why on earth would someone close these blinds? I stepped back and shivered again. Well, I knew that Hudson hated working in the heat of the day. And he definitely kept the temperature cool in here. He probably just didn't want the hot sun warming up the great room. But seriously . . . it was really cold. I looked around for the thermostat as I wrapped my arms around myself. If he wanted me to make myself at home, it needed to be a few degrees or ten warmer. *I should have brought a sweatshirt . . .*

There didn't seem to be a thermostat in the main room. Honestly, there wasn't much of anything in the living room, just a white couch that looked like it had never even been sat on. I had expected the place to be a little messier. *God, I hope he won't be mad at me for wearing shoes inside.* Maybe he was a really careful tenant.

I wandered into the kitchen. I didn't think the thermostat would be in there, but another idea had popped into my head. If I were cooking, I wouldn't notice the chill in the air. Hudson had offered to make me dinner, but it would be a lot nicer for him to come back to a home-cooked meal after a long day of work. And the top-of-the-line appliances looked like they'd never been touched. They were practically dying to be used.

I opened the fridge and stared at the empty shelves.

What the . . . ?

I opened up the freezer door.

Nothing.

His whole refrigerator was empty. And so was the pantry. And so was almost every other cabinet I opened. He barely even had any dishes. Who had absolutely nothing in their kitchen? *A bachelor, I guess.* I sighed and closed the last drawer. So much for the nice gesture, which would have been even nicer, since it seemed like Hudson probably ate out most nights. Actually, going out sounded kind of fun. I hadn't even left this neighborhood yet. Hudson probably knew all the best places on the island. And maybe a restaurant would be a little warmer than this rental . . .

It was possible there was a place to eat within walking distance. Being this close to the beach almost ensured it. I pulled out my phone to call him, but before I clicked on his name, I heard the front door open.

Hudson whistled through the entranceway. I smelled the delicious aroma of takeout before he even turned the corner into the kitchen.

"Welcome home," I said.

He smiled as he set down the bags of food. Then he grabbed my hand, pulling me into his chest. "I guess I should have yelled 'Honey, I'm home!' when I walked in."

"Except I'm not a perfect housewife from the fifties. You know . . . since your whole kitchen is empty."

"Confession." His hands settled on my lower back. "I don't actually know how to cook anything. But I did pick up dinner."

I smiled at him. "I think that'll do. Please tell me you have something to drink, though. I'm in desperate need of a glass of wine. Or three."

He laughed. "I'm no wine connoisseur, but I'm sure I can find something suitable in the wine cellar."

"Oh." I didn't want him to have to take something from the owners that he'd have to replace. Renting this place was probably expensive enough. The bottles in their wine cellar likely cost thousands. After all . . . they were fancy enough to have a wine cellar. "I mean, I don't really need a drink. That seems like a hassle."

"It's not like you asked me to drive across town. It's just in the basement. I'll be right back."

I pressed my lips together. If he was offering . . . I guessed it was okay.

He wandered off to go find a bottle. I grabbed plates and utensils that I'd found earlier and pulled out the take-out containers. I smiled as I opened the first one. Chicken lo mein. I hadn't had good Chinese takeout since leaving New York. This looked freaking delicious. I put heaping servings on two plates and slid them down the long kitchen counter toward the stools at the other end. They landed perfectly in place.

I knew I'd seen a couple of wineglasses somewhere too. It took me only two tries to find them. As I was pulling them out, Hudson shouted something from the basement about red or white.

One of the glasses fell out of my hand, and the stem snapped off on the side of the counter. The rest of the glass shattered into a million pieces on the floor. *Shit!*

I bent down to clean it up.

"Don't touch it," Hudson said sternly.

I froze.

"Just leave it," he said. His casual smile from earlier was gone. He looked really pissed. Honestly, he kind of looked like Mr. Remington right now.

"I'll just—" I reached out to pick up a piece of the glass, but he grabbed my hand to stop me.

"I don't want you to cut yourself," he said.

Oh. He wasn't mad. He was just concerned. But still . . . I felt horrible. "I'm so, so sorry, Hudson. First me demanding expensive wine and now this? I'll pay to replace it. The glass and the wine. Or maybe just skip the wine because I probably can't afford it."

"What are you talking about?"

"I don't want you to get in trouble."

"With . . . who, exactly?"

"The owners of this house." I tried to grab a shard of glass again, but he pulled me to my feet so that I couldn't.

He laughed as he moved me away from the glass. But he stopped when he realized I wasn't laughing too. "Oh. You thought . . ." His voice trailed off. "Hazel, I own this house."

I laughed.

"Why are you laughing?" But he was smiling too.

"Because you're lying. You're, like, twenty. You're a student. You don't own this estate."

"I don't not own this estate."

That didn't make any sense. "You said you come to town in the summers because your uncle hooked you up with a landscaping and pool-cleaning gig."

"Yeah. I like doing landscaping in my free time."

"Free time . . . as in your summers off from school?"

He shrugged.

"Hudson, you don't own this house. You're clearly renting it."

"Why would you say that?"

"Beyond what I already said about you not being able to afford it? There aren't any pictures of you. It barely looks like you live here at all."

"Well, yeah, I don't live here full time. I like to travel."

"You're lying."

He laughed. "I'm not lying. I love to travel."

"That's not what I think you're lying about."

"Why would I need pictures? I'm perfectly familiar with my own face."

I'd never heard anyone describe pictures of themselves that way. "But they're memories. And your face isn't always going to look the same."

He shrugged.

"And, again, that's not what I'm talking about. You don't seriously own this estate. How did you afford it?"

"You're suddenly very curious about my finances."

I gaped at him.

"I only come here in the summer. I spend most of my time abroad. It's the closest thing I have to a home, but yeah . . . I guess I could use some help decorating."

"What do you do when you're not traveling or doing hobby landscaping?"

He laughed. "My family is wealthy. Did you not get that from how snooty my uncle is?"

"No. I didn't get that at all." Yeah, his uncle was snooty, but . . . he was Athena Quinn's assistant. He lived in her house. "Does your uncle work for Athena Quinn as a hobby too?"

"Yeah, that's definitely a hobby."

The way he said it made me think that banging Athena Quinn on the regular was the hobby he was referring to. "So you're all just independently wealthy?"

"You saw those old family portraits. My ancestors came over on the *Mayflower* and made a fortune in the New World."

In the New World. The only time I'd ever heard anyone say that was in Disney's *Pocahontas*. I just stared at him.

"Stop looking at me like that," he said.

"Like what?"

"Like I'm an alien. This is why I didn't tell you."

I definitely didn't think that *this* was his secret. I wasn't unreasonable. "I'm not. I just . . . Why did you lie to me? I wouldn't have judged you in any way."

"Really?" He stared at me skeptically.

"Really."

"Well, I didn't lie. I simply omitted the entire truth."

"Saying that you're a pool boy and that your uncle hooked you up with a landscaping gig is pretty far from the truth, Hudson."

"I mean . . . all of that is true."

"You're not a pool boy. You're a rich . . . traveler."

He shrugged. "I'm also pretty good with investments. We should probably eat. Dinner's getting cold." He grabbed another glass from the cupboard and maneuvered me around the shards on the floor. "Seriously, just leave the glass. The only thing I can't afford is for you to cut yourself."

If he could afford this house, he could definitely afford Band-Aids. Half of the things he said made no sense at all. But if he thought I was going to drop this . . . he was sorely mistaken.

I needed to know how, exactly, the Remingtons gained their fortune. It might be the key to everything.

CHAPTER 21

Monday—September 5

"Are you not hungry?" I asked as I polished off my second glass of wine. I'd finished my food a long time ago, but we were still sitting at the kitchen counter because Hudson had barely touched his meal.

Hudson pushed his plate to the side. "Not really."

He and his uncle didn't like to eat much at dinner. "I bet Atlas is sitting at that long dining room table right now, all alone and scowling." He'd asked me a while ago to stop calling his uncle Mr. Remington. And I was a little worried that when I saw Atlas next, I'd accidentally call him by his first name.

Hudson glanced at his watch before pouring me another glass of wine. "Probably not. It's past nine."

"Is it?" I hadn't realized how long we'd been sitting here talking. "Ah, then maybe he's moved on to berating Miss Serrano or something."

"Could we maybe stop talking about my uncle?"

I opened my mouth and then closed it. Had I been talking a lot about Atlas? I certainly had been complaining about my job for a while . . . Based on the fact that it was after nine o'clock, I'd been doing it for hours. And complaining about my job really meant complaining about Atlas. I didn't even realize I was doing it. "Sorry, I didn't mean to talk about work."

"It's fine." But it didn't really sound fine. He sounded a little pissed.

I cleared my throat. "Tell me about your ancestors. What did they do to amass their fortune when they moved here?"

"Mostly agriculture. Trade. That sort of thing."

"What did they grow?"

"I really don't like talking about it." He ran his thumb down the condensation on the side of his untouched wineglass.

It almost looked like he was remembering something. Like he'd actually been there. I remembered first driving up to Athena Quinn's mansion. I could so easily picture someone in a petticoat running out the front door to greet me. The house looked like it belonged on a southern plantation. I knew there were lots of plantations down here. I'd driven past other neighborhoods with "Plantation" at the end of their names.

If Hudson's ancestors had lived down here, they may have run one. Lots of southerners had gotten rich through cash crops. "Did they grow tobacco?" I asked.

"Some." He shrugged. "What about you? How did your ancestors amass their fortune?"

I laughed. "What fortune?"

He smiled. "I just meant, what do your parents do?"

"Both my parents were English teachers."

"Were?"

"Yeah. They passed away right before I went to college. A car accident." I kept talking so I wouldn't get emotional. Words, I'd found, were a great way to silence the heartache. That was one of the reasons why I loved writing. "I think that's why Kehlani and I are so close. My freshman roommate somehow became my only family. And it's because of my parents that I've always loved reading. They instilled it in me when I was young. It's why I hope to be an author one day. It makes me feel close to them, you know?"

"Hazel, I'm really sorry."

"It's okay." I don't know why I always said that. It wasn't okay. But what the hell else was I supposed to say?

He stared at me. "It's not."

I pressed my lips together.

"I know it's not the same," he said, "but I never knew my mom. She died giving birth to me."

Oh my God. I didn't think dying during childbirth was very common anymore, but it did still happen. I reached out and grabbed his hand. No, it wasn't the same as my situation. In some ways, I thought, it was worse. At least I'd had time with my mom. He'd never gotten to know his. "That must have been really hard for you and your dad."

"My father definitely took it hard. He blamed himself."

"Why?" What could he have done to help? At least he didn't blame his son.

"I don't know." He cleared his throat. "So that's why you're here, though? Because you love Athena Quinn's writing and wanted a behind-the-scenes look?"

I laughed, happy about the lighter topic. "No, not really. She had a few good books, but she's kind of lost her touch."

Hudson laughed. "Don't tell her that."

"I would never. And I know she is a good writer. She just . . ." I let my voice trail off. "I've seen the hate mail she receives. She started listening to hateful trolls instead of her actual fans. She's releasing books with no substance because she's scared. I think that's why she hides in that house all day too. I think she's just hurting. And, yeah, I was hoping that by working with her, I'd become a better writer. Except I'm not even allowed to meet her."

"Yeah, well, Athena Quinn's a dick."

I laughed. "I can't believe you've gotten to meet her and I haven't."

"Trust me, you're not missing anything. And it's kind of you to think she's scared instead of what it really is."

"That she's just a dick?" I said with a laugh.

"Exactly."

I stared at him. "Was she rude to you? Rumor has it that she's known to have *outbursts*." That was what Atlas had said. That Miss Serrano was tired of Athena Quinn's *outbursts*.

"No, it's not that. It's more of . . . this air of superiority. She's condescending. Snooty. She thinks she's better than everyone else. And she always thinks she's right. It's hard to even have a conversation with her."

"No wonder she and Atlas get along."

Hudson laughed. "Yeah. A match made in hell."

"Do you think he loves her?"

"Why would you ask that?"

"He didn't have a bed in his room. It's almost like his room is just for show. I'm pretty sure he sleeps with her."

"You really shouldn't have gone into his bedroom."

I pressed my lips together. I was rambling. I'd definitely had a little too much to drink. "He didn't invite me in or anything like that. I snuck in. I thought he was hiding something."

He stared at me. "I mean, he's your boss. There should be some kind of line, right? Between your work life and private life?"

"Yeah, but . . ."

"Hazel, are you asking me if my uncle is in love with Athena Quinn because you want to know if he's single?"

"No," I said with a laugh.

"Are you sure? Because we've pretty much talked about Atlas the entire night. And by that, I mean *you* talked about him. I mostly just listened."

I cringed. "I know, I'm sorry. He's just so frustrating."

He stared at me. "To answer your question, I think love and hate are a fine line."

So Atlas hated Athena Quinn? Or was Hudson saying Atlas hated me? And that hate was close to love regarding Atlas's relationship with me? I shook away the thought. *Relationship?* We weren't in a relationship. But Atlas did hate me. And if love and hate were a fine line . . .

"It's late," Hudson said, "and I have to be up early. Let me show you to the guest room." He'd never been so formal with me before.

"Hudson, I'm sorry . . ."

"It's fine." He stood up and started walking away from me.

It definitely didn't seem fine.

"Hudson," I said and ran after him.

He was walking up the stairs.

I took them two at a time and grabbed his hand to prevent him from walking any farther down the hall.

He looked down at our joined hands. "It really is okay. It's better to waste a little time figuring out what you want than to waste a lifetime. Because you only have one, Hazel. Make the best of it."

We both had only one lifetime. And I wasn't wasting Hudson's time. I did like him. But my feelings toward his uncle were stronger—he was right about that. Not in the direction of love, though. Much more in the direction of hate. I hated Atlas Remington. He was a pompous asshole. And yet . . . I couldn't stop talking about him. Or thinking about him. He'd even taken over my dreams. And the story I was trying to write.

Hudson dropped my hand and opened the door behind him.

I didn't have anything else to say. I was worried that he was right. "Are you sure it's okay that I still spend the night?"

"Of course. I told you to make yourself at home." The corner of his mouth ticked up, but it didn't look like his normal smile.

"Thanks, Hudson." I stood on my tiptoes and kissed his cheek.

"Good night, Hazel." He stepped back from me and disappeared through the doorway down the hall.

I knew I'd ruined our night by talking nonstop about Atlas. But a part of me wondered if Hudson didn't invite me into his room because he secretly didn't have a bed either. I shook the thought away and closed the door of the guest bedroom behind me. I heard Atlas's words in the back of my head: *Make sure you lock your door tonight.* I locked the door and collapsed backward onto the bed.

I closed my eyes and pictured Atlas staring at me intently.

Why?

Why did I keep seeing him?

I squeezed my eyes shut tighter as all the thoughts in my head swirled around. Guilt, exhaustion, and confusion pushed through me in waves, and I felt the effects of the wine on top of everything. I needed to be up early for work, and I didn't know how well I could sleep at this house, even if it wasn't as creepy as Athena's estate. I yawned as I thought about the list I'd made outlining Atlas's peculiarities. Some of the points fit Hudson too.

1. Uses old-fashioned words and phrases.
2. Southern gentleman.
3. No bed in his room.
4. Cold hands.
5. Strict about Athena Quinn's rules.
6. Angry about tomato sauce and then . . . hid it?
7. Won't let me meet our boss.
8. Gentle when he touches me.

I mentally added a ninth item: *Hates the heat of the day.*

I yawned again.

The heat of the day. That was so random. Who hated hot weather and chose to live on a beach? I pictured the closed blinds in Hudson's house. What if it wasn't about the heat of the day? What if Hudson didn't like the sun? He always hurried off before the clouds parted, saying it would be too hot. But it was all based on where the sun was in the sky.

Had I ever seen Atlas outside during the day when it wasn't overcast? He ate breakfast in the day kitchen, where there were no windows. And he ate dinner in the dining room past seven, when the sun had set. And *ate* was generous. Atlas and Hudson rarely ever took a bite of food.

They both had cold hands.

They were both old-fashioned southern gentlemen, although Hudson hid it better.

Neither had much of an appetite at meals.

I was starting to think that Hudson didn't have a bed either.

And maybe they both hated the sun? I mean, I was pale too, but I just used sunscreen . . .

I yawned again as I pictured Atlas eating alone in the dark dining room. The scowl on his face. The intensity in his eyes as he stared at me. Almost like he wanted to devour every inch of me.

I sat up with a start.

The cold hands.

The weird old phrases.

Not going out in the sun.

My heart started pounding as I stared at the locked door. I knew something that fit that description. I knew why Hudson and Atlas both kept warning me about the other. Why I shouldn't roam around the beach at night. Why Athena Quinn's mansion was dangerous past dusk.

The Remingtons were . . .

I shook my head. But I couldn't shake away the thought that had suddenly taken hold.

Cold to the touch.

Old-fashioned.

Scared of the sun.

Everything clicked into place in my head, even though I no longer wanted the pieces of the puzzle to fit together. My heart beat faster. It was like I could feel the blood pumping through my veins. And that was a huge problem. Because I was pretty sure the Remingtons were vampires.

CHAPTER 22

I stared at the locked door in horror.

Vampires? The word echoed around in my head. Vampires weren't real. I knew that, and yet . . .

I pictured the old portraits of the Remingtons' ancestors. The canvases were covered in cobwebs, like they'd been sitting there for a century. I'd believed Hudson when he said that the subjects of the paintings were his ancestors. But now? That man in the picture . . . he looked exactly the same as Atlas. Exactly the freaking same. And it all made sense now. That wasn't Atlas's great-great-great-grandfather in those old portraits. It was him. Just like I'd originally thought.

Atlas and Hudson . . . were both vampires.

The thought took hold in my mind and wouldn't let go.

And the more I thought about it, the more the puzzle pieces fit together.

Atlas said weird things and was so formal because he was actually from another time period. He'd been alive for centuries, according to the old portraits.

His hands were freezing. And when he touched me, he was so gentle because he was probably worried about his superhuman vampire strength. He was worried he could break me. Because he could.

163

Maybe Atlas was having an affair with Athena Quinn. Or maybe he had already killed her. But neither of those were the reasons why he didn't have a bed in his room. He probably had a coffin somewhere. Or didn't sleep at all.

Hudson practically ran whenever the clouds parted. His yard was overgrown with foliage to ensure that it was always shaded. He couldn't let the sun touch his skin.

I thought about how everyone at that party on the beach had asked if I was *all alone*. And I had thought they kept looking at my lips. But what if I was wrong? What if they'd been looking at my *neck*? They wanted me all alone to . . .

I stood up.

I had to get the hell away from here. Not just away from Hudson and Atlas but away from this fucking island. I knew something wasn't right. I knew everyone seemed off.

I took a step toward the locked door. And then a step back. If Hudson didn't sleep . . . he'd hear me leave if I just walked out. I turned to the window. And what the hell was I going to do if I did leave? I didn't have my car keys. Because Atlas had taken them . . .

God, I'd been so worried about him setting me up for the murder of Athena Quinn. I'd never really considered the fact that he was about to murder me.

I pulled my phone out of my purse. My hands were shaking as I hit Kehlani's name. I had to escape out the window, right? I couldn't risk bumping into Hudson in the middle of the night. I walked over to the window and pushed the blinds to the side. It wasn't *that* high . . .

Kehlani picked up after only one ring. "If you're calling me, that means you're not having wild, kinky sex with Little Remington. Was he actually little?"

I wanted to laugh, but I was much closer to crying than anything. "Kehlani?" I whispered.

"Girl, why are you whispering?"

"I think I'm in trouble."

"What's going on?"

I crouched in front of the window and tried to push it up, but it was locked. "I . . ."

I heard a creaking noise coming from the hallway. I clasped my hand over my mouth so I wouldn't scream.

A shadow appeared in the middle of the light pouring in beneath the door.

"Hazel?" Kehlani said.

Hudson was standing out there. Listening. Waiting. My knees buckled, and I sank to the floor. *I don't want to die.*

"Hazel, tell me what's wrong!" Kehlani yelled.

My hands were shaking so badly that I almost dropped my phone as I lowered the volume. Did vampires have good hearing? *Please, please don't let Hudson have heard that.*

"Hazel, I swear to God," she said.

The floorboards creaked again as the shadow shifted. For a moment, there was only light beneath the door. And then it was all dark. Hudson must have switched off the lights. To pretend he was asleep or something. I breathed a sigh of relief. But for a few seconds, I just sat there, staring at the dark sliver beneath the door.

"Hazel!"

Kehlani's voice shook me out of my trance. There was no way I was going to let a vampire suck my blood. I stood back up. "I need you to google how to hot-wire a car," I said. I took a deep breath, trying to calm my nerves.

"What?!"

"You probably have, like, five minutes to figure it out while I figure out how to climb out the second-story window and not die."

"Can we back up for a second?" Kehlani asked. "Whose car are you stealing? And why are you jumping out of a window?"

"I'm not stealing anything," I whispered. I found the latch on the window and slowly pushed it up. The sea breeze usually calmed me down. But now it just reminded me that this entire island was infested with monsters. "Atlas stole my keys. I think. I don't know. Maybe I just misplaced them. But I gotta get out of here."

"So you want to hot-wire your own car? Was the date that bad?"

Earlier I'd told Kehlani all about Hudson's excuses for Atlas being creepy. She'd believed him. Hell, I'd believed him too. Or else I wouldn't be in his guest room waiting to be murdered. "Hudson lied."

"About what?"

"Everything." My hand froze on the windowsill as I peered out at the overgrown bushes below. I heard Hudson's words echoing around in my head. What he'd said to me when I'd tried to clean up the broken glass: *"The only thing I can't afford is for you to cut yourself."* Hudson would lose control if I cut myself and bled. That was what he'd been talking about. I'd just been too overwhelmed to understand. He'd given me so many clues, and I couldn't even fathom the truth.

I looked down at the steep decline. If I cut myself falling out the window . . . he'd kill me, right? He wouldn't be able to help himself when he smelled my blood. He'd already warned me. I pictured a pool of blood and Hudson descending upon me.

Blood.

A chill ran down my spine.

It felt like the last piece of the puzzle clicked into place. "Vampires don't like garlic," I said.

"Um . . . yeah, I guess not," Kehlani said. "I'm sorry, but what does this have to do with anything?"

"Hudson said that Atlas was allergic to garlic. That he bought some special tomato sauce out of town or something. *Allergic to garlic.* Hudson laughed about it. And I didn't understand what was so funny. But he's been giving me clues this whole time."

"I'm sorry," Kehlani said. "I'm not following."

"He was making a joke," I said. I pictured the container of tomato sauce in my hands. It wasn't about garlic. It was a hint about what the Remingtons were. Hudson was just having fun fucking with me. Throwing me off the scent and toying with me at the same time. Giving me hints and watching my head spin. Because the truth wasn't fathomable. They drank blood. That was why they never ate anything at meals.

Blood.

Oh my God.

"There were so many containers," I said. "The whole freezer was full of them."

"What? The tomato sauce containers? Hazel, you're not making any sense."

I pictured the way the sauce had tilted in the container when Atlas grabbed it out of my hands. It was off. All of it was off. Especially since Atlas didn't ever freaking eat anything. "Kehlani, I don't think it was tomato sauce."

"Then what was it?" she asked.

The red liquid was so thin.

It was such a dark red.

It was . . .

"What the hell was it?" Kehlani asked again.

"Blood." My voice cracked.

"Ew, what?"

"I really think it was blood." I looked back out the window. "Kehlani, they're vampires."

She laughed.

"I'm serious," I said.

"You're drunk. Or high or something."

"I'm not that drunk. And they don't sleep, Kehlani. I don't think Hudson has a bed, or else I'd probably be in it. And Atlas definitely doesn't have a bed."

"But we've been over this. It's because Atlas is sleeping with Athena Quinn. Not because he's a vampire. You know . . . since vampires aren't a real thing. And maybe Hudson just isn't that into you."

"Rude." But I didn't have time to be insulted. "The first night I was here, Atlas was wondering if I was touring the grounds in the middle of the night, which was a very weird assumption. But it's because he doesn't sleep. *Period.* And they're both really pale, despite the fact that they live on a beach." My eyes gravitated to the pale white sheets. *Bingo.* I'd read somewhere that if you tied sheets together, they formed a perfect makeshift rope.

"Hazel . . ."

"And I was right about those portraits," I said as I pulled the sheets off the bed. "It was Atlas in them. I know it. He's hundreds of years old. That's why he uses all those old phrases. And thinks I love dalliances." *Vampire asshole.* I tied the top sheet to the fitted one and then looked around for what might be strong enough to hold my weight.

"I'm sorry, what?"

I tied the end of one of the sheets to a dresser leg. "And I've never seen either one of them outside on a sunny day. And they never eat anything at meals because they drink blood. And they have freezing-cold skin. And I'm about to die if you don't tell me how to hot-wire a car." I tossed the sheets out the window. Since my homespun rope consisted of only two sheets tied together, it didn't go down very far. But it was better than just jumping out the window.

"You're serious? Hazel, vampires don't exist."

"Were you not listening to anything I just said?"

"I am listening," she said. "But you also said you aren't *that drunk,* which means you have been drinking . . ."

"I thought you, of all people, would believe me," I said as I climbed up onto the ledge.

"What is that supposed to mean?"

I tugged on my makeshift rope. It seemed secure enough. "You love Athena Quinn's novels. You believe in love at first sight. And love triangles. And all things revolving around love."

"Believing in happily-ever-afters is the exact opposite of believing in vampires," Kehlani said.

"Is it, though?" I asked.

"If your point is that they're both fairy tales, well . . . you're basically admitting that vampires aren't real either. But if you want to admit that true love exists, maybe I can admit that vampires do too."

"This is really not the time to have this discussion," I said. "And you were just trying to get me to leave that creepy house. Why do you suddenly believe it's not creepy?"

"I do think it's creepy," Kehlani said. "But not vampirically creepy. Just murderously creepy."

"Will you believe me if I jump out a window to get away from Hudson?"

"Hazel, you've lost it. Maybe you've had too much sweet tea down there or something."

"Well, I haven't had any sweet tea. It was probably invented way after the Remingtons were born."

"Hazel . . ." Her voice trailed off. "Is this maybe about your parents?"

"What are you talking about?" How did this have anything to do with them? Why did she think every idea in my head was based solely on what had happened to my mom and dad? The Remingtons being vampires was a completely rational conclusion. Literally every single strange thing pointed to them being vampires.

"You know . . . because vampires are immortal."

"So you do believe me?!"

"No," Kehlani said. "I'm saying that maybe you hope Hudson and Mr. Remington are vampires. Because then they'd be immortal. And if you fell in love with one of them . . . he'd never leave you."

I opened my mouth and closed it. "That's not what this is about." But now I wanted to cry because I was scared and my chest hurt.

"Okay," she said. "But maybe, just maybe . . ."

"I'm not crazy. I'm not playing make-believe because I miss my parents. I'm in real danger here." I peered out the window. "Now, are you going to help me or not?"

"Of course I'm going to help you. I've had a YouTube video about hot-wiring a car playing in the background this whole time. And if you're somehow right about vampires existing . . . I really don't want it to be my fault that one of them sucks your blood."

I shivered. "Good." I tossed my shoes and my purse out the window. They landed gently in the bush below. "And I am right about them being vampires." I grabbed on to the end of the rope and swung one leg over the ledge. *Here goes nothing.* I swung the other leg over and jumped before I could chicken out.

"But . . . ," Kehlani started.

I didn't hear what she said because my makeshift rope was not tied tightly enough. Something snapped. Or maybe I was just too heavy for the dresser. But I fell hard and fast, somehow avoiding the soft-looking bush that my shoes and purse had landed in. *Ow.* Wherever I'd read that sheets make a great rope, it was 100 percent wrong. Or maybe I just sucked at tying knots.

"Hazel, did you hear me?" Kehlani asked.

"What?" I groaned as I pushed myself up out of the grass. *That really hurt.*

"You need tools and stuff to hot-wire a car. Like a screwdriver. I don't think you can do it unless you get the necessary supplies."

I reached out to grab my purse. Not being able to hot-wire my car was suddenly the least of my problems. I looked down at the blood dribbling down my wrist. *Shit.*

CHAPTER 23

Monday—September 5

"Kehlani," I whispered, "I'm bleeding."

"That's the one thing you're not supposed to do around vampires, Hazel!"

"I know that." I tried to wipe off my scratch in the dewy grass, but I just spread the blood around. I looked up at the second-story window. If the dresser had moved, Hudson may have heard it. He may have already been coming downstairs to find me. Or maybe the scent of blood would entice him down. "How far away can vampires smell blood?"

"One sec—let me google it."

I grabbed my purse to look for something to stop the bleeding. Why had I packed a toothbrush but no tissues?

"Good Lord, according to this, vampires can smell blood from several miles away."

"What?!" I hissed. I looked over my shoulder. If that were true, it wasn't just Hudson I had to worry about. I pictured all the people down on the beach the other night. What if I had been right about them staring at my neck? I swallowed hard. Everyone in this neighborhood might be a vampire.

"Or maybe ten meters?" Kehlani said. "I'm not sure how accurate Reddit posts are . . ."

"Why are you giving me measurements in meters?" I said. "I don't even know how far one meter is, let alone ten."

"Looks like a meter is about a yard. So, like . . . thirty feet or so?"

I wasn't confident that Hudson was thirty feet away from me. And he definitely wasn't several miles away. "Isn't there something more concrete than Reddit posts?"

"There're no known facts about vampires! This was the first thing that popped up."

Gah. I went to wipe my hand off on my dress, but running around with blood on my dress somehow seemed like a worse idea. "What am I going to do? I don't have anything to stop the bleeding. And if I make a run for it, will the scent kinda spread in the wind or something?"

"I don't know about wind patterns," Kehlani said. "But you need to wrap something around it to hide the smell and make it stop bleeding. Tear off a piece of your outfit."

I looked down at my dress. "I don't have superhuman vampire strength. I can't just rip fabric in half."

"Try it."

I grabbed the hem of my dress and tried to tear it in two. Nothing happened. "I can't tear the dress—it's too well made . . ." I looked down at my thighs. "Wait, I have a small piece of fabric." I lifted my skirt and pulled off my thong. I wrapped the stretchy material around my scraped palm and balled my hand into a fist, hoping the compression would help. "I'm so glad I wore underwear tonight."

"You wrapped your underwear around your hand?" Kehlani asked.

"What else was I supposed to do?"

"I don't know!"

"Did you figure out the car situation?" I asked as I stood up and grabbed my shoes and purse. I ran toward the road and stopped when I saw all the gravel. If I ran through that barefoot, I'd have bloody feet too. I guessed I was making a run for it in my wedges. I strapped my shoes back on.

"Do you know anything about starter cables?" she asked.

I started running down the gravel road, cringing with every loud step. "What do you think?"

"Well, you don't have a screwdriver, so I think we need to go with the cables. There's two brown and two red . . ."

"How do I even get into the car in the first place?"

"I don't know. Last time I lost my keys, I called the fire department," Kehlani said.

"Not helpful." I ran past Hudson's neighbor's house and saw a light turn on upstairs. Did a vampire live in that mansion? Did they smell my blood? I clenched my fist harder.

"What about getting an Uber?" Kehlani asked.

"I don't know who I can trust on this island. I don't think the Remingtons are the only vampires. Tell me more about those wires. Where are they located?"

"Crap," Kehlani said. "For the starter-cable method, it says you need insulated gloves and wire cutters. I'm guessing you don't have those under your dress?"

"Unfortunately not." I was out of breath by the time I reached Athena Quinn's long drive. Running in heels was not an easy task. I was lucky I hadn't twisted my ankle.

"Hazel, you could electrocute yourself. Every way to do this requires tools and . . ."

"It's better than being eaten alive." I ducked behind a bush and stared at Athena Quinn's mansion. It was pitch black. Everyone was asleep . . . or pretending to be. I pictured myself walking up to her front door on my first day. Excited and naive, just like the protagonist of Athena Quinn's work in progress. And I wondered if Athena Quinn was the one who'd wanted me to find her manuscript. She'd written about something dark and sinister in the house. She'd meant this house. She'd tried to warn me. And I was too stupid to realize I was her character until it was too late.

"It says you should really consult your car's manual," Kehlani said, pulling me out of my thoughts.

"Kehlani, I don't have time to read my car's manual." I looked down at my hand. It seemed like the bleeding had stopped. At least that was a good sign. I peered around the bush and stared at my car. "Can you break a car window with your elbow?"

"I think I've seen that on TV before."

"Me too." I stayed low as I crept up to my car. *Here goes nothing . . .* "Hazel . . ."

I slammed my elbow into the driver's-side window. *Son of a bitch.* I winced in pain and grabbed my elbow. "I think it's broken," I croaked.

"I was just going to say that I don't think that's a good idea. You need something stronger than bone."

"You think?" I gritted out. I moved my arm. My elbow hurt, but it did still move, so that was probably a good thing.

"Do you have a baseball bat?" Kehlani asked.

"No, I don't have a freaking baseball bat! Or wire cutters. Or a screwdriver. I don't have anything!"

"Calm down. We'll figure this out. You said there were statues in the gardens . . ."

"They're huge, Kehlani. I couldn't possibly lift one." I scanned the gravel drive and saw a few bigger rocks by the entrance to Athena Quinn's mansion. "Will a large rock do?"

"I bet it will."

I hurried over and picked up a rock. Right when I did, the front lights turned on. I froze, and the rock slipped out of my hand. Had someone turned those lights on? Or were there motion sensors? *Screw this.* I wasn't waiting to find out. I picked the rock back up, ran over to my car, and threw it as hard as I could through the driver's-side window.

The glass shattered. "I did it . . ." My voice died away as the car alarm started blaring and the lights started flashing.

Shit. Shit, shit, shit!

"What did you do?!" Kehlani screamed through the phone.

"Google how to turn a car alarm off!" I yelled back. I reached in through the broken glass to try to unlock the door from the inside, but the glass was so jagged. I didn't want to cut myself again. And I couldn't reach the lock. Usually when I set off my alarm, I just hit the button on my remote key. But I didn't have my freaking keys.

It seemed like the alarm grew louder with every second that passed.

"I think there should be a little button by the steering wheel to stop it," Kehlani said. "But it depends on the make and model of your car."

I pressed the phone a little tighter between my shoulder and ear as I reached farther into the car. If I could just hit the unlock button on the car door . . .

"Miss Fox?"

I hadn't heard Mr. Remington approach because of the alarm. I froze, and my phone somehow slipped from its secure spot and landed with a sickening crunch on the gravel. *No. Kehlani was my only hope.* I could have sworn that my heart stopped beating.

"What in heaven's name did someone do to your motorcar?" he asked.

At least he thought someone else had done this. And didn't suspect me of trying to run. But I couldn't make my mouth open and respond to him. I just . . . couldn't move at all. I stared into my car, willing my hand to move down to the lock. But what was the point? I didn't know how to hot-wire it.

"Miss Fox, are you all right?" he asked.

Vampires were hunters, right? Which meant that I was his prey. I was frozen in place, but that was good, I thought. Didn't most prey freeze in hopes that the predator wouldn't be able to see them? Did that work with vampires?

This time I heard his shoes on the gravel, approaching me.

Of course it didn't work with vampires. I wasn't camouflaged, and I had blood on my palm.

He lifted the hood of my car, and a moment later, the alarm and flashing lights stopped.

And I still just stood there with my arm halfway in the car, hoping he'd magically walk away. Because magic did exist, right? If he was a vampire, anything was possible.

But I wasn't that lucky. He stepped up to me, staring directly into my eyes.

"Careful," he said and grabbed my arm.

I didn't realize that my arm had been shaking.

"The last thing we want is for you to cut yourself."

It was a little late for that. But this time I heard the warning loud and clear. It was practically a confession of what he was.

He slowly pulled my arm out of the way of the shattered glass. His eyes fell to the thong wrapped around my palm. He didn't say a word, but his fingers tightened on my forearm. They grew tighter and tighter, digging into my skin as he stared at my palm.

My life flashed before my eyes. I waited for him to take a step forward and finish the job.

But nothing happened. My mind was as frozen as my body. I stared at the water dripping from the ends of his hair. This wasn't the first time I'd caught him looking like he'd just walked out of the ocean. His wet T-shirt clung to every muscle on his torso.

Monsters shouldn't look so perfect.

"You already cut yourself on the glass?" he asked. His voice was lower than usual, his southern accent more pronounced.

And I had no idea why, but I felt myself leaning closer to him.

"Miss Fox?" he said again.

I shook my head. My voice was still not working. I wondered if the rest of my body would oblige. If I could knee him in the junk . . . I let the thought trail off as I watched his eyebrows lower.

He was staring at me so intensely.

I didn't really want to knee him in the groin. I felt myself leaning closer to him again. What the hell was my body doing? Freezing hadn't worked. I should have been running. But where was I supposed to run? Especially if all I wanted to do was lean closer.

"Did Hudson hurt you?" He sounded sincerely worried.

I shook my head again.

His grip on my arm loosened as his fingers trailed along the inside of my forearm and down to my wrist. He lifted my palm to inspect it.

"Athena Quinn is writing about me," I said. I wasn't sure why those were the first words out of my mouth. But it was as good of a last confession as any. I thought he should know that the woman he was living with couldn't be trusted to keep his secrets.

"And why would you say that?" he asked. His eyes finally met mine. His irises looked a darker shade of brown than before. Or maybe it was just because we were standing alone in the dark. He released his grip on my wrist.

I moved my arm behind my back, trying to get the blood as far away from him as possible. "She tried to warn me." I felt myself leaning closer still. Or maybe he was tilting his head closer to my neck. "I'm the fool in her story."

"I don't think you're a fool, Miss Fox."

I swallowed hard. "Aren't I, though?"

He shook his head. "No. But there is one way to test your theory about Athena Quinn writing about you." He leaned closer still. Our lips were only a fraction of an inch apart.

"How?" Could he tell that I was still trembling?

"Do something unexpected. And see if she writes about it."

"What would be unexpected?" My heart was pounding so fast. I willed it to calm down. I did not need my blood pumping any faster.

"Well, you're clearly scared of . . . *something*. What was your first instinct when that fear gripped you?"

I would have protested, but I knew I was easy to read. I was scared. Of *him*. Of his nephew. Of everyone I'd met on this island. Of the island itself. And I knew that he knew that. The way he'd said "something"—he knew I was scared of him. My first instinct had been to run. I was pretty sure that was as clear to him as the fact that I was scared. But I didn't want to say it out loud. I didn't want him to stop me from succeeding.

His eyes searched mine. "Whatever it was, it would be unexpected to do the opposite. Far more interesting for her story."

It would certainly be unexpected to stay and bide my time. To continue working here despite my terror. But it would also be ill-advised. I'd be playing into the notion that I was a dumb, naive girl, just like she'd said.

He reached up and ran his fingers down the side of my neck.

Fuck. The opposite of being scared of a vampire was giving in to one. Surrendering. Letting one suck your blood. My breath caught in my throat when I met his gaze. I wanted to slap his perfect face. But I was frozen all over again. His hand slid back, wrapping behind my neck. All he had to do was pull forward and he'd have perfect access.

"Mr. Remington." My voice quivered.

"Do the unexpected, Miss Fox." He was so close that a droplet of salt water fell from his hair and onto my cheek.

I took a deep breath. There was no choice to run or stay. My fate was in his hands. But there was one thing I wanted just as much as I wanted to run. I'd wanted it ever since I set eyes on him. Something I'd been fighting. If I was about to be killed anyway . . . I might as well have this one last desire satiated. And it was definitely unexpected.

I reached up and ran my fingers through his wet, unruly hair.

He leaned forward, closing the small distance between us.

I closed my eyes and cringed, waiting for the devil himself to bite me. But his lips didn't meet my neck. They crashed against mine.

CHAPTER 24

Monday—September 5

Mr. Remington kissing me was definitely unexpected. But he was probably as surprised as I was that I buried my fingers in his hair.

Maybe Hudson was right. Love and hate were a fine line. Mr. Remington had consumed my thoughts all night and all day. During the day . . . I hated the man. But at night? In my dreams? I'd dreamed of this. I'd tossed and turned every night since I'd arrived, desiring this exact moment.

So when Mr. Remington's tongue slid against my lips, I opened my mouth to him.

It was reckless.

But what was the point of wasting time when he could so easily take my life?

He groaned and tilted my head back, exposing my neck even more. I wanted to blame the fear in my chest for pulling him closer. To believe that kissing him was just a way of distracting him from biting my neck.

But that wasn't it at all. I needed more of . . . *him*. My hands skated down his wet T-shirt, tracing the muscles of his back. I pictured him devouring me. Feasting on my blood. And that same intensity was there, but it wasn't scary. It was just a kiss. An innocent kiss. Well, not really innocent. It was so fucking hot. He kissed me like he'd been dreaming of this moment too.

Mr. Remington was always in control. But he wasn't kissing me like he was in control right now. He was kissing me like he'd lost it. Maybe we both had. He bit down on my lower lip.

Fuck.

I let my hands push up the back of his shirt, pulling him closer still. His cold skin sent shivers down my spine. I pushed his shirt up even more as he deepened the kiss. God, this was so much better than in my dreams.

A siren bleeping made me open my eyes. The dark sky was suddenly lit up by flashing red-and-blue lights. The police car's tires spit out gravel as it came to a stop right next to us.

I took a step back from Mr. Remington. The distance from him made my head stop spinning. And I realized my mouth tasted of blood. I reached up and touched a cut on my lip. *He bit me.* So hard he'd made me bleed. And I hadn't even flinched. I'd just pulled him closer. I pressed my lips together to stop the bleeding. Why hadn't that made me scream? My heart started pounding against my chest. Why had I liked it?

Two cops exited the car.

Seeing them didn't ease my rapid heartbeat. Not even in the slightest. Because I recognized the shorter one from the beach party the other night. He was one of the guys who had asked if I was *all alone.* He'd stared at my neck.

I hadn't caught the cop's name. But our conversation had stuck vividly in my head. *"Oh, you're Mr. Remington's?"* I'd thought he misspoke. But maybe he'd actually meant what he said. That I belonged to Mr. Remington.

I glanced at Mr. Remington out of the corner of my eye. Yes, he'd bitten my lip. But he hadn't exactly sucked my blood. I didn't know what that meant. And my mind was spinning again. Was he a vampire? Was the creepy shorter officer a vampire? Were all three of them?

"Ma'am," said the taller one in a southern drawl, "are you all right?" He lowered his eyebrows when he saw my car's broken window.

"We're quite all right," Mr. Remington said and stepped forward.

"We both know he wasn't talking to you," the shorter cop said. "He was talking to the lady." He walked up to me.

Mr. Remington rolled his eyes behind the guy's back.

Probably because he wasn't at all worried about these cops taking him to jail. The shorter cop knew him. And I wasn't sure why he was pretending that he didn't. Everything about this situation made me uncomfortable. It was like they were all playing a game, and I'd never learned the rules.

The shorter cop stopped in front of me.

I could have sworn that his eyes fell to my neck again. I crossed my arms in front of my chest, trying to hide my injured hand from him. I pressed my lips together, pulling the cut deeper into my mouth. I did not want either of these cops smelling blood on me.

"We got a call from a concerned young woman," he said.

I knew Kehlani had my back. But this was a mistake. I'd told her that I didn't trust anyone on this stupid island. And one of the creepiest guys I'd met had shown up.

"She said . . ." His voice trailed off. "You're shaking." He reached out and put his hand on my shoulder. It felt just as cool as Mr. Remington's touch. And it had me shivering all over again.

Even if I was 100 percent sure that these were normal cops, I wasn't sure I'd tell them that I was scared of Mr. Remington. Because if Mr. Remington was a vampire and they weren't? He'd probably just kill these cops and then me. And if these cops were vampires too . . . I'd much rather die staring into Mr. Remington's eyes.

"The woman on the phone said you were in trouble. How about you come with us?"

His words from the party echoed through my head. *All alone.* He wanted me all alone. To do . . . what, exactly?

"That won't be necessary," Mr. Remington said.

The cop ignored him.

I did not want to go with these men. I licked the cut on my lip. I was pretty sure it had stopped bleeding. "I'm fine," I said.

"You're still shaking."

I nodded. "The fall air is finally here, don't you think?" It honestly wasn't that cold. But I doubted that someone whose skin was so cold could really tell the difference.

"Indeed," he said.

The tall cop was inspecting the car. His shoes crunched on the broken glass. "What happened here?"

"I think it was burglarized," I said quickly. A lie seemed better than the truth. "We heard a noise from inside and both ran out. But whoever broke the window was long gone."

He stared at me. "That's not what the woman on the phone said happened."

"I was hysterical when I called her. She probably didn't understand a word I was saying." I needed to think of a way to get rid of these guys. The shorter cop had basically said I belonged to Mr. Remington. Maybe if I leaned into that, they'd leave me be.

"This neighborhood is usually so safe," I said as I put my arm around Mr. Remington's waist, hoping to convey that we were happily together. That I wasn't being assaulted or anything. That I belonged to him.

Mr. Remington wrapped his arm protectively around my back.

I looked up at him. And I didn't understand the expression on his face at all. It almost seemed like a combination of anger and . . . sadness?

"Isn't that right, dear?" I said.

He lowered his eyebrows as he stared down at me. If there had been a hint of sadness there before, it was gone. He just looked pissed.

Did he want me to go off with these cops? Did our kiss mean so little to him that he wanted me gone? I quickly looked away and cleared my throat.

The two cops stopped examining the car and turned to stare at us.

"Dear?" the shorter one said. "Interesting."

"Very interesting," the taller one agreed.

Why was that so *interesting*?

"I appreciate you coming out at this hour," Mr. Remington said, "but as you can see . . . we have everything under control."

The shorter cop stared at him.

Maybe the two of them didn't know each other. Maybe the cop just knew *of* Mr. Remington.

"I really think the young lady should come with us," the taller cop said. "Just until we sort it out."

Mr. Remington's fingers tightened on my hip. "How about I call Captain Vega and see what he thinks of the situation?"

The two cops stared at each other uneasily.

I was pretty sure I looked just as uncomfortable. Of course Mr. Remington had the police department in his pocket. Suddenly Mr. Remington's arm around me didn't feel as comforting. Having the police on your side was convenient as a vampire. It would certainly help when you sucked the blood of innocent people. What kind of mess was I in here?

The taller cop nodded. "That's not necessary. We'll be off, then."

"Have a *pleasant* evening," the shorter one said. His eyes traveled to my neck again.

He really made that sound like an *unpleasant* evening. And I really wished he'd said, "See you around." Or something that made it seem like I'd be alive tomorrow. And I wished I'd listened to Mr. Remington in the first place and locked myself in my room at night. I wasn't sure I'd get another chance to follow his instructions.

Athena Quinn had tried to warn me . . .

Shit, Athena Quinn. I turned to look at the sprawling mansion. Did the commotion wake her? Was she even still alive? I wanted to say something to the cops. Tell them of my suspicions. But they weren't cops I could trust. I couldn't trust anyone here.

The cops climbed back into their car. The siren bleeped once more as they backed up.

I stared as the car disappeared into the darkness. The sound of crunching gravel faded with them until all I could hear was the cicadas humming.

Mr. Remington's grip on my hip slowly eased. His fingers trailed along my lower back and fell to my elbow. They slid down my forearm until he reached my hand.

My bloody hand.

He lifted it up.

I held my breath as I waited to see what he'd do next.

"He wanted you," he said as he stared down at my hand.

"What?" I tried to hide the quiver of my voice but failed.

"The shorter cop. He wanted you." He ran his thumb down my palm, pulling on the thong to reveal my cut.

I didn't know what to say to that. And I was much more focused on the fact that he was staring at the dried blood.

"He wanted you," Mr. Remington said. "Just like Hudson wanted you." He dragged my thong slowly down my fingers.

I swallowed hard. "Just like you want me?" I was pretty sure there wasn't enough oxygen going to my brain.

His eyes met mine. "Clean your wound and cover it."

"I thought you were trained to be a doctor." I pictured the way he'd gingerly tended to the bruise on my hip. After he'd gotten me half-naked.

"It turns out I'm not so great around blood," he said as he dropped my hand.

Because it made him faint? Or because he loved it? By the way he was staring at me . . . it seemed like the latter. His jaw looked tight, his posture equally rigid. He didn't look like a man who would ever faint. He looked like he was seconds away from losing control, though.

And I just wanted to run. Run from him. Run toward him. I didn't even know anymore.

"What did you do when you opened the hood of my car?" I asked.

"I disconnected the battery. You won't be going anywhere tonight, Miss Fox. Please wash your cut. And lock your door."

The wind blew, and I smelled the salt water on his skin.

It looked like whatever he smelled in the air wasn't as alluring, though. Because he took a step back from me. "We'll discuss what happened in the morning." He turned on his heels and walked back up to the mansion.

My heart was still pounding in my chest, even though the door had closed behind him.

What the hell had just happened? I glanced at my car. I didn't know how to hot-wire a car, and I definitely didn't know a thing about batteries. I was stuck here. It wasn't like the cops were going to help me. I was so fucked.

I ran my fingers across my lips. So why didn't I feel like I was doomed? I grabbed my phone off the ground. The screen was cracked, and there were a dozen missed calls from Kehlani.

But it wasn't my phone that was alarming. The thong I'd used to wrap around my palm was gone. I knew Mr. Remington had pulled it off my fingers. I looked around on the ground, but it was nowhere in sight.

Had he kept it? I imagined him sliding it into his pocket. I stared at the front door of the estate. I no longer felt frozen. I no longer wanted to run.

I knew full well that it was the last thing I should do, but I walked willingly back into the mansion.

CHAPTER 25

Friday—September 9

I'd expected everything to be different once I kissed Mr. Remington. I thought that maybe I'd feel a little safer in this empty mansion.

But, if anything, I was even more isolated than before. Because I hadn't seen Mr. Remington since the night he'd kissed me.

Every morning I came down to breakfast expecting him to be there, only to be greeted by an empty table and an assignment jotted down on a piece of paper. Every night I did the same, sitting at the long dining room table all alone.

All alone.

The words rattled around in my head.

I had no idea where Mr. Remington was.

I still hadn't met Athena Quinn.

I hadn't even seen Miss Serrano for four days.

And Hudson had texted me to tell me he was leaving the morning after I'd jumped out his window.

For four days I'd been completely alone. Or maybe not quite . . . I looked up from my computer at the curtain that had just moved behind a second-story window.

No, I definitely wasn't alone. I felt eyes on me at every turn. Or maybe I was just hyperaware of any movement because I was hoping it was Mr. Remington.

Kehlani thought I was foolish to stay. Hell, I thought I was foolish to stay. And I couldn't quite explain why I was still here.

This wasn't the dream job I'd been promised.

And I was scared of my boss. I truly was. Even if he wasn't a vampire, the man still unnerved me. The more distance there was between us, though, the less I believed he was a vampire.

Because mythical creatures didn't exist, for one.

And because I was still alive, for two. That meant something. Besides, in the bright light of day, I thought about how lots of things could be explained away. Those old portraits could be of his ancestors. The containers of blood . . . maybe they were actually tomato sauce.

And for three, maybe Kehlani was a little right about my parents. Before I'd met her in college, I'd felt so alone. I didn't want to ever feel that way again. And what would be better than dating an immortal vampire? It was a fantasy I didn't even realize I had. It was as comforting as it was horrifying.

I saw the curtain move again out of the corner of my eye.

Or he was biding his time. The thrill of the chase. I stared back down at my computer. I'd finished the busywork I was supposed to do hours ago. I'd finished my work early every day this week. And in the afternoons, I worked on my manuscript. I'd write until the sun dipped below the horizon. I always felt safest here when I was out in the sun.

I would have felt bad for taking Athena Quinn's money to work on my own book, but it was hard to feel bad for a person who refused to meet you. I looked back up at the room where the curtain had moved. What was she doing in there? Was she writing about me? It was ironic that I was worried about it, since I was most definitely writing about her.

There were mysteries in this house.

She'd said so herself in her manuscript.

And I didn't care that our books were similar. I cared about the truth. But right now I wasn't uncovering the truth in reality or in my manuscript. My thriller had taken a rather romantic turn. I stared at my last few lines. The ones inspired by that searing kiss:

Mr. Remington gripped my hair, tugging it so that my neck was completely exposed to him. His lips traced the soft flesh.

I should have trembled. I should have pushed him away. But I needed him—however he wanted me.

"I bet you taste as sweet as you look." His teeth grazed my skin. "Just one taste, Miss Fox."

And . . . now I was writing a vampire romance? I groaned and slammed my laptop shut. I hadn't even bothered to change the names. It was like I was consumed by Mr. Remington's kiss. It was all I could think about. The more time we spent apart, the more obsessed I became. And my manuscript was quickly becoming X rated.

God, what was I doing? I needed to focus on the mystery. A lot of the vampire stuff could be edited out for more of a serial-killer vibe. After all . . . my employer was more likely a murderer than a vampire.

My phone started to ring. "Hey, Kehlani," I said as I stood up and stretched. I was glad for the distraction. Besides, the sun would set soon, and I didn't want to be out here after dark.

"Hey, my friend got back to me," she said.

"And?" I headed back inside, doing my best not to shiver at the drop in temperature.

"It's a dead end."

What? I hurried up to my room and locked the door. "The LLC has to belong to someone," I said. The fact that Hudson owned a property right down the street had stuck in my head. Mr. Remington was wealthy. So why was he living with Athena Quinn? Or . . . did she live with him? I'd tried researching it myself, but the LLC was owned by another corporation.

"Right. It belongs to a company. And that company belongs to another company . . ." Her voice trailed off. "And so on and so on."

"He couldn't find out who owns any of the corporations?"

"No, I'm sorry. Apparently you can file an information request with the state."

"How long will that take?"

"For them to get back to you? I'm assuming it's not fast. Why don't you just ask Mr. Remington?"

I sighed.

"What, has he still not made an appearance?"

"No." *Not unless you count last night in my dreams. Or in my steamy manuscript.* "And he never answers my questions anyway. I don't think he'd be pleased that I've been snooping around behind his back." But that was pretty much all I'd done since I'd arrived here. "I think I need to try to find those containers again. To see what's really inside them. I didn't get to inspect enough in that creepy servants' corridor."

"Please don't," Kehlani said.

"But . . ."

"Look, you clearly like the guy, or you would have left as soon as you thought he might be a vampire. So just ask him. The truth will set you free."

I laughed. "I think the truth is much more likely to kill me."

"Seriously, stop freaking me out and come home."

I opened my closet and ran my fingers along the clothes that Mr. Remington had given me. I wanted to look my best the next time I saw him. But I had no idea when that would be. I quickly changed into one of the shorter dresses as Kehlani droned on and on about the dangers of vampires.

"And they have hypnotic effects on their victims," Kehlani said.

She'd already told me all this. "I thought you didn't believe in vampires."

"And I thought you did," she said.

"You were right about the other night. I'd been drinking. I jumped to a hasty conclusion. It's the author in me trying to find a plot twist." *And maybe I do feel a little isolated here. Maybe I'm tired of being alone.*

"You're only saying that because you haven't seen Mr. Remington in days. You don't remember how vampiric he is."

I ran my finger along my lower lip, remembering how he'd bitten me. The taste of blood. How intense his gaze had been. *"I'm not so great around blood."*

"I think he's hypnotizing you," Kehlani said. "Putting you under his spell so you don't leave."

I pressed my lips together.

"You paused," she said. "Look, Hazel, I don't know if vampires exist. But I know when someone is being creepy. And Mr. Remington is really freaking creepy."

"He's just old-fashioned."

"You called me at one in the morning, jumped out a window, and smashed your car window with a rock to get away from him. Trust your instincts."

"But I'd been . . ."

"Drinking, I know," Kehlani said. "I'm just really worried."

"If he was going to hurt me, he would have already." I knew I was being reckless. Kehlani had a right to be worried. I honestly didn't know why I hadn't left yet. My mind was screaming at me to leave. But something stronger was making me stay.

"You don't know that."

I didn't. But I hoped it was true. "He knows I tell you everything. He'd never get away with murdering me."

"But what if you just . . . disappear."

A chill ran down my spine. "Stop it. You're freaking me out."

"*You're* freaking *me* out!"

I pulled the hair tie out of my hair, letting the strands fall down my back. "Everything is going to be fine," I said. "I have to get down to dinner. Just in case he comes."

"Will you please keep texting me? I swear, you're going to give me a heart attack."

"I promise to text you before I go to sleep," I said.

"Good."

"And I'll call you tomorrow when I go back in the servants' corridor. Byyyye!"

"What? Hazel!"

I hung up the phone. She'd be fine. I was the one in danger, not her. And I wouldn't really be in danger until I continued my snooping tomorrow.

Unless Mr. Remington showed up to dinner tonight and ended me. Just thinking about seeing him again had my heart racing. And I didn't know if it was because I was scared or excited.

I walked into the hall, locked my bedroom door behind me, and hurried down the stairs. My bare feet padded across the marble toward the dining room.

I had a million questions running around in my head.

Does Mr. Remington regret kissing me?

Does he have any news about Athena writing about me and him?

Does he own this house?

Is he a freaking vampire?

I walked into the empty dining room and my heart sank. Of course he wasn't here. But there was something unusual. There was a wrapped package with a bow sitting next to my silver cloche.

I sat down and picked up the envelope that was tucked beneath the bow. Mr. Remington had already bought me clothes for which I couldn't repay him. What on earth was in this small box? I pulled out the handwritten note.

Miss Fox,

I'm sorry about the other night.

—Mr. Remington

He was sorry?

For what, exactly? Kissing me? Scaring me? Avoiding me for four days?

I pulled on an edge of the bow and unwrapped the package. It was a brand-new cell phone. My screen had cracked the other night when he sneaked up on me. Right before our kiss.

Was he apologizing for breaking my phone?

Or for the kiss itself?

I stared at his empty seat.

He was probably apologizing for both. And I had my answer. He regretted it. He was avoiding me because he didn't want to face me.

I pushed the phone aside. I didn't want a new phone. I just wanted to speak to him in person. I needed to look into his eyes and see what he was thinking.

But if he were coming to dinner, he would have just brought the present himself instead of placing it here ahead of time.

How could he regret our kiss so much? It was the best kiss I'd ever had. He had to have felt it too.

I sighed and lifted the cloche. But there wasn't an elegant meal beneath it. There was a manila envelope. I looked toward the archway to see if anyone was watching me. And then I slid the contents out of the envelope.

It was more pages of Athena Quinn's manuscript. My eyes scanned the first page.

> She felt the coolness in the air.
> The coolness of his touch.

The coolness in his stare.

But she didn't realize it was death staring back at her until it was too late. She'd waited too long. She tried to run when the truth caught up to her. But he already had his claws in her. There was no escape.

I'd know. I'd been trying to escape for years.

I wasn't as naive as her. I'd run. Five times in total, I'd run. And every time, he pulled me back. Locked me in this house with his demons. Locked me in this room, where I couldn't warn her.

I watched her from my window when she tried to run.

I tried to call out to her, but my voice was silenced long ago. The only voice I now have is my written words. And soon they will be stifled too.

Her fate lies parallel to my own. If she can uncover the truth, maybe it will set us both free.

But I've seen this play out before. She's going to push away her fears for one intoxicating touch. It is always the things that are bad for us that feel the best. And only time can teach you such lessons.

I called it as soon as she stepped out of her car. She was naive when the world around her was dark.

We are both doomed.

"She didn't write about us," Mr. Remington said.

I jumped, dropping the pages and scattering them all over the floor.

CHAPTER 26

Friday—September 9

Mr. Remington crouched down at the same time I leaned over. We reached for the same page, and his fingers touched my wrist.

I forced myself not to shiver.

For a second, neither of us moved. He stared into my eyes.

"It was death staring back." I couldn't stop my shivers this time as I thought about Athena Quinn's words. Did I see death in his eyes? I wasn't sure that was what it was. I saw . . . torment. He looked conflicted. Like he was trying to control himself around me. But was that because he liked me or because he was worried he was about to kill me?

He dropped my gaze as he grabbed another sheet of the manuscript.

I stared at him as he picked up the pages. He was wearing a vest with his dress shirt sleeves rolled up to his elbows. It was the vest I thought I'd seen in one of the portraits. Even though that wasn't possible. It couldn't be.

When he'd grabbed all the pages, I thought he'd stand up. Instead, he slowly reached out his hand, tracing his thumb along my ankle. "You remembered to go barefoot."

The lightest of touches shouldn't have made my heart race as fast as it did. I shouldn't have been leaning closer. It was like Kehlani had said . . . There was something hypnotizing about him.

194

"She's going to push away her fears for one intoxicating touch." I tucked my foot beneath my chair. Athena Quinn thought I was a fool, but I wasn't. I was still here because I wanted answers.

Mr. Remington cleared his throat and stood up. His eyes scanned the first page. He'd said that Athena Quinn hadn't written about us. So he had seen these words. I figured that he'd placed them beneath the cloche. But he was looking at them like he was surprised they were there. Like he was surprised Athena Quinn was sharing them with me.

I swallowed hard as I stared at him. I had a hunch based off that first page. *"My voice was silenced long ago. The only voice I now have is my written words. And soon they will be stifled too."*

Mr. Remington had said that Miss Serrano couldn't speak. Was it possible . . . I shook the thought away, but it refused to be dismissed. Was it possible that Miss Serrano was Athena Quinn? That she left the manuscript under the cloche? She was the one who brought the food out. She could have easily slipped it in.

Mr. Remington handed the pages back to me. "I thought that you might be right," he said. "That Athena Quinn was writing about you. About me. But there's nothing about us in those pages."

Is that what he thought? Because to me, it very much seemed like she was writing about us. The three of us. Like she was watching from the window as I made mistake after mistake with Mr. Remington. I pictured the curtains moving whenever I was outside. How the hair on the back of my neck rose whenever I walked into a new room. She was watching me. I knew she was. She was probably watching me right now.

"You look pale," he said. "Are you all right?"

"I'm fine."

"You need to eat." He turned toward the doorway. "Miss Serrano!"

She hurried in with two plates.

I hadn't seen her in days. I wasn't sure if she'd been avoiding me. But now everything seemed even more twisted. Maybe she wasn't hiding at all. Maybe she was dying for me to put the pieces together. Waiting for me to help her. To save her from this hell. I had so many questions.

But Miss Serrano hurried off without making eye contact. Why did she always run from me?

I turned to look up at Mr. Remington. He was still standing by my chair and didn't seem at all inclined to go over to his side of the table.

"Why doesn't she speak?" I asked.

"It's a long, sad story."

I waited for him to go on. Instead, he just stared down at me. And I felt it again . . . this hypnotic pull toward him. I blinked and picked up my fork. I expected him to move to his side of the table, but he still didn't budge. After all . . . what was the point? He wasn't going to eat that food. It was much more likely that he was going to eat me.

He watched as I took a bite of mashed potatoes. Normally a comfort food, it felt more sinful than anything as he looked on.

I stared up at him instead of taking another bite. "Did you put the manuscript on the table?" I asked. But I knew he hadn't. I could tell. Well, kind of. Honestly, I had trouble reading the man.

"No. I've been trying to persuade Athena Quinn to let you do more work."

Had he really? I didn't believe a word of it.

"And it appears as though she finally listened."

"Thank you. For helping me get access." I was pretty sure, though, that he had been preventing it. "But you've already read this section?"

He nodded.

"And you don't think it has anything to do with us?"

"How could it? It's about a woman trapped in a house. Are you trapped, Miss Fox?"

"Well, my car window is smashed. And you disconnected the battery."

Mr. Remington smiled. It was rare for him to show any expression at all, and for some reason it made me smile too.

"I told you I'd fix it," he said.

He had left a note on my pile of work Tuesday morning. But as far as I could tell, my car had been untouched. And my keys were still missing. I'd searched for them everywhere. Except the servants' corridor. It was possible I'd had them with me there. I may have dropped them when I got scared.

"I just haven't had time to leave the house this week," he said.

It had been unseasonably warm all week. The sun bright and not a cloud in the sky. He couldn't leave. Or maybe he was just busy. "Were you a mechanic in another lifetime too?"

He lowered his eyebrows as he stared at me.

"You said you studied to be a doctor. A lifetime ago."

"It's an expression, Miss Fox."

In this context, I didn't think it was. I did think he actually was a doctor. I did think he'd done a lot of things if he'd been alive since the 1600s. Maybe he was a doctor before he became a vampire. He'd said he wasn't good around blood. Becoming a vampire may have forced him to change professions to . . . what? What else had he been doing for four hundred years? And why, of all things, would he choose to be someone's assistant if he had the time to be anything?

I stared at the man, who looked like he was in his thirties. Probably because he was just in his thirties. *I'm losing my mind.*

"Hudson told me about your ancestors," I said. Barely. He'd given me just enough information to have me dying for more. But Mr. Remington didn't know that. For all he knew, I was now aware of all their secrets.

"Is that all you and Hudson did the other night? Talk about me?" He looked amused by this news.

I pressed my lips together. Technically they were Hudson's ancestors too. But Hudson had been annoyed that all I could do was talk about Mr. Remington. Hudson could tell how much I liked his uncle, even if I'd been trying hard to hide it. "I told you it was none of your business."

"He left," Mr. Remington said. "I'm simply asking why."

Hudson had texted me the night after I sneaked out to say that he'd decided to take the fall classes he'd signed up for. He hadn't asked me about jumping out the window. But he must have known something odd happened. I left that bedroom door locked. He knew I was suspicious of his lineage. Maybe he wanted to be long gone before I outed him for what he truly was.

That was how it felt. Like I was about to tell the whole world the Remingtons were monsters. But Mr. Remington didn't seem like a monster. It was easy to forget how captivating he was when he'd been ignoring me. But here in his presence again? It really didn't seem like he wanted to hurt me.

"Miss Fox?" he said.

"What?" I hadn't realized he'd asked me a question.

"Why did my nephew suddenly leave?"

I'd told Mr. Remington it wasn't his business. But technically it was his business if I desperately wanted him to kiss me again. *Desperately?* Was that really so? My head felt scrambled around him. But it was true. I wanted him to kiss me. I wanted to see if he'd draw blood again. "Because there was no reason for him to stay."

"None at all?"

"No." I'd asked Mr. Remington lots of questions, but he'd deflected them all. Yet here I was, basically telling him I liked him. How was he so easily able to get information from me? I wanted to ask him if he was seeing Athena Quinn. But something about the way he was staring at me made my voice get caught in my throat.

He put his hand out for me, but he didn't say a word. And I didn't know if taking his hand meant that we were about to dance around the dining room or that I was consenting to let him bite my neck. But I didn't care. I just wanted to feel his skin against mine again. I slid my hand into his.

He pulled me to my feet.

But he didn't whisk me into his arms for a dance. Instead, he stared down at me, the intensity in his eyes growing.

"Sit on the edge of the table," he said.

I moved back, letting my butt hit the edge of the table.

"I like when you follow my instructions, Miss Fox."

I swallowed hard.

"Spread your legs."

I didn't even hesitate. I spread my thighs, and he grabbed one, wrapping it around his waist.

He leaned forward. I expected him to kiss me again, but his mouth moved to my ear. "Do you see the picture of the setting sun on the wall?"

I nodded because my voice was still lost. All I could feel was the coolness of his skin against mine. *"One intoxicating touch."* Athena Quinn was right. I was lost whenever he touched me. I could barely pay attention to his words. I just wanted his lips on mine again.

"There's a camera on the top right corner of the golden frame. There are cameras in most of the rooms. She's watching us right now."

A chill ran down my spine, but this time it wasn't because of his touch. I knew she was watching. I could feel it.

"You want to know if she writes about you." His fingers traced lightly down the side of my neck. "Do you want to test that theory again?"

My heart started hammering against my rib cage as his thumb pressed against the base of my neck.

"You're shaking," he said. He went to take a step back, but I grabbed his hand, keeping it on my thigh.

He looked down at the contact.

Was he doing this only because he was curious to see if Athena Quinn would write about it? Or because he wanted to? I needed to know if this was just for show. But more than anything, I needed him to kiss me again.

"Stay," I said. I hated that there was a tremor in my voice.

He didn't move.

"Your note said that you were sorry. Were you sorry that you kissed me?"

He just stared at me.

"Is that why you avoided me all week?"

He was so still that he almost looked like one of Athena Quinn's sculptures, hidden in a room where no one ever saw them.

Maybe it wasn't Athena Quinn who was trapped in this house. Maybe it was him. Maybe he was scared to leave because he thought he might hurt someone. By accident. I couldn't imagine him doing it on purpose. I didn't believe for a second that he was a monster.

"I'm not scared of you, Mr. Remington."

He finally moved, his hand sliding up my thigh until it rested on my hip. "Yes, you are, Miss Fox."

I didn't have time to process his words before his lips crashed against mine.

He leaned forward, and my hand landed in my plate of food. I had the strangest urge to smash the mashed potatoes into his face. I'd never heard the man laugh.

He groaned as his fingers dug into the skin of my hip.

Screw laughing. I wanted to hear him groan again. I tightened my legs around him as his lips fell from mine.

I thought he was going to pull away, but instead he traced kisses along my jawline. I tried not to tense when his lips dropped to my neck. My head fell back as he gently sucked on my exposed skin. He wasn't biting me. Just sucking on my flesh. Marking me.

I would have buried my fingers in his hair if not for the mess it would have made. Instead, I stayed completely still as his hand slid up my side. He stopped right before he reached my breast.

A moan escaped my throat.

And he immediately took a step back from me. His eyes were wild. He took another step back. I would have thought he was scared if he weren't staring at me like he wanted to devour every inch of me.

Could he tell that it hurt me when he always backed away after our kisses? Did he regret it again? "How could she resist writing about that?" I asked, trying to pretend I wasn't affected by his actions. That I was just doing it to test my theory too. That my heart wasn't invested in the outcome, even though it was all a lie.

He didn't respond, but his eyes dropped to where my skirt had bunched up at my waist. I pressed my thighs back together.

"I guess we shall see."

My heart hammered against my rib cage again. "I guess we shall." I lifted my hand out of the mashed potatoes.

"I'll leave you to your dinner."

"Aren't you hungry?" I was. I licked some of the potatoes off my finger, but I stopped when I saw his Adam's apple rise and then fall.

"I'm starving, Miss Fox." It looked like he wanted to step back toward me. But instead he turned around and disappeared through the archway.

Starving? Then why hadn't he touched his food? The only thing he'd feasted on was the side of my neck. I touched the spot with my clean hand. The skin was already ginger from a bruise forming.

It was just like Athena Quinn had said. He'd unraveled me with one intoxicating touch. But I was pretty sure I was unraveling him too.

Yes, his touch was distracting. My heart was still pounding. But his touch wasn't distracting enough to stop me from continuing to investigate what he and Athena Quinn were hiding. I needed to talk to Miss Serrano, even if all she could do was write.

I grabbed my new phone and walked into the day kitchen. The phone was a nice gesture. But, honestly, I was so suspicious of Mr. Remington that I didn't trust the new device. For all I knew, it was bugged. And I didn't want him listening to every word I spoke.

I quickly washed my hands, grabbed a sticky note, and wrote to Miss Serrano. I kept the note discreet. I just said we needed to talk. And I asked her to meet me outside Monday afternoon while I worked. She'd know it was me. I was the only one who left the house.

Besides, I was almost positive she'd been waiting for me to reach out. I lifted a plate on the drying rack and placed the note down, then covered it with the plate. Miss Serrano was the only person who did the dishes. She'd find it. I just hoped she was ready to talk. Because even though I'd tried, neither Little nor Big Remington had let very much slip.

Big Remington. I sighed. I knew what I'd be dreaming of tonight.

CHAPTER 27

Miss Serrano did not show up outside on Monday. I'd left her another note, and she'd ignored my request again. And again.

I knew that she'd found them. I'd checked, and they were gone. And she'd made herself scarce again. As had Mr. Remington.

Every time he kissed me, he pulled back. Maybe I was just a bad kisser.

I sighed and rested my chin on my knee as I read through the last chapter I'd written. It had ended with the hero taking me right there on the dining room table. A fantasy. This hero was as smitten as the heroine. Definitely a fantasy. I was pretty sure Mr. Remington cared only about testing theories and sticking to strict rules.

I frowned as I read through the scene. My thriller had turned to mush. Hell, my brain had turned to mush. I saved my manuscript and closed the lid to my computer, then stared out at the crashing waves.

But my current work in progress wasn't really mush. I felt the words because I'd lived them. But my relationship with Mr. Remington—or lack thereof—was completely one sided. If Mr. Remington liked me, he wouldn't avoid me for days at a time. He'd want to give in to the temptation just as badly as I did.

I stared out at the setting sun. Despite what everyone thought, I wasn't the fool in this story. The fool was the vampire who chose to reside on a sunny beach, of all places. And I wasn't going to sit around waiting for him anymore. I needed a night out.

I grabbed my phone, but it wouldn't turn on. *Shit.* I must have damaged more than just the screen when I'd dropped it. Which meant I'd have to use the phone Mr. Remington had bought me. I pushed myself up out of the lounge chair and made my way inside. While my new phone charged, I pulled off my work clothes and opened the closet. All the expensive clothes that Mr. Remington had bought stared back at me. I shut the doors and opened one of the dresser drawers. My favorite pair of cutoff jean shorts and a tank top were much better suited for a night out in a beach town.

I changed and freshened up my makeup. I pushed my hair over my shoulder and stared at the bruise on my neck. It was starting to fade, but it was still evident. I dabbed some concealer onto it. Honestly, it barely helped to hide it. Did I even want to cover it? Something about Mr. Remington marking me had my heart racing all over again. He must have known my neck would bruise beneath his lips. He must have done it on purpose.

So why hadn't he spoken to me since? I let my hair fall back into place. I just needed him out of my head for one night. Maybe some distance would clear my mind. I walked back out of the bathroom and grabbed my new phone. It charged so much faster than my old one. Maybe there were perks to dating a rich, older man. Seriously, what was wrong with me? *"He already had his claws in her. There was no escape."* I hated how Athena Quinn's words kept echoing around in my head. I needed them out just as much as I needed Mr. Remington out.

I unhooked my new phone from the charger and accessed my contacts list. I wasn't sure how Mr. Remington had synced my old phone with my new one, but all my contacts were already there. The only one I really cared about was Kehlani. But I found myself scrolling down to Mr. Remington. I knew it was silly that I didn't have him as Atlas in my phone. But he didn't like when I called him by his first name. And I really loved the way that "Mr. Remington" rolled off my tongue. *Stop.* Tonight wasn't about Mr. Remington.

I needed to relax. Have fun. I was living at the beach, and I was acting like I was being tortured. This was an experience. And I didn't want to look back and regret a second of it.

I grabbed my purse and googled local restaurants. It looked like there was a bar and grill about a mile outside the gates of the neighborhood. That would be perfect because I still hadn't found my car keys, and I had no idea whether Mr. Remington had fixed my car yet.

I had planned to go into the servants' corridor again to look for my keys and more clues. But when I'd called Kehlani a few days ago, she'd refused to stay on the line with me if I went in there again. I wasn't sure if she was more freaked out by the corridor itself or by the fact that I'd told her Athena Quinn had cameras everywhere. Were they in the corridor too?

I wanted answers . . . but I was a little scared of that creepy corridor and the cameras too. If Mr. Remington was telling the truth about them . . . Athena Quinn probably knew I was searching the house. So why hadn't she stopped me? Maybe she wanted Mr. Remington to tell me about the cameras. So he could warn me and force me to stop looking for answers.

I stopped at the top of the stairwell and stared down Athena Quinn's corridor. *What do you want from me? Why won't you speak with me?*

For one night, I was going to try to not think of the answers I was seeking. I made my way downstairs. I didn't even bother to look into the dining room. It would be empty. It was always empty, especially on days I wished it wasn't.

I made my way outside and pulled on my flip-flops. I paused on the steps and stared at where my car usually sat. It was gone. The shattered glass was gone too. It was like my car had never been there at all. Mr. Remington must have called someone to fix it. I wasn't sure how I was going to pay him back for that. I hadn't really been joking the other night . . . I kind of figured he knew a lot about mechanics if he'd been alive so long. I hated when things broke. If I had ten lives, I'd learn how to fix things too.

I tried to push all the thoughts of Mr. Remington out of my head as I made my way down the gravel drive. I passed by Hudson's estate. The overgrown foliage looked even more wild than it had a week ago. A perfect hiding spot for a vampire.

Stop it. Seriously, stop it.

Vampires don't exist.

They just . . . don't.

I reached the front gate and waved at the man on duty.

He did not wave back.

When I'd first arrived, he'd been unfriendly. When I'd told him I was going to work for Athena Quinn, he'd seemed surprised. What had he said? *"You're in for quite the surprise if you think you're going to see her."*

I walked up to his window and knocked.

He lifted his gaze from the newspaper he was reading, but he didn't open the window.

"I have a question," I said and motioned for him to slide open the glass.

He slowly set his paper down and slid the glass to the side.

"Have you ever seen Athena Quinn leave the neighborhood?"

"Ma'am, how did you get through the gates?"

Did he seriously not recognize me? I'd arrived less than a month ago. "I . . ."

"We don't allow reporters on the premises. I'm going to have to ask you to leave."

"I'm not a reporter. I'm Hazel Fox, Athena Quinn's new assistant."

He stared at me.

"Hazel Fox," I said again.

"I heard you the first time, ma'am." He grabbed a clipboard and flipped back a few pages, scanning it.

I just stared at him. Was he trying to dismiss me? Or was he waiting for me to ask my question? I leaned forward to catch the name on his name tag. Serrano. *Wait . . . what?* "Mr. Serrano?"

"No," he said and let the pages flutter back in place on his clipboard.

"No that's not your name or no . . ."

"No, Athena Quinn hasn't left her estate any time recently. Have a good night."

He went to close the glass window, but I stuck out my hand to stop it. "Your last name is Serrano?" I asked.

He stared at me.

"Are you related to Athena Quinn's live-in maid and personal chef?"

"Her live-in maid?"

"Yeah . . . Miss Serrano."

"*Mrs.* Serrano is my wife. And she certainly doesn't live with Athena Quinn."

But I'd never seen her leave the premises either. I'd never seen another car . . . I eyed the patrol car next to the security building. *Oh.* He must pick her up after work. "Why doesn't she speak?"

He just stared at me like I wasn't making any sense.

"She doesn't speak," I repeated.

"Maybe she doesn't speak to you," he huffed under his breath and picked up his newspaper again.

"No, Mr. Remington told me she doesn't speak at all. That there was some long, sad story about . . ."

"I think I know my own wife."

I opened my mouth and then closed it again. God, Mr. Remington really was trying to scare me. Why? Why did he so desperately want me to fear him? What the hell was his game? "So she *can* talk?"

"I don't know what you think you're doing, but spreading rumors about my wife . . ."

"Is she Athena Quinn?"

He glared at me. "Ma'am, are you intoxicated?"

Why did everyone always ask me if I was drunk? "No." At least, not yet. After this conversation I really needed a drink.

"You're off in the head. You best be going." He slammed the glass partition closed and hit something to make the front gates swing open.

Was I off in the head? I walked through the gates. Mr. Remington *had* said those things about Miss Serrano. I wasn't just making it up. He'd said it several times. I wasn't mistaken.

I looked back as the gates swung shut behind me. *"Off in the head."* I wasn't off in the head. Everyone else behind those gates was. And seriously . . . where was everyone else? I hadn't seen a single sign of life in any of those houses except for a light flickering on in one.

I walked down the worn path on the side of the road. Not a single car drove past me until I turned the corner to a busier street. Really, why were there no other cars in the neighborhood? Why was there no one around? And why did Mr. Remington lie to me about every freaking thing?

I needed a drink.

⊙≫⊙

If the sign hadn't been in lime green, I would have missed the bar. Just like the other structures on the island, the building was brown and blended into the scenery flawlessly. I opened the door and was relieved to feel a blast of air-conditioning. Fall refused to hit the island, and the mile-long walk felt longer with the setting sun hot on the back of my neck.

"Table for two?" the hostess asked.

Why would she assume that? "No. It's just me. Could I sit at the bar?"

"Of course. Right this way." We walked past several full tables to the bar. There were only a handful of empty seats. I sat down in one as she handed me a menu. I didn't expect a Wednesday night in September to be so crowded. But the bar was full of energy. It reminded me a little of New York. No matter what time of day or what day of the week, the night life was electric.

I ordered a burger and fries and sipped on my Long Island iced tea. I'd missed this. Night after night all alone was getting to my head. Maybe even more than I realized. *"You're off in the head."*

It didn't take long for my order to come out. Miss Serrano was a great cook, but I'd missed fast, greasy food. Sorry, *Mrs.* Serrano. I was on my second drink now, and I didn't know if the bar was rowdier because I was tipsy or because it actually was louder.

But I could feel the beat of the music reverberating in my chest as I sipped on my drink.

"Do you need another?" someone asked and slid into the seat beside mine.

He didn't give off the same creepy vibes as the other people I'd met on the island. Or maybe I was just too relaxed to notice or care. "I would love another."

He waved the bartender over.

As my third drink was placed in front of me, I felt the hairs on the back of my neck rise.

I didn't need to turn around to know who had just walked into the bar.

CHAPTER 28

Wednesday—September 14

I tried to discreetly peer over my shoulder. Mr. Remington was chatting to the hostess. He was dressed more casually than I'd ever seen him, in a white V-neck tee and a pair of faded blue jeans. He was dressed like he was trying to fit in here. But he couldn't blend in even if he tried.

Maybe it was a coincidence that he was here. But it didn't feel like it. One night to myself. One night was all I was asking. But Mr. Remington had followed me. How did he even know where I was?

"Are you okay?" the guy who had just bought me a drink asked.

"I'm great," I said sarcastically.

He laughed. "You sound anything but great."

"It's nothing." I did my best to keep my eyes trained on him and ignore Mr. Remington. "My boss just walked in."

He turned to look over at the front door. "Do you want to get out of here? My place is just around the corner."

Whoa, that was not at all what I was suggesting. "No, I just want to sip my drink and pretend he's not here."

"We can definitely do that," he said with a smile. "So what do you do for work?"

"I'm an assistant to an author."

"That guy's an author?"

"No, not him," I said with a laugh. I couldn't imagine Mr. Remington writing a book. It would be so stiff and lifeless. *And hot.* I pictured his lips against my neck. *Stop it.* "Athena Quinn. The romance novelist."

"Yeah, I think I've heard of her. Pretty sure my sister reads her books. Is she nice?"

"I wouldn't know. I haven't gotten to meet her. My boss keeps giving me busywork instead of anything remotely interesting."

"And your boss is the guy coming toward us?"

Wait, what? I turned around to see Mr. Remington prowling toward me, a scowl plastered to his face. He looked just like he had when he'd asked me if I was having a dalliance with his nephew. Almost as if he were jealous. *No. Hell no.* He wasn't allowed to be jealous when he ignored me for days on end. And I definitely wasn't going to allow him to reprimand me in public.

I grabbed my new friend's hand and pulled him to the dance floor. He didn't even hesitate to put his hands on my hips.

I placed my hand on his shoulder as I tried to peer around him to see where Mr. Remington had gone. But I couldn't find him.

Maybe I'd misread the situation. Maybe he wasn't even here because of me. I closed my eyes and moved my hips to the beat of the music. I just wanted one night away from him. From my constant nagging thoughts. Whenever he was nearby, I couldn't think clearly.

I thought about what the guard at the front gate had told me. If Mrs. Serrano really did speak . . . why had Mr. Remington lied? Why did he keep messing with my head? I needed distance. Just one night out of that house, away from him.

I spun around, pressing my backside to my dance partner. I focused on the music and tried my best to get lost in it.

Just pretend he isn't here. Just listen to the music.

When I opened my eyes again, Mr. Remington was standing at the bar all alone, staring at me. He slowly sipped his drink without breaking eye contact with me. It was certainly possible he'd come in here to have a drink alone. Same as me. But it was much more likely that he'd followed me. Especially since he was staring daggers at the man whose hands were on my waist.

I dipped it low, staring at Mr. Remington the whole time. It was probably the drinks that made me do it. Possibly the fact that I actually did kind of like when Mr. Remington scowled at me, which he was currently doing. It looked like he was holding his glass so tightly that it might shatter.

I reached behind me and ran my hand down my dance partner's neck. Mr. Remington's eyes bored into mine.

And I just stared back. As I danced against the stranger, I wished he were Mr. Remington. But Mr. Remington stayed firmly in his spot at the bar. He probably didn't know how to dance like this. He grew up doing . . . what were they doing hundreds of years ago? Choreographed line dances or something?

It was a shame. Because I would have loved his hands to be on my hips right now. Could he see it in my eyes? How desperately I wanted him?

A bead of sweat ran down the center of my chest, and I watched as Mr. Remington's eyes traced its path.

The way he was staring at me made me feel desired. But if he desired me . . . why did he kiss me only when he was testing a theory? Why did he keep avoiding me? Hell, he was avoiding me right now. Just staring.

The beat of the music sped up, and I felt it in my chest. It seemed like my heart was ricocheting around faster than normal. I felt hot all over, and the air in the bar was suddenly stifling. I wanted to run over to Mr. Remington, jump into his arms, and kiss him senselessly. But there was nothing about his posture that said he wanted that. He just looked . . . pissed.

I stopped moving my hips. I'd had it right when he'd walked in. He wasn't here to drink and dance and have fun. He was here to scold me. Or to tell me I was a courtesan or whatever old-fashioned term he used for a slut. That was what he thought about me, right? That I was loose?

And it certainly didn't help that I was staring provocatively at him as I grinded my butt against another man. What was I doing? I stepped away from my dance partner.

He reached out for me, but I took another step away.

"Sorry, I forgot I have . . . a thing." I hurried off the dance floor, past the tables, and out into the fresh air.

The salty air felt heavy tonight. The alcohol had gotten to my head. My fantasies about Mr. Remington had gotten to my head even more. I wasn't this girl. I didn't want to make him jealous. I wanted him to want me for me. I didn't need to play games. I just needed Mr. Remington out of my thoughts.

I folded my arms across my chest and started walking back toward Athena Quinn's estate. Tonight was supposed to clear my head, but now I was more confused than ever.

A sleek black car with tinted windows pulled up beside me. The window slowly rolled down.

"Get in," Mr. Remington said.

Of course his car windows were tinted. I didn't turn to look at him. I just kept walking.

The car moved forward. "Miss Fox, get in the car."

"I'm perfectly capable of walking myself home."

"Miss Fox, I'm not going to ask you again . . ."

I stopped and stared at him through the open window. "Maybe I'd want to get in the car with you if you stopped being formal for one second and used my first name. If you didn't avoid me for days every time you kissed me. If you acted . . . human." I shouldn't have said that last thing. I shook my head and kept walking.

The car inched up again.

"Hazel, get in the car."

I froze. He'd used my first name. He hadn't acknowledged the rest of what I said, but . . . that was something. And, honestly, I didn't feel that comfortable walking back to the estate when it was so dark out. *Screw it.* I opened the car door and slid in.

"Put your safety restraint on," he said.

Did he mean *seat belt? I was just about to do that.* I really hated when he bossed me around. But I found myself clicking my seat belt into place anyway.

He put his foot down on the gas pedal without another word.

I thought he might acknowledge the rest of what I'd said. The kissing. The human comment.

Mr. Remington just kept driving.

Was he really not even going to talk about the fact that he'd followed me to that bar? Or that he'd watched me dance like he was a stalker?

Apparently not. The gates opened to the neighborhood, and all I could hear was the gravel spitting out from beneath the tires. He pulled into Athena Quinn's long drive and cut the engine where my car had been parked.

Was he not even going to mention where my car was?

He climbed out and closed the door.

Asshole. He really had nothing to say to me at all?

He walked around the car like he was going to help me out. But I didn't need his help. I climbed out and slammed the door closed.

He didn't say a word to me as I walked past him.

"Miss Fox," he finally called after me.

Back to being formal? I wasn't interested. And I didn't want to go into that house. I didn't want to close my eyes and dream of that infuriating man. So I walked past the front door and around the side of the house. I didn't stop until I was standing on the edge of the pool.

I closed my eyes and breathed in the salty air and listened to the waves crashing in the distance. My heart rate slowly returned to normal. What was it about Mr. Remington that pissed me off so much? And why was I being openly rude to him? That didn't seem like a good idea, since there was a chance he wanted to suck my blood. I pictured him sucking on my neck, and I almost wanted to cry.

Why did he keep avoiding me?

"Miss Fox?"

I looked up to see him standing right next to me.

He cleared his throat. "I wanted to surprise you."

I just stared at him. What was he talking about? Surprise me at the bar?

"It just arrived tonight." He pulled a set of car keys out of his pocket. But they weren't mine.

"I don't understand."

"The car I picked you up in. It's yours."

"What?"

"To replace your broken one," he said.

"My window was broken, not my whole damned car."

"It was a death trap. You shouldn't be driving around in that old thing."

God, if he told me what to do one more time . . . "I don't want you to buy me a new freaking car!" *I just want you to talk to me.*

"I think it's best if you—"

I didn't hear the rest of what he said because I pushed him into the pool.

He caught my wrist at the last second, pulling me in with him. I screamed as we fell into the water.

We came up for air at the same time, our limbs a tangled mess.

When he broke the surface, he laughed. A deep, rolling chuckle. It sounded almost magical to my ears. And I couldn't help but laugh too.

He rubbed the water out of his eyes, keeping one hand around my waist. He made a face. "I hate chlorine water."

"I hate when you ignore me." I swallowed hard. I hadn't meant to say it. It just kind of tumbled out.

He placed his wet hand against my cheek.

I almost felt sick for his touch. Like I needed it. Like I needed him.

His eyes searched mine. "Okay," he finally said.

"Okay?"

"I won't ignore you anymore."

I didn't know what he meant by that, exactly. But I didn't even care. At least it was something. And anything at this point felt like progress. "You're driving me wild."

"I wasn't the one dancing with someone else." He lowered his forehead to mine and took a deep breath, like he was breathing me in.

"I won't do it again," I said. "If you stop seeing Athena Quinn."

He lifted his head from mine. "Athena Quinn? I thought you realized that I'm not one to partake in dalliances, Miss Fox."

I laughed and splashed him with water.

He looked completely shocked but then splashed me back.

I tried to swim away from him, but he caught my ankle and pulled me back toward him. I squealed as he brought me in close. His chest rose and fell, spreading the wet fabric of his V-neck. "I like this version of you, Atlas."

He smiled. "What version?"

I shrugged. I didn't know how to describe it. The fun version. The version that liked me back.

He touched the side of my neck.

I was just thinking that this was going straight into my novel when he kissed me.

I wrapped my legs around his waist as he pushed my back against the side of the pool.

I didn't know what secrets he was hiding. But I didn't care if being with him meant kissing in the pool at night instead of during the day. The best things happened after the sun fell anyway.

CHAPTER 29

The phone rang several times before Kehlani finally picked up. "Kehlani speaking."

"Hey, it's me," I said as I changed into a pair of warm, comfy pajamas.

"Hazel?" There was a long pause. "Whose phone are you calling from?"

"Oh," I said with a laugh. "My new one." I wrung my hair out in the sink. Maybe Mr. Remington disliked the smell of chlorine, but I'd forever associate it with him now.

"Does that mean you got a raise for all the crap work that Mr. Remington is making you do?"

"Not exactly. It was a gift from Mr. Remington. Atlas, I mean." I wanted to start calling him Atlas now. It had made him smile when I'd done it earlier. And then he'd kissed me senseless. I collapsed onto my bed with the biggest smile on my face.

"Another gift? Hazel, I'm not sure you should be accepting all this stuff from a guy you barely know."

"Then it's probably a bad time to tell you he also bought me a car."

There was another long pause.

"Are you still there?" I asked.

"Yeah." Another pause. "Don't you think he's expecting something in return for all these extravagant gifts? First the clothes, then a phone . . . and now a car? Who buys a complete stranger a car?"

"He's not a complete stranger. I know things about him." *Some things.* "And he's just being generous. I don't even know if I'm going to accept the car. But it was sweet of him. He was worried that my old one wasn't safe. I think that maybe this is how he's used to showing emotion."

"By buying people off?"

I laughed. "No."

"Are you okay?" she asked. "You sound weird."

Weird? Maybe. I'd never really felt this way before. "I don't know how to explain it, Kehlani. But everything feels different with him. Bigger. More important."

"Are you drunk right now?"

"I'm not *not* drunk. But no matter how much I've had to drink, I know without a doubt that I'm falling in love with him." I held my breath as I waited for her to respond.

"Hazel," she said.

"Kehlani," I said back.

"It wasn't but a week ago that you thought the man was a vampire and were terrified of him. You *still* think he's a vampire, which brings me to what I wanted to talk about. You need to force-feed him garlic. Or shove him into the sun. Or stab him in the heart with a wooden stake."

"I'm not going to stab him."

"Then do one of the other two."

"Kehlani, didn't you hear anything I just said? I'm falling in love with him. I just went out for dinner, and he followed me. I don't know how he knew where I was, but that's beside the point. You should have seen the way he stared at me when I was dancing with another man. It was so possessive and so hot."

"You're wasted."

"If anything, I'm tipsy. You're not listening . . . I . . ."

"He's dangerous, Hazel."

I pressed my lips together.

"He probably put a tracking device on that new phone he gave you. What he's doing isn't romantic. It's controlling."

Was that how he'd found me? Had he bugged my phone? I shook my head. "You're the one who's always telling me to go on dates and . . ."

"With normal men. Not creepy older vampires!"

"I think I misjudged him."

Kehlani sighed. "Or maybe you had it right the first time. Your gut reaction was to fear him. Gut reactions are usually correct."

"Then why did you keep talking about love triangles and egg me on?"

"I know, I'm sorry, but I've been doing so much research on vampires now. I'll admit, I may have fallen into a bit of a rabbit hole on the internet. I think vampires might actually exist. I mean . . . how do you explain all the creepy stuff in the house? All the things that don't add up? Something is off about him."

The smile faded from my lips. "I thought you of all people would be happy for me. You love romance novels. You read every Athena Quinn release."

"It's all make-believe, though. They're stories. Fantasies. They're not real."

I didn't know what to say. But maybe I was a little tipsier than I realized because, just like that, my excitement over the evening was gone. God, the last hour felt like an emotional roller coaster. Tears slid from my eyes and into my hair as I stared up at the ceiling.

"Are you still there?" Kehlani asked.

"Yeah," I sniffled.

"Girl, I didn't mean to make you cry."

"I think I'm in over my head. I was so wrapped up in uncovering his secrets. And now I'm just wrapped up in him. It's like he's taken over all my thoughts. I don't think I could get him out of my head even if I wanted to. I . . ."

"You're in love with him," Kehlani said. "I think maybe it's time you told him that."

"I can't tell him that. He spooks easily."

She laughed. "He's not a horse."

"Right, just a vampire. So you want me to push him into the sunshine and then tell him I'm obsessed with him if he doesn't burn up?"

"Answer me one question—do you feel safe around him now?"

Yes. Most of the time. Despite what Mr. Remington believed, I wasn't scared of him. He'd had so many opportunities to end my life. But he hadn't. I didn't think there was anything to fear. "Yes," I finally said. "He doesn't scare me."

"Then maybe I'm being dramatic. Damn it, just because my fairy tale hasn't happened yet doesn't mean you can't have yours."

I smiled again.

"But you have to ask him all the questions swimming around in your head. You need to make him give you straight answers."

"Or I could go into the servants' corridor again . . ."

"You're not an investigative journalist, Hazel. You're a fiction writer. Stop snooping and spying and flat out ask the man if he's a vampire."

"That seems like a dangerous proposition."

"Preface it with: 'Kehlani and I both think you might be a vampire.' That way, he knows that I know too."

"So if he kills me, he'll kill you too?"

"Well . . . no. I'm hoping it will ward him off killing either of us."

"Maybe." I didn't think coming right out and asking him was the best approach. There had to be a more subtle way.

"Can I say one more thing?"

I nodded and realized she couldn't see me. "Yes."

"I told you so."

I groaned.

"I totally knew you were smitten with him the whole time!"

"I wasn't—"

"Don't even lie," Kehlani said. "You one hundred percent were. It just took you a while to get out of your head for once."

I smiled up at the ceiling.

"You promise you'll ask him about the whole vampire thing?"

I had more questions than just the vampire thing. And I would ask him eventually. But for a little while longer . . . I wanted to live in whatever happy bubble I'd just created. "I promise," I said. But I was worried that as soon as I asked, the bubble would pop.

CHAPTER 30

After breakfast, Atlas caught my hand and pulled me into the pantry. He leaned down and kissed me in the darkness.

I sank my fingers into his hair.

He'd done what he'd promised. He hadn't ignored me at all after our kiss in the pool. For weeks, my days had been full of stolen kisses. He kissed me whenever we walked past each other in the halls. And he was always pulling me into dark, tight spaces like this. I loved that the most.

My elbow hit one of the shelves, and a box of something fell over. But I didn't care. All I cared about was the fact that he was kissing me. Pulling me closer. The only thing he hadn't done was touch me where I needed him most.

It was probably the southern gentleman in him. His old-fashioned nature. But he'd have to cave soon, right? How many weeks could just kissing last?

"I should get back to work," he said, his lips falling from mine way too soon.

I moaned a protest.

And I could barely make out his smile in the darkness. He did that more now too. Smile. It still caught me off guard whenever it happened, though. It felt like he reserved those smiles just for me.

"Maybe we could go for a quick walk," I said. A walk along the beach right now would be lovely. And proof that he could venture out on a sunny day. Last week I'd kept my nose in my own business. But this week? I'd been trying to do what Kehlani had asked. All my suspicions and curiousness about Atlas were still there. It was hard to shut them off. But every time I asked him to go outside, his response was a resounding *no*.

"I'm behind on a few pressing tasks," he said.

Okay. I needed to get him around garlic, then. "Well, what if we go out tonight?"

"I don't—"

"Just for dinner," I quickly said before he could shut me down. "We can go somewhere other than that bar. I know you don't like to dance or anything."

"What gave you the notion that I don't like to dance?"

I laughed. "The fact that you just stared at me a few weeks ago instead of dancing with me."

"Hmm." He reached out and ran his fingers down a strand of my hair.

"Is that a yes to dinner?"

"We have everything we need right here. I don't want to go out."

There was something distant about his response. Like he was already checked out of the conversation. Like he found my request a nuisance. "Okay. Well, then, maybe we can go for that walk? Relationships are about compromise."

He let go of my waist. Like the word *relationship* had offended him. "I'll be inaccessible for the rest of the day," he said formally. "But I'll see you at dinner."

I slowly died inside every time he pulled back from me. And when he told me no. Did he have any idea how close I was to pushing him out into the sun like Kehlani wanted? "Okay," I said. I felt as dejected as I did that Athena Quinn *still* didn't want to meet me. Or had Atlas killed her? I stared up at him. He wouldn't. I didn't believe he'd hurt anyone.

He gave me one last kiss and exited the pantry.

"Atlas?" I said before he closed the door. "Do you promise you'll be at dinner?" Some nights he still didn't show up to the dining room. And I never got a reason why. Not one excuse. What was he doing on those nights? Not that I could really be upset. He gave me plenty of attention whenever he did see me.

"I promise, Hazel." And with that, he walked away, leaving me alone in the darkness.

I smiled to myself. He still called me Miss Fox more than Hazel. Whenever he used my first name, it made me feel . . . loved. I shook the thought away. Yes, I was falling for him. But in love with him? How could I be? Kehlani was right—I barely knew him.

Asking him to go for walks was the only thing I'd done as far as trying to get answers. I didn't know him any better than I had before we started whatever it was we'd started. He didn't label it. All it amounted to was him not ignoring me.

I shook away my pesky thoughts. That wasn't true. It was certainly more than that. He couldn't keep his hands off me. He was completely different than he had been when I first met him. For one, he actually smiled now. Occasionally, he even laughed. And God, I loved that sound more than anything.

I knelt down to pick up the box I'd knocked over. Hopefully Mrs. Serrano wouldn't be too angry about a little spilled rice. *Mrs. Serrano.* Maybe I could start there. Just rip the Band-Aid off and ask Atlas about Mrs. Serrano. I would have asked her . . . but she'd made herself even more scarce over the past weeks. Almost as if he'd told her to.

There were a lot of nagging questions in the back of my head. But the Mrs. Serrano thing? Atlas had completely lied to me about her. I could definitely ask him about that. Tonight. I'd do it at dinner.

"I don't understand what you're waiting for," Kehlani said. "Just play a game of this or that. List two things and make him choose which one he prefers. Rapid-fire pace so he doesn't have time to think. Ask a few normal things: Night owl or early bird? Mountains or ocean? Hot or cold? And then slip in: Ice cream or blood? Easy. Done."

"Why ice cream?" I said with a laugh.

"It was the first thing that popped into my head."

"They're nothing alike."

"None of the things are alike. They're usually complete opposites. Like cats and dogs."

"And you think ice cream is the opposite of blood?" I was just messing with her. Buying time because I knew she was right. I just needed to talk to Atlas. I pulled out one of the dresses I hadn't worn yet.

"I mean, I know I'd say ice cream," Kehlani said.

"Fair."

"Plus, ice cream is one of my favorite things. And I'm assuming that blood is one of Mr. Remington's favorite things. And he kept his blood in the freezer. Same place ice cream is stored. Boom. I'm a genius."

I laughed. "You are. And I have been trying. I've been bugging him to go for a walk, and he always refuses."

"It's been sunny down there this week, right?"

"Yeah." I sighed. "But, Kehlani, he hasn't once tried to hurt me. Since our first kiss, there has been zero blood drawn."

"He's making you feel comfortable."

"He's never once hurt me," I said again.

"Because he has dozens of containers of stored blood hidden somewhere in that creepy estate. He doesn't need you. *Yet.*"

I shivered. I definitely didn't love the idea of him running out of his food source. "I am going to ask him," I said as I changed into the dress I'd picked out. I added a shawl. There was a chill in the air tonight. But I didn't think it was the weather that was bothering me. Every time I pictured those containers, I remembered the way the liquid had tilted in them. It wasn't tomato sauce. It just . . . wasn't.

"I've gotta go," I said. "I don't want to be late."

"Good luck. Remember, make sure he knows that I know. And bring a garlic clove with you."

I was not doing that last part. But I would do the first one. "Thanks. I'll call you later and tell you how it goes."

I made my way downstairs and into the dining room. There was only one place setting tonight. My heart sank.

I went to sit down but stopped. *Screw this.* Yes, Atlas didn't ignore me during the day. And he showed up to dinner half the time. But he wasn't allowed to ignore me the other half of the time. Especially without an excuse.

I walked back upstairs and down the hall to his room. I knocked.

No answer.

I knocked louder.

Still no answer.

I pressed my ear to the door, hoping to hear the shower running or something. But it was eerily quiet.

I stared down the hall toward Athena Quinn's private wing. Atlas had told me he wasn't sleeping with her. But he'd lied about Mrs. Serrano. Was he lying about this too?

CHAPTER 31

I hadn't seen Atlas all day. Normally, when he didn't show up for dinner, he'd at least show up for breakfast. Or I'd see him during my lunch break. At first, I was annoyed, but now I was getting worried.

I pushed my sandwich aside and stared up at Athena Quinn's estate. A curtain fell back into place behind a window on her private wing. She was watching me. Always watching.

What if I'd had it all wrong when I thought Atlas was suspicious?

What if Athena Quinn was actually the one with all the secrets? She was definitely hiding something if she refused to meet me. What if she was keeping Atlas here? Trapped in *her* claws, not the other way around? When I'd first arrived, I'd been so suspicious of her. But when I became infatuated with Atlas, I'd gotten tunnel vision. What if Athena Quinn had done something to him? What if he was the one in trouble?

I'd never texted him before. He didn't seem like the kind of person who loved technology. But I wanted to make sure everything was all right. I pulled out my new phone and shot him a quick text: Are you okay?

His response came almost immediately: Yes. Apologies. I was up late.

Up late doing what? Screwing Athena Quinn? Because he certainly hadn't been in his room. The thought made me feel sick to my stomach.

Why did he love pulling me into dark, confined spaces to kiss? I'd been so swept up in all of it that I thought this was hot and sexy and forbidden. But . . . what if he was trying to avoid Athena Quinn's cameras? What if he was sneaking around with me behind Athena Quinn's back?

Or maybe he wasn't saying that at all. He was probably up late working. Doing edits for Athena Quinn or something, not sleeping with her.

I shot him another text: If you need help with any of your work, I'm almost done with mine for the day. I'd love more responsibility. I'd gotten a new garbage bag full of hate mail to sort through this week, and it was starting to weigh me down too. I could read only one more letter saying that Athena Quinn was a terrible writer before I lost my mind. Why did people have to be so hateful? And so vocal about their hate? The death threats were the worst. They were shocking and horrifying. Athena Quinn was just trying to share her gift with the world. Her art. She shouldn't have been subjected to all this.

My phone buzzed. I grabbed it to see his response: It's not work related.

His words made my stomach churn. So what the fuck was he doing late at night that was not work related but required him to be somewhere other than in his own room?

He's cheating on me.

I shook my head. He couldn't cheat on me. We weren't exclusive. It was much more likely that I was the other woman. I texted him back: I'm glad everything is all right. Enjoy your non-work-related project.

I will.

He will? What the . . . If the phone I was holding hadn't been brand new, I would have thrown it in the pool. He did not seriously just tell me he would *enjoy it.* Next time I saw him, I was going to slap him.

I tore open another envelope and scanned the letter. *More trash.* I tossed it into a pile with all the other rejected mail, even though a small piece of me wanted Athena Quinn to see it. I wanted her to feel as shitty as I did today. And any one of these awful letters would do.

I read another super-rude piece of fan mail. I was starting to believe the drivel. Athena Quinn was the freaking worst.

I sighed. That wasn't true. If Atlas really was seeing both of us . . . that was *his* fault. Not hers. He was the bad guy here. And hadn't I known that all along? I leaned back in the lounge chair.

⸎

All day long I'd gone back and forth between fuming and wanting to curl up in a ball and cry. This was the exact reason I'd focused on my studies in college instead of going out. Dating wasn't fun. It was like throwing your heart into oncoming traffic and hoping that it wouldn't be run over.

But that was the problem right there. Atlas and I weren't dating. The only time I'd ever mentioned the word *relationship*, he'd immediately paled.

I trudged upstairs as my thoughts turned even more sour. I was investing too much time in a man who couldn't even go for a freaking walk in the sunshine. Who wouldn't answer any of my questions point-blank. What was I doing? Seriously, what on earth was I doing?

I froze when I spotted a large box sitting outside my bedroom door. It had the same red satin bow as the boxes that Atlas had delivered the first week I arrived here. If he would just talk to me, he'd know that I didn't want gifts. I wanted time with him. I didn't want to share him.

I tucked the box under my arm and opened the door. No, I didn't want gifts. I didn't need a new phone or a new car or more clothes. I dropped the box on my bed and stared at it. There could be nothing in there that would make up for the fact that he was sneaking around. He was up to no good. He was no good.

But I didn't really believe that. Because I'd seen him smile and laugh and let me in . . . even if only just a little. I pulled the card loose from the bow.

Meet me in the foyer at 7. I'll show you how grand a night in can be.

—Mr. Remington

I laughed that he'd signed his name Mr. Remington instead of Atlas. Ever so formal. And grand, huh? That meant he'd listened. He knew I wanted to go out to dinner with him. Maybe he would bring dinner to us . . .

I tugged on one end of the bow to undo it and lifted the lid of the box. *Wow.* I picked up the emerald-green dress inside and let the fabric cascade to the floor. The layers of the skirt were sheer, but there were enough of them so it wouldn't be see-through. And the top was corseted. It almost looked like a modern version of a dress that someone would have worn in this house when it was first built.

It was too much. Everything Atlas did was too much. But I could feel all the worries from earlier dissipating.

It was already almost seven. And despite the fact that Atlas loved to stand me up, I rather liked being punctual. I changed as quickly as I could, doing my best to tie the corset tight behind my back. The bottom of the dress just dusted the tops of my bare feet. I somehow felt sophisticated and like a little girl at the same time. I just wanted to twirl around in a circle and let my skirt flare out. Or run along the beach barefoot, letting all the fabric get picked up by the wind.

Maybe after a formal dinner, I could finally convince Atlas to venture out on that walk. After all, the sun had already set.

I walked into the hall and paused at the top of the stairs. Atlas stood at the bottom in a fitted suit, his back turned to me.

And even though it was a silly thing to feel, I felt like a princess as I walked down the stairs.

He turned and smiled up at me as he watched me descend. Before I reached the last step, he put his hand out for me. "You look breathtaking."

I could feel the heat rising to my cheeks. "You clean up nice your-self. I especially like this." I reached out and touched his perfectly knot-ted bow tie.

He smiled down at me. "One last thing," he said and dropped my hand. He reached into his inside jacket pocket.

And for just a second . . . I could picture him getting down on one knee. I could picture myself saying yes. But of course he didn't drop to one knee. And the box he pulled out was long instead of square.

He opened it, and a beautiful diamond necklace stared back at me. "Atlas, I can't accept . . ."

"Don't be ridiculous," he said and grabbed the necklace. "It will look perfect on you."

I didn't even know what to say. It was too much. All of it.

"Turn around, my lady."

How could I say no to that perfect southern drawl? I turned as he draped the expensive ice around my neck. But it wasn't long, as I at first thought it would be. He clasped it tight. I lifted my hand to feel the diamonds on the choker. And I couldn't help but wonder if it was meant to remind him to stay away from my neck.

"Actually, there is one more thing . . . ," he said.

"Atlas!" I said with a laugh.

"Close your eyes."

I stared at him, the laughter still on my lips.

He reached out and lightly traced his fingertips below my new choker. "Miss Fox, you know I don't like asking for things more than once."

A chill ran down my spine. I'd noticed that he called me Miss Fox only when I perturbed him. He was bothered by me not following his instructions. And just like most days, my brain was begging me to run. But my heart was begging me to stay. For the first time in my life, my heart was guiding my every move. I closed my eyes.

He draped something silky soft over my eyes, and I felt him tighten it behind my head.

I opened my eyes and was greeted by darkness. "What are you doing?" I said with a laugh. I reached up and touched the blindfold.

"I have a surprise for you. Come with me." He grabbed my hand and pulled me forward.

I put out my other hand like I might hit something, even though I knew the foyer was empty.

"Trust me," Atlas said. "I won't let you fall."

I did trust him. I didn't care if that made me the fool in Athena Quinn's story. I didn't care if she was watching our every move. I didn't care about any of it. All I cared about was that Atlas was here, choosing me.

He put his hand on my back and guided me forward. I was glad I was barefoot, because I was pretty sure I'd be tripping if I were in heels.

"Where are we going?" I asked. It seemed like we'd walked too long to be heading toward the dining room.

"It's a surprise," Atlas said.

We kept walking. And walking. I could feel the coolness of his touch, even through the fabric of my dress. And I had the oddest sense of calm. Even if he was walking me toward my death, at least I'd gotten to kiss him. At least he'd given me just a few weeks of blissful happiness.

We finally came to a stop. He dropped his hands from me, and I heard the sound of a key turning in a lock. Since we hadn't gone toward the dining room, we must have entered Athena Quinn's wing. Was he finally going to let me meet her?

My heart started pounding against my chest. He grabbed my hand and led me into the room. The air felt different in here. Heavy and silent. And it smelled strangely of fresh paint. The floor felt different beneath my feet too. It wasn't the cold marble in the rest of the downstairs. It seemed warmer somehow.

"Are you ready to see your surprise, Hazel?" he whispered in my ear.

I felt like a lamb being led to slaughter. And still I nodded. I wanted anything he'd give me.

Atlas tugged on the back of my blindfold. We were standing in a huge empty room. I blinked as my eyes adjusted to the light. Atlas touched the bottom of my chin to direct my gaze upward.

I gasped out loud. An intricate painting of the night sky traveled up the walls and scattered stars across the ceiling. It was like we were standing outside on a cloudless night. I could have sworn that some of the stars even twinkled. It took my breath away.

The sound of string instruments filled the silence. I spun around and saw that a string quartet was set up on a stage in the corner. And they weren't playing some old-fashioned tune. They were playing modern music. One of the songs I'd danced to with that stranger at the bar. But the quartet somehow captured every second of it without any words.

"I've been working on restoring the old ballroom for quite some time," Atlas said. "But you inspired me to finish it."

I turned back to him to see him staring up at the painted starry sky. "You painted this?"

"I thought you'd realized by now that I have many hidden talents."

I laughed. *Several lifetimes of them.*

"May I have this dance?" he asked and put his hand out for me. "I do like to dance. Just . . . in a different way. If you'll allow me to show you."

He'd been insulted when I said I knew he didn't like to dance. He did. But of course he didn't like how I'd danced in the bar. He needed a whole string quartet. I smiled as I slid my hand into his. "I don't know how to waltz. Or whatever it is you're about to do."

"Follow my lead," he said as he lifted my hand to his shoulder.

He took a step forward, and I took a step back. I mimicked his movement to the side and back again. He twirled me around, letting my skirt spin up around me. I laughed. It was exactly what I'd wanted to do.

I'd expected Atlas to be stiff and formal while dancing. But he was anything but. It honestly may have been the most relaxed I'd ever seen him, aside from when I'd pushed him into the pool.

I followed his movements all around the ballroom, alternating between looking into his eyes and staring at the starry sky. The tempo of the music escalated, almost making me feel dizzy.

The stars blurred in the sky as he spun me again. It took several songs, but I finally got the hang of it. It was like we were floating around the ballroom. And I could so easily picture it a century ago, filled with people dancing and laughing. The old estate suddenly seemed full of life. I wondered if one day it could be like that again.

Atlas grabbed my waist and lifted me into the air. He held me up as he spun around.

I laughed and looked up at the painted sky. I felt like I was flying.

He slowly lowered me, keeping me close to his chest.

The song ended, and the next tune was eerily quiet in the large ballroom. I knew there were musicians, but he was staring down at me like we were all alone.

"So this is what you were doing on our nights apart?" I asked. "Painting?" I'd assumed the worst. But this? I knew he said he'd been restoring it for a while. But I'd inspired him to finish. He'd done all this for me.

He nodded.

"I didn't know you were an artist too."

"I went to London to study art after I dropped out of med school."

"A doctor. An artist. A dancer."

He laughed.

"Why are you working as Athena Quinn's assistant?" I asked. "With everything else you've done, why have you settled on this?"

"Why have you?"

"I haven't. I want to be an author one day. And I thought I'd learn by working with one of the best. Even though I haven't met Athena Quinn, I think I have learned a bit by living here. With you."

"How so?"

"Full confession," I said. "I think you're my muse. I've been writing about you. About our time together. I won't do anything with it if you don't want me to . . ." My voice trailed off when he didn't respond. "You can read it if you want. It's almost finished."

He was still just staring at me.

"Maybe I'm your muse too?" I said and looked up at the stars. It felt like wishful thinking. Like I was staring at the stars, hoping one would shoot across the sky, and my wish would come true.

"How could you possibly fill up a whole novel about me?" he finally said.

I was surprised by how serious he sounded. I smiled at him. "Oh, you'd be surprised, Mr. Remington. There's so much beyond the old-fashioned facade you put on." I reached out and touched the chain of his pocket watch.

He didn't look amused by my words.

God, why had I brought any of this up? But if he was already upset . . . maybe now was the best time to talk about what was bothering me. "Hudson told me about your ancestors. About how your family made its fortune in agriculture. How you have all the money in the world but chose to follow your heart and work here. Why is that, Atlas? Why do you live here with Athena Quinn when you could live anywhere in the world? *Do* anything in the world? Why this house? And that woman? Are you in love with her?" The words poured out of me before I could stop them.

"I've already answered this question, Miss Fox." He took a step back from me.

Miss Fox. He was definitely upset with me. But I just wanted the truth. "I talked to the man at the front gate. He's married to Miss Serrano. *Mrs.* Serrano, I mean. He said she talks . . ."

"Miss Fox . . ."

"Did you direct her not to speak to me? Or was it Athena Quinn who told her to give me the silent treatment?"

He took another step back.

"I don't understand, Atlas. Are you trying to scare me off? Or win me over? Because grand gestures like this are the complete opposite of the lies. And I'm so confused. I just want you to talk to me. Answer my questions. Give me anything . . ."

"Anything? I did this for you." He pointed to the ceiling. "All of this." He gestured to the string quartet, who'd just awkwardly hit a string wrong, piercing the air with discord. "I've given you all that I can. What else do you want from me?"

"More than this." And that was the truth. This wasn't enough. I didn't want pieces of him. I wanted all of him. "I deserve more than fragments of the truth. You're hiding something from me. I've been snooping around the house for clues because you won't talk to me . . ."

"You're incorrigible," he said, cutting me off.

I'd only really heard someone use that word in a lighthearted way. As a joke. But he wasn't joking around. "I didn't realize you were trying to manage me."

"I am your boss, Miss Fox."

"Is that all you think you are to me? Is that why those police officers looked surprised when I called you 'dear'?" I didn't even realize that I'd still been holding on to that. I'd said it only to get them to leave. But the looks on their faces . . . like they believed Atlas wasn't capable of love. "Do you always hire help and discard them? Is that what's going on here?"

"I think it's best if we both retire for the evening. I'm sorry you didn't enjoy your surprise." He turned and started to walk away.

I could feel tears welling in my eyes. I'd loved my surprise. I loved him. That was the whole problem. "And which wing are you spending the rest of your night in?" I called after him.

He kept walking. The door closed with an echoing thud, leaving me all alone. Well, not alone. A whole string quartet was staring at me in uncomfortable silence. I looked up at the painted sky again. The stars blurred as my tears spilled over. I wanted to go back in time and keep dancing.

I knew I'd pushed Atlas. I knew he didn't want me to ask him the questions swirling around in my mind. But enough was enough. And I wasn't done with him tonight.

CHAPTER 32

Friday—September 30

There was no answer when I knocked on his door. My heart actually hurt. But maybe he was in there and just ignoring me. I tried to ignore Athena Quinn's words in my head. *Fool.* It wasn't foolish to fall in love. It wasn't.

I went back to my room and shot Atlas a quick text: Rumor has it that the beach is dangerous after nightfall. Meet me down there so I'm not in harm's way.

I tossed my phone on the bed. If he cared at all, he'd follow me down there. He wouldn't want me on the beach all alone.

I ignored how sinister the words *all alone* had become in my head. As I made my way outside, I looked up at the starry sky. Atlas truly had captured it perfectly. *For me.* And I'd ruined everything. I shook away the thought. Me asking questions about him and his life shouldn't have aggravated him like that. And I had no intention of stopping. Honestly, I was luring him down here to get more answers. I wasn't taking no for an answer.

The last of the summer heat was dissipating, but the breeze was still warm. I made my way slowly down the steps. They were lit up tonight. They had been every night since I'd hurt myself on them. I'd noticed it from my balcony. I knew Atlas had turned them on just in case. Because he didn't want me to injure myself again. It was a sweet gesture. But for every sweet thing he did, he did something else to ruin it.

I hoped I'd hear his footsteps behind me, but all I could hear were the waves crashing. My feet touched the sand, and I let go of the skirt of my dress. It lifted in the breeze. It felt just like it had when I was dancing with Atlas. And I wondered if I'd ever be able to go to a beach again without thinking of him. Dance again without thinking of him. Write again without thinking of him.

Because this was it. His last chance to come clean.

I wasn't sure how long I waited, but he didn't come. I stood there staring at the ocean, wondering what to do. I knew what Kehlani would tell me: run. I took a slow, deep breath. The salty air filled my lungs, and I couldn't help but want to cry.

Maybe I shouldn't have pushed him tonight. I should have just danced. I shook away the thought. I'd never been very patient. I wasn't the kind of girl who sat around waiting for someone to open up. I'd lost myself a little here. And I was proud of myself for trying to get answers. I just wished it didn't hurt so damn much.

Atlas was done with me.

Athena Quinn never wanted to meet me.

I was done here. I'd done my best. It was time to leave. I reached up and touched the choker on my neck. That was when I finally felt his presence. The little hairs on the back of my neck rose, and I spun around.

Atlas was standing there without his suit jacket, his sleeves rolled up and his bow tie untied. He looked even more handsome like this.

I could have just caved. Done what he wanted. But I think he needed someone to push him just as much as I needed someone to push me. Because I'd certainly never felt this way before. And if I wanted the truth from him, he deserved the truth from me.

"I'm pretty sure I've fallen in love with you," I said.

He didn't respond.

But, honestly, I hadn't expected him to. I stood up a little taller. "We're going to play a game."

He just stared at me, the wind blowing his hair.

"I'm going to ask you a series of questions. I want you to nod yes or shake your head no. And every time you do, I'm going to undo a row of hooks on my corset."

We'd only ever kissed. But I'd told him I needed more. I needed this.

"Did you lie about Mrs. Serrano not being able to speak?"

For a second he just studied me, but then he finally nodded.

I wished I hadn't said it was just yes-or-no questions. I unknotted my corset. I wanted to hear why. I wanted an excuse that was more than one syllable long. But I'd set the rules. "Were you trying to scare me?"

His eyes searched mine. He slowly nodded.

I unhooked a row. *Why? Why were you trying to scare me?* But his lips were sealed. "Are you sleeping with Athena Quinn?"

He shook his head.

Then why didn't he have a bed in his room? I reached behind my back and unhooked another row. There had to be a way to get closer to the truth. "Did you put the broken bobby pin on my vanity?"

He looked down at his feet in the sand. Finally his gaze met mine again. He nodded.

So he knew that I knew he didn't have a bed in his room? Had he wanted me to know that? I slowly unhooked another row from my corset. I only had a few questions left. "Then why don't you have a bed in your room?"

"That's not a yes-or-no question," he said.

"And you think *I'm* incorrigible?"

He stared at me. "I don't sleep well, Hazel." He took a step toward me. "I've battled with insomnia my whole life. When I do sleep, it's usually in my office."

His office? I'd never thought about him having one. But that made sense. Of course he did. I unhooked another row. The fabric started to fall forward. I put one arm across my chest and stared at him.

I didn't want to push him, so I thought of another yes-or-no question. "You seemed cold toward Hudson. Do you not get along with his father?"

"I'm not the cold one. My brother is."

Something about the way he said it made a chill run down my spine. I had a lot more questions about that. I couldn't imagine someone more rigid and strict than Atlas. But now didn't seem like the appropriate time to dive deeper into that. "Does this house belong to you?"

He nodded.

He wasn't sleeping with Athena Quinn. He wasn't in a relationship with her. So why was he letting her live with him? I thought about all the hate mail Athena Quinn received. She was broken. Worn down. Maybe the two of them were just friends. Maybe he was supporting her when no one else would. I unhooked another row on my corset.

I had two questions left. "So that library upstairs and the room full of sculptures—those belong to you?"

Atlas nodded and walked forward, closing the distance between us. I put my hand up to stop him from reaching out to me. Our game wasn't done yet. I had one question left. And I knew what it needed to be. Even if it meant the death of me.

"Are you a vampire?" I asked.

"You have quite the imagination, Hazel."

"That's not an answer, Atlas."

"And what, pray tell, makes you think I'm a vampire?"

He wasn't answering the question. And wasn't that answer enough? "I think you weren't upset that I went into Athena Quinn's freezer. I think you were mad that I found your stash of blood."

His face held no expression.

"I know vampires are portrayed in different ways, but I think that maybe they're beautiful. And that's how I'd describe you. Your face is perfect. Your body is perfect. At least what I've seen of it."

He didn't react to that either. Not even a smile at the compliment.

"I don't think the old portraits in your basement are of your ancestors. I think they're of you. From different time periods."

He didn't even blink.

"You use old-fashioned phrases. You wear a pocket watch. You don't have a bed." I knew he'd already touched on that last point. But . . . still. "I've never seen you eat more than a few bites at meals, even though you have an intensity to your gaze, like you're hungry. You're pale. Your skin is so cold. Every time you touch me, I shiver."

His Adam's apple rose and then fell.

"And when you first kissed me, you bit me so hard that you made my lip bleed." My heart thumped against my rib cage. I willed it to calm down as he stared at me.

"I'm allergic to garlic," he said.

That did not at all quell my suspicion. He must have realized that . . .

"I get a special tomato sauce from a local place. I buy it in bulk."

That was what Hudson had said. Maybe they'd rehearsed their lies.

"My bloodline is strong. I don't look exactly like my male ancestors, but yes, I see the resemblance. I take most of my meals in my office too. And I am old-fashioned. I like old things. That doesn't make me a monster."

"Then why did you try to scare me away? It's almost like you wanted me to think you were a monster." I had heard his excuses. I wanted to believe him. And yet . . . he'd never flat out denied it.

"You're out of questions, Hazel." He reached behind me and unhooked the last row.

My dress fell to the sand. I didn't want to be out of questions. "Then why don't you ever go outside on sunny days?" I asked.

He ignored me as he slowly unbuttoned his shirt. My question disappeared from my mind as he undid his belt. I'd wanted this moment for so long. All those stolen kisses and heated glances. I needed this almost as much as I needed answers.

"Take the rest off." His voice had dropped an octave.

And I found myself reaching back and unhooking my bra. His eyes fell to my exposed breasts in the moonlight.

"I said all of it, Hazel."

I grabbed the sides of my thong. "Answer my question, Atlas."

"I will. After you do what I say."

I couldn't really argue with that. I pulled my thong down my thighs and kicked it off my ankle.

He finished undressing, taking the time to fold his pants before he discarded them in the sand. But he never once looked away from me.

"Now tell me why I'd want to come down here on a sunny day," he said, "when the privacy of night is so much more fun."

I squealed as he reached down and lifted me into his arms.

"Atlas!" I screamed as he carried me into the freezing-cold water.

He went under a wave, silencing my protests. And when we both came up for air, we were laughing. He pulled me against his chest, and I wrapped my legs around his waist.

"Tell me this isn't better than the daytime." He cupped my cheek in his hand, and for once his hand felt warm in comparison to the cold water.

"It's better," I confessed. I stared into his eyes.

"Tell me what you said before. When you saw that I'd come down to the beach."

"I'm pretty sure I've fallen in love with you," I said.

He closed his eyes like it was almost painful for him to hear.

"It was a lie," I said.

He opened his eyes.

"I know, without a shadow of a doubt, that I love you. I'm in love with you, Atlas."

His lips crashed against mine. He kissed me like he always did. Like he was trying to take everything from me. But he already had. He buried his fingers in my hair as his free hand traced up my thigh.

"Tell me to stop and I will," he whispered against my lips.

I didn't need him to be a southern gentleman right now. I just needed him. "Don't make me beg you."

"I don't hate the image of you on your knees." His thumb lightly brushed against my clit.

"Atlas."

His index finger slid inside me.

Fuck. I held on to his shoulders. I'd written about him touching me. I'd dreamed about it. But this was the first time he'd ever caved in real life.

"Say it again," he said as his mouth moved to my neck.

"I love you." It was like he was starved to hear the words. And I thought I understood. This was his house. He was the one who had made it haunted. He chose to live this way. He chose to push people away. But he wasn't pushing me away right now.

His finger pulsed inside me as his thumb kept pace with slow circles around my clit, driving me wild.

"Atlas, please."

"Tell me what you want," he said.

I repeated his words from our first kiss. "The unexpected."

"Nothing that's happened between us has been unexpected," he said.

"I don't think falling in love was on my to-do list."

He stared down at me. "You're right. I never expected to fall in love with you."

I held my breath.

"But I did," he said. "I'm in love with you too."

I wanted to cry. But my emotion quickly changed when he thrust inside me.

Fuck. My fingernails dug into his back. It felt like I was flying under the stars again.

I knew he came down here at night. That he swam in the darkness. His skin always smelled of ocean salt. His hair always looked windswept. It was like he'd welcomed me into his heart.

I'd tried so hard to fight off my feelings. But I knew a part of me had fallen for him as soon as I met him that first day. He was nothing like I'd expected but everything I needed.

And maybe I still wanted to cry. I just wanted to stay in this moment forever.

He pulled on my hair, tilting my head back. His mouth kissed down my neck and dipped to my right breast. He swirled his tongue around my hard nipple.

Jesus. I tightened my legs around his waist, and he groaned.

He kissed between my breasts. "I never thought I'd find love," he whispered so softly that I barely heard him.

His words broke my heart. Why did he think he was so unlovable? He thrust again, pushing my thoughts aside.

"Atlas," I moaned.

His fingers tightened on my hips as he thrust faster.

I grabbed the back of his neck, pulling his lips down to mine. When I was dancing with him earlier, I thought I'd never be able to top that feeling. The only thing better than dancing under the stars was making love under them.

I couldn't get enough of him.

He bit down on my earlobe, and I felt myself clench around him.

"Hazel," he groaned as we both lost control.

When I finally caught my breath, I laughed and let my forehead fall to his.

"I love you," he whispered.

"I love you too. But I'm so freaking cold."

He laughed and carried me out of the water.

CHAPTER 33

Friday—September 30

"You can spend the night," I said when we reached my bedroom door. "Maybe sleeping next to me will help your insomnia."

"I'd love to take you up on your offer." He tucked a strand of wet hair behind my ear. "But I'm a little behind on a deadline. My surprise for you took me away from work."

"Well, I appreciated it. You're a wonderful painter, Atlas. And dancer." I stood up on my tiptoes and kissed him.

"Is that all I'm good at?" he asked with a smile.

I lightly shoved his shoulder.

"I'll see you in the morning, Hazel."

I nodded.

"Sweet dreams."

I smiled and opened my bedroom door.

"And change out of that wet dress. I don't want you to catch a cold. I know I'm in much need of a hot shower."

"Yes, sir." I hadn't even realized I was cold until he reminded me that my dress was wet. I was a little more preoccupied with my feelings toward him.

He smiled at me.

I closed my bedroom door. *Sweet dreams.* I knew exactly what I'd be dreaming of. My mind was going to reenact every second of our time in the ocean. And it was going to be sinful, if anything. I went to take off the dress that I'd somehow managed to get back into with wet skin. But I froze when I saw my reflection in the mirror.

I touched the diamond choker. I hadn't seen what it looked like on me until that moment. It somehow combined my normal style with the more sophisticated look Atlas preferred. I could tell he'd taken the time to pick it out in the hope that I'd like it. I couldn't believe I'd worn it into the ocean. I needed to take better care of it.

I unclasped the chain. It was a little heavier than I expected, and my cold, shaking hands dropped it onto the floor. *Shit.* I leaned over. It had somehow managed to slide beneath the dresser. I reached under to grab it, and as I pulled it out, I felt how rough the wooden floor was against my hand.

Atlas had answered my questions with one-word answers. But I hadn't gotten a chance to ask the *why* of things. He'd admitted that he put the broken bobby pin on my vanity. He'd admitted that he was trying to scare me.

But . . . *why?*

I ran my fingers along the scratch in the floor.

I stood up and pushed the dresser to the side. I figured it would be hard to move, but it was surprisingly light. Like it was meant to be easily moved.

I'd looked for uneven wallpaper in my room, but I hadn't looked behind the dresser. I stared at the edge curling up right in the middle of the wall. I pushed, and the wall gave way, swinging back. Another entrance to the servants' corridor.

Unlike at the entrance I'd found weeks ago, no puff of dust went up in my face. It was almost like it had been used recently. I pressed my lips together.

I'd been on my best behavior ever since I'd decided I liked Atlas. And I'd gotten everything I wanted. Atlas. Answers. I shook my head.

Some answers. But I still didn't know what the hell was going on with Athena Quinn. I just needed to speak with her. Or at least find one clue that made sense of everything.

I put the necklace down on my bed and grabbed my phone and a recently acquired screwdriver. Fine, I hadn't been *completely* on my best behavior. I'd studied YouTube videos about how to open locked doors more easily. A screwdriver was almost as good as a key. And I'd found one in the shed by the gardens.

I turned on my phone's flashlight feature and ducked into the narrow corridor. I wanted to call Kehlani, but I knew she'd tell me to turn around. To abort the mission. To do anything but this.

But I needed to do this. Someone had been sneaking into my room. Yes, Atlas had confessed to doing it once. But that didn't mean it was only him. Athena Quinn was the one with cameras watching our every move. I trusted Atlas, but I didn't trust her.

The old floorboards creaked under my feet as I made my way down the stairs. I could faintly make out footprints in the dust. And it wasn't just one set coming and going. I squinted in the darkness, but it was hard to tell if they were the same size.

I looked all around the floor, searching for my car keys. Had Atlas stolen them to make sure I'd stay? I didn't even remember bringing them in here. It was much more likely that he'd sneaked into my room and taken them. Or Athena Quinn had taken them. Or Mrs. Serrano had sneaked in and stolen them.

Maybe Athena Quinn was jealous of my relationship with Atlas. Threatened somehow. I stopped at the dumbwaiter that was in Athena Quinn's wing. I had this wild idea that maybe I could climb up the shaft.

Why hadn't I taken the time to change? I hitched up my dress like I was about to jump into the dumbwaiter. But the empty space was small. I put my phone into it, lighting up the way to the second story. There was no way in hell I would fit. And even if I could, the old rope inside looked like it was seconds away from splitting in two.

"Athena!" I yelled. "Can you hear me?!"

I wasn't worried about Atlas hearing me. He had said he was going to shower before getting back to work. And he was in a completely different wing. "Athena!"

But no head popped out to see what the ruckus was.

Damn it. There were at least ten rooms in her private wing. She must have been in a different one. I was hoping that since the dumbwaiter went up there, it was her room.

I wandered down the stairs into the basement. I hadn't found a freezer down here before, but I wanted to see if I'd missed something. And I wanted another look at those portraits.

I pulled the cloth off one, but it wasn't the one I wanted to see. I'd been picturing it in my head. The woman in one of them looked so familiar.

I pulled off another white sheet and stared at the portrait I'd been looking for. Atlas's ancestor who looked just like him. And a woman who looked familiar too.

Why did she look familiar? It wasn't possible that I knew this woman. Had I seen someone else like her on the island? Maybe at that beach party?

I shook my head. I didn't think so. I searched the picture and saw the book she was holding. I leaned down and squinted. I could only just make out the name on the book: Luca Armani. The poet. One of the three authors in Atlas's private library. Atlas owned dozens of first editions of his work. Some duplicates. Why did he have so many? Had his family been friends with Luca Armani?

The man in the picture looked like Atlas. He looked just like him.

I typed "Luca Armani" into my phone's Google search bar. The Wikipedia article that came up didn't contain any pictures. I typed in the name of one of the other authors featured in his library: Finn Bauer. An article on Finn Bauer did have a picture, and it was Atlas. Or . . .

I pulled a few more white sheets off. *Him. It was him.* I stared at the image of Atlas's ancestor in the portraits.

Was Atlas related to the poet and the thriller author? Or was it possible that all these men were just . . . Atlas? That he really had lived centuries?

He was a painter and a doctor. Who was to say he wasn't an author too?

I walked back to the original portrait I'd been looking for. And it finally hit me. The woman's face. It looked like one of the sculptures. I glanced back down at the book in her hand. All the sculptures were of women weeping over novels. Maybe the man in this picture was a famous sculptor?

I knew Atlas painted. Was it possible that he was a sculptor too? Because these men didn't look like distant relatives. They looked exactly like him. How strong could his bloodline possibly be?

I wished Hudson had pictures of his father in his house. The other man portrayed in some of the portraits had similarities to Hudson. But I had no idea what his father looked like.

Wait. I searched on my phone to see if Finn Bauer had a brother. I stared at the image that came up and then back at the portrait. It was the same man. The exact same. It just wasn't possible. It wasn't . . .

He had told me he wasn't a vampire. Kind of. But that didn't mean he wasn't something else. Like a time traveler or . . .

God, what the fuck was I doing down here spying? Atlas was finally talking to me. I just needed to ask him.

I pulled all the cloths back in place and made my way up the rickety old stairs. But it didn't matter how far away I walked. The images in those portraits were seared into my brain. I went to go back to my room but paused.

Who was to say Atlas would ever tell me the truth? Maybe he'd never let me meet Athena Quinn. Maybe I just needed to do what I'd come in here to do.

I walked over to the door I'd found the first time I was here. The one to which the footprints led. I pulled out my screwdriver.

It didn't take long for the doorknob to fall off. I pushed open the door. It didn't resist at all. Someone had been using it regularly. The room was dark. I stepped in and lifted my phone.

I blinked as I stared at the wall. It looked just like something you'd see in a murderer's lair. There were pictures and index cards tacked up to the walls, with red yarn connecting everything. And I recognized the name of one of the characters from Athena Quinn's manuscript.

I took a step forward. A picture of Mr. Remington was under the name on the wall. I followed one of the lines of yarn and stared at the picture of me. Under the name of the heroine.

The characters . . . they were . . . us.

There was another piece of yarn connected to mine. I followed the line to see a picture of Hudson. The three of us formed a perfect triangle. *Son of a bitch.*

Atlas had told me she was watching. But this? This was a little extreme. Writing about our personal lives for her own entertainment. This was why she didn't want to meet me. She'd never invited me here to be her assistant. She just wanted to write about me.

I moved my light and saw tons of computer screens. I looked around for the power button. I hit a button, and nothing happened. I hit another, and the monitors lit up. Camera angles. Of everything. I stared at a video feed of my bed and felt my bottom lip trembling.

This was sick.

She was sick.

I looked back at the wall with the pictures of us. The triangle. The stupid freaking love triangle. I wanted to rip down the pictures. I wanted to smash the screens that invaded my privacy.

And Atlas thought she wasn't writing about us? I wanted to laugh. I wasn't the naive one. He was. I didn't even know the woman. I couldn't imagine how he'd feel once he realized that his friend had betrayed his trust.

I flashed the light onto some of the pages on her desk. There were some notes jotted down.

Grand gesture.

Jewelry.

Dancing.

I swallowed hard. She must have just written this. Watching us. I looked back over at the monitors. There wasn't a feed of the ballroom, but there was one of the foyer. And if she and Atlas were friends . . . maybe he had told her what was going on. Told her he was falling for me.

I felt like I was going to be sick. It wasn't just an invasion of my privacy. It was an invasion of his. No, there weren't cameras in his private room, but . . . *still*. She was using him for a stupid story.

I backed up, and my legs collided with something. I fell backward onto something soft. As I turned, the light from my phone lit up a couch. There was a blanket and a pillow, like Athena Quinn spent restless nights here when she was writing. About *us*.

Atlas needed to know what was going on. As I fired off a text, I was somehow able to breathe a little easier. Just thinking about him made the saltwater smell on his skin return to me. I loved the smell of his skin.

We need to talk, I texted. **It's about Athena Quinn.** I hit "Send."

A buzzing sound came from Athena Quinn's desk.

I walked over to her desk and opened the drawer from which the noise had come. I picked up her phone. My text was staring back at me. *What?*

I clicked on it. My whole text message thread with Atlas was there.

I looked back at the security cameras. This was his house. Why would he allow cameras to be put in? Unless . . .

I glanced back at the notes on the desk. I recognized that handwriting. And the smell of salt air. It was all around me. This room smelled like him. *"I've battled with insomnia my whole life. When I do sleep, it's usually in my office."*

I dropped the phone, and it landed back in the drawer next to my thong. The one he'd stolen after our first kiss.

Atlas Remington was Athena Quinn. And his manuscript was true. I was a fucking fool.

CHAPTER 34

Friday—September 30

I felt my dress snag on something, but I kept running. I'd never cared about the stupid clothes. All I'd wanted was for Atlas to be honest with me.

The worn stairs creaked under my feet. I was out of time. Atlas would be returning to his office soon. And as soon as he did, he'd see me fleeing on his security system.

I ran into my room, not bothering to close the hidden door. I wanted him to know that I knew. But I didn't want to face him to tell him.

I grabbed all my things, leaving the clothes that Atlas had bought me. It was like he'd been playing dress-up with a doll. Watching me. Ordering me around. Using me.

Tears burned my eyes as I slammed my suitcase closed.

God, I was so stupid. I'd known he was no good. I'd known it and trusted him anyway.

I grabbed the keys to the new car he'd given me. I'd return it to him somehow. But right now, I needed it. I just wanted to go home.

I peered out my bedroom door. The coast was clear, which meant that either Atlas was still showering or I was definitely about to be caught. I ran as fast as I could, pulling my suitcase behind me.

No one yelled at me to stop. Or begged me to stay.

A part of me thought that Atlas was already watching me. And he didn't fucking care. I tried to wipe the tears from my eyes, but they just kept falling.

I shouldn't have been crying over a man who'd never actually loved me. It was all just a game. I opened the front door and stared back at the foyer. Based on the direction of the video feed from Atlas's office . . .

I turned toward the left corner and flipped off the camera. I slammed the door behind me, threw my suitcase in the car, and peeled backward out of the driveway in record time.

Normally, the sound of gravel spitting up and hitting the car would have bothered me. But I didn't care if this car got covered in little dents. Honestly, I hoped it would.

I didn't bother to open my window and play nice with the security guard.

I laid on the horn.

The gates opened just enough that I wouldn't ram my car straight through them.

I felt better the farther away I drove.

Even better when I crossed the bridge off the island.

I thought about going to the airport, but the wind in my hair and the music blasting on the radio somehow soothed my soul. Probably because I was screaming at the top of my lungs to the rap music.

My phone buzzed. I glanced down for a second to see his name lighting up my screen.

Fuck. You.

I put my foot down harder on the gas.

Shit, if Kehlani was right, Atlas had a tracking app on my phone. I would have chucked it out the window, but not having a phone on the highway sounded like a bad scenario.

Besides, Atlas knew where I lived. It was on all those damned documents I'd signed . . .

My thoughts trailed away from the song on the radio. And I laughed. I laughed because he had probably told me what he was going to do in the contract. It was probably all there in black and white so I couldn't sue his rich ass.

Arrogant.

Asshole.

"Fuck!" I screamed at the top of my lungs.

I hit my fist against the steering wheel as my tears started to fall even faster.

Why was I crying?

I hit my fist on the steering wheel again.

Stop crying. He's not worth it.

I turned the music up louder and sang at the top of my lungs. I just wanted the sadness out. I rolled down the windows the rest of the way, hoping all my anger would somehow get lost in the breeze. But the air still smelled salty. It smelled like him. And it just made me cry harder.

❧

I drove all night and all morning. I just kept going and going, not stopping once. I was pretty sure I was severely dehydrated from my tears. And my throat hurt from screaming and singing at the top of my lungs.

I cut the engine outside the apartment I'd shared with Kehlani. It was the middle of the afternoon. Kehlani always spent Saturday afternoons running errands. She wouldn't be home until dinnertime. But luckily I still had my key.

No one gave my ripped dress or tearstained face a second glance as I tugged my suitcase out of the back seat. It was the welcome home I'd expected from NYC.

I don't know how I was able to pull my suitcase up that many flights of stairs. But I couldn't really feel my body anymore. I was just . . . nothing.

And that thought alone made the stupid tears start falling again.

I ignored my buzzing phone as I made my way into the apartment. Atlas had called me several times during my getaway. But if he thought I was going to speak to him, he was dead wrong. In the car, I'd just turned up the music so I couldn't hear my phone. And now my ears were still ringing.

I collapsed face-first onto Kehlani's couch, wishing my heart could be as numb as the rest of my body.

CHAPTER 35

Saturday—October 1

Kehlani's screaming made me sit up with a start.

She was wielding a frying pan, and it looked like she was seconds away from whacking me across the face with it. But she lowered it as soon as she saw who I was. "Hazel? You scared me half to death. I thought you were an intruder. What in the ever-living hell . . ." Her voice trailed off as she stared at me.

"I . . ." My voice was so dry that the word came out scratchy and weird. "Water," I croaked.

Kehlani dropped the pan on her counter and poured me a glass of water.

I downed the whole thing in practically one gulp. I lifted the glass for more. She didn't seem to mind my temporarily using her as my waitstaff.

She filled my glass back up and handed it to me.

I tried to drink a little slower this time. I hadn't had anything to eat or drink since . . . I didn't even think I'd had dinner last night. "Pizza," I said.

"Are you not going to tell me what happened?"

"Pizza."

Kehlani pulled out her phone and ordered a pizza while I drank the rest of my water.

She sat down next to me, pushing some of the dirty layers of my dress out of her way. "No more one-word answers. Tell me what happened. You look like a runaway bride."

I looked down at the beautiful dress I'd ruined. I pictured how the skirt had flared up when Atlas was dancing with me. I pictured the wind whipping it around down on the beach. I just wanted to go back to last night before I found out the truth. But there was no going back. I sniffled. "He was lying to me," I said.

"No shit. He's a freaking vampire."

I laughed, but it came out forced. "Not that." I paused. "Well, maybe that. I don't really know for sure."

"He was lying about something else too?"

I nodded. "You know how I told you it always felt like someone was watching me? It was Atlas. He brought me there to write about me. Not to be his stupid assistant."

"Wait, he's an author too?"

"Yeah. He lied about everything. Kehlani, *he's* Athena Quinn."

Kehlani laughed. But she stopped as soon as she saw that I was serious. "Athena Quinn is, like, a seventy-year-old woman. Haven't you ever seen her picture?"

"Yeah, that one headshot? The same one that's been used for years? Haven't you ever wondered why she never goes to any book signings? She didn't even go to the premiere of her own movie. She's super private. It's all because she's not a *she*. It's Atlas's pen name."

"You're serious right now? Athena Quinn is Atlas Remington?"

"He had all these cameras watching me. And he had this notebook full of the things he was planning on doing. To 'woo' me or whatever ridiculous phrase he used."

"Are you sure?"

"He didn't let me meet Athena Quinn because there was no one to meet. Or . . . I'd already met him. Or whatever. God, do you know what

Hudson called Athena Quinn? He said she was a dick. A *dick*, Kehlani. What a turn of phrase!"

Kehlani laughed.

"It's not funny."

"I know it's not funny. But it is a little funny that Hudson kind of did tell you that Athena Quinn was a man."

"Ha. Ha. Hilarious." I shook my head. I'd been so consumed with figuring out if sunshine would kill Atlas that I hadn't seen what was right in front of me. I shook my head. "I insulted her in front of him. When I first met him. I said Athena Quinn had lost her touch. He was so pissed. He . . ." My voice trailed off. I thought about all the hate mail that was actually his. I shouldn't have felt bad. But all those hateful words directed at him? No wonder he stayed alone in that big house. He felt like the world despised him.

"He what?" Kehlani asked.

"He was so cold when I met him. But he changed over the past few weeks. He really did." No, he hadn't opened up to me. He'd lied a ton. But what if he was just scared to pour his heart into something else, only for it to be thrown back in his face. Just like with his latest novels.

My phone buzzed. I looked down to see his name flashing across the screen. I declined the call.

"What did he say when you confronted him about this?" Kehlani asked.

"I didn't. I broke into his office and saw what he was up to, and then I ran away."

"You drove all night and all morning and haven't answered a single one of his"—she picked up my phone—"eleven missed calls?"

I nodded.

"Make that an even dozen," she said and handed my phone back when it buzzed again. "Maybe you just need to speak to him."

"And say what? 'I was in love with you, but it was all a lie because you're a creepy pervert'?"

Kehlani laughed. "I don't think he's a pervert."

"There was a camera pointed at my bed."

"Which you slept in. It wasn't like he was watching you hook up with another man or something. It's only weird when it tips the line into voyeurism."

I just stared at her. "You're seriously saying that you wouldn't be upset if the guy you were dating lied about who he was and watched you sleep?"

"Honestly?" She scrunched her mouth to the side as she thought it over. "I've never been with a man who hasn't lied about something. And I think it's kind of hot that he watched you. I mean . . . he's basically obsessed with you. Why is that such a bad thing?"

"You're as twisted as him."

There was a knock on the door.

"That delivery was fast," Kehlani said. "You'll definitely feel better once you eat all the pizza."

I wasn't sure that was true. But cheese would certainly help. Maybe I could get the delivery guy to go get me some ice cream too.

"Ummm . . ." Kehlani turned around after looking through the peephole. "It's not pizza. I'm pretty sure it's Mr. Remington."

"What?" I stood up. "Atlas is here? As in standing outside our door?"

She turned back and looked out the peephole. "Or it's a very handsome, very apologetic-looking stranger delivering a huge bouquet of flowers." She looked over her shoulder at me. "And I'm not dating anyone."

I ran over to the door and peered out at Atlas. I swallowed hard. He did look sorry. Or guilty. His eyes met mine through the peephole. I knew he couldn't see me. But his gaze did something strange to my chest. What was he doing here?

"That's exactly how I pictured him looking," Kehlani said. "He's so hot. Let's hear him out, shall we?"

"What? No." I swatted her hand away from the doorknob. "I don't want to speak with him. He's a dick."

"But he came all this way to see you. And he brought flowers. Which means he's going to apologize for lying and being a bit of a voyeur."

"You said he wasn't a voyeur."

"I mean . . . we don't know for sure he wasn't aroused by watching you, unless we take the time to ask." She reached for the doorknob again.

"Stop it. I'm wearing the same dress that he broke my heart in. I can't let him see me like this. Get him to leave."

"And what, exactly, should I tell him? The door is thin. He's probably already heard this whole conversation."

"Then tell him he's a dick!" I yelled at the door. "And that I'm showering." I ran to the bathroom. She'd get rid of him. I knew she would. But just in case he tried to storm in and see me, I turned on the shower, stripped out of my dress, and stepped under the hot stream.

Even though it felt amazing, I instantly regretted my choice. I should have just crouched behind the kitchen island or something so I could spy on their whole conversation.

I closed my eyes and let the water run down my face.

Atlas had come to New York.

For me.

He rarely ever left his house. This wasn't just a coincidence. He'd come for me. And he must have driven all night long too.

I couldn't help but smile as I rinsed the shampoo out of my hair. I kind of thought he'd just let me leave. That he'd easily move on with his life. That all his feelings toward me weren't genuine.

But why else would he have driven all this way if he didn't love me back?

God, what was I doing? I needed to hear what he had to say. I turned off the shower, wrapped a towel around myself, and ran out of the bathroom.

CHAPTER 36

Saturday—October 1

Kehlani was sitting on the couch all by herself, reading a magazine. As if nothing had just happened.

"He's gone?" I asked.

She looked up at me and nodded.

"Back home? Or is he staying in the city somewhere?"

"Apparently his brother lives in the city." She tossed her magazine to the side. "He said he'd be staying with him. As long as it takes to win you back." Her smile grew with each word out of her mouth.

"He said that?"

"He did."

"What else did he say?"

"You just ran out here like you wanted to speak to him," Kehlani said. "Tell me what *you* wanted to say to *him*. And then I'll tell you what he said."

I took a deep breath.

"Don't think," Kehlani said. "Just say what you were going to say."

"I would have said he betrayed my trust."

She nodded.

"But that I understand that maybe his actions came from a place of hurt. I read those awful letters from his fans. How could he not

260

be hurting? And I know he probably had a good reason for doing what he did." I pressed my lips together. "That he thought he'd lost his touch with writing. That he was just hoping to find it again. And that it all got really messy when he fell for me. Because it got messy for me too."

Kehlani smiled.

"But I'd definitely tell him that I'm still mad. That I gave him so many opportunities to tell me the truth. And he has a lot of explaining to do." I took another deep breath. "Now tell me what he said."

Kehlani's smile grew.

"I said that I knew I betrayed your trust," said a deep voice.

I spun around, and Atlas stepped out from behind the huge bouquet of flowers. Kehlani had totally set me up.

"But I never meant to," he said. "You pegged me just right when we met. I have lost my touch. I needed inspiration. And you were full of it."

I knew it was a compliment, but I just glared at him.

"I'm going to give you two a moment," Kehlani said and hurried out of the room. But there was no way she wasn't still going to eavesdrop on our every word.

"I never brought you to my estate to fall in love with me. I wasn't trying to manipulate you on my behalf. My nephew was in town, and I figured if I hired a young, attractive woman . . . then maybe the two of you would hit it off. And I could write about it."

"You did manipulate me for your benefit. *You* wanted a story. How is that not for your benefit? You do realize how fucked up that is."

He nodded. "But you signed all the consent forms saying it was okay for me to draw inspiration from your time on the estate . . ."

"Inspiration? Spying on me is not inspiration! It's an invasion of privacy!"

"I know that. And I also know that there were a lot of forms to fill out. I purposely misled you."

I just stared at him.

"But I didn't have all those cameras at first. I added them because . . ." His voice trailed off. "I wanted to know what you did in your free time. I wanted to know everything."

"You could have just asked me, Atlas."

"You were dating my nephew . . ."

"For the past few weeks, I wasn't! I told you I loved you. I stood in that ballroom and told you that I was writing about you. That you were my muse. Why the hell didn't you confess then?"

"I knew you were writing about me. But the timing of your confession still caught me off guard. I did plan on telling you the truth, but not yet. I was worried about how you'd react, even though you were doing the same thing—writing about me."

"But I wasn't spying on you, Atlas!"

"I know, but—"

"Wait," I said, cutting him off. "What do you mean you already knew I was writing about you?"

"You were connected to my Wi-Fi. I had access to all your documents."

"So when I told you about my novel, you'd already read it?"

He nodded.

I could feel my stupid tears trying to fall again. I blinked fast. "That was private."

"You said I could read it . . ."

"But I didn't know you were reading my every word the whole time!" I shook my head. I thought about the words I'd written. The characters had admitted they were in love a long time before I'd confessed my feelings to Atlas. "You knew how I felt about you before I even told you."

"I thought you said it was fiction?" He smiled. As if that could erase everything he'd just said.

"Was any of it real?"

"Any of what?" he asked.

"Everything that happened between us. Or was it all just some plot point in your novel?"

He took a step toward me. "How could you possibly think that?"

"How could I not? I saw the notes on your desk. You thought out everything we ever did."

"I'm a planner, Hazel. I plot everything out. That's just how my mind works."

"Even your life? You intricately wove the perfect lie. None of this was real."

He reached out and wiped his thumbs beneath my eyes, removing the tears I didn't even realize I'd shed. "All of it was real. I should have told you sooner. But that's why I didn't. Because I didn't want to lose you."

"Well, you did lose me." I pushed his hands off me.

He shook his head. "No, I didn't."

I glared at him. "Yes, you did."

"You're still in love with me, Miss Fox."

"You arrogant bastard."

He laughed. That gorgeous sound that I'd grown so addicted to.

And I could tell I was smiling too. I tried to hide it. "You haven't even properly apologized."

"Do you want me to get on my knees and beg you for forgiveness? Because I will."

It was impossible to hide my smile now.

He didn't get down on his knees, but he did grab my hands and squeeze them.

"I owe you my sincerest apologies," he said. "Without a doubt, I should have told you the truth sooner. But I was nervous. I was concerned that everything we had would break. You're the best thing that's happened to me in a really long time. I didn't mean to mess it up before it even began."

I stared into his eyes.

"I put my work before your feelings. I won't do that again. You know the rest of my flaws. And I know you have doubts about what kind of man I am. But I'm giving you what's left of my heart."

"What's left?"

He lifted my hand and put it to his chest. "You're the only person who's ever been able to see the hurt. The pain. And you didn't run screaming. You ran toward me."

There had been so many times that I'd wanted to run away screaming. But something always made me stay. "You wanted me to run, though. You constantly pushed me away. And you nodded yes down on the beach, when I asked if you were trying to scare me. You told Mrs. Serrano not to speak to me. You told me Athena Quinn was watching us."

"Well, I was watching you."

I lowered my eyebrows at him. "You know what I meant."

"Yes, I was trying to scare you. At first. My latest manuscript is more of a romantic thriller. I wanted to see your reactions when things were creepy, so I had Mrs. Serrano play along. She seemed rather fond of it, honestly. I asked her not to speak. She threw in acting like she was terrified of you all on her own. She's quite the actress." Humor danced in his eyes.

I glared at him. This wasn't funny. God, of course Mrs. Serrano was part of it. Her not being able to speak was a long, sad story? *Yeah right.*

"And yes, I made it seem like Athena Quinn was warning you. Trying to get you to escape."

I'd seen only truth in it. But of course it was fiction. He'd written it to scare me. "What other things did you do to purposely frighten me?"

He nodded. "I had this old skeleton from Halloween that I used. I put a wig on it and set the office chair up with a remote control. I told you not to go into any of the rooms that first night, hoping that you actually would. When you opened the door to her office, I hit a button that made the chair turn, just enough so you'd think Athena Quinn really existed."

I'd forgotten about that. I had seen her. Or . . . he'd made me believe I had. "I remember. You slammed the door closed before it turned all the way. You were already watching me that first day?"

"My research started as soon as you drove up to the estate."

I shook my head. "So you did cut the power that first night?"

"Yes."

He'd orchestrated every second of our time together. But I knew it had become more than that. I knew he was telling the truth. I knew he was sorry. "And the tomato sauce and stuff? Did you want me to think you were a vampire?"

He shook his head. "No. I definitely didn't plan for you to come to that conclusion. But you did make it easier for me to scare you once I read that in your novel."

"A lot of the creepy things you did happened way before I wrote about any of my suspicions."

He shrugged.

That was not an answer. "The books in your library. And the room full of those beautiful sculptures."

He smiled when I said they were beautiful. As if I were complimenting him.

"Are you Finn Bauer? And Luca Armani? And do you sculpt and paint? Because that picture of Finn Bauer in your basement looks just like you."

He tilted his head to the side as he stared down at me. "I have a strong bloodline. But are you really suggesting that my writing is so similar to theirs?"

"You just said you were writing a romantic *thriller*. Finn Bauer was a famous thriller author. And everything you say is pretty poetic, like Luca Armani. And I know you're an artist."

"If I were all those men . . . that would make me . . . close to four hundred years old, Hazel."

That wasn't an answer either. "Did you put a tracking app on my phone? Or were you able to track me down based on the scent of my blood?"

He laughed and put his hand on the side of my neck. "I promise I don't bite. Unless you want me to." His thumb traced down to my clavicle. "I'll never hurt you again. You have my word."

That was all I really cared about. "You swear?"

"I swear it. And because I do plot everything out . . . do you want to know what happens next?"

I smiled up at him. "You whisk me away, back to your creepy estate, and make love to me?"

"Well, yes. But I actually meant what happens next in my novel . . . or, I should say, *our* novel."

What?

He reached behind him on the counter and handed me a huge stack of papers.

"I should have told you yesterday in the ballroom," he said. "You are my muse, Hazel. You and your writing. I want to combine our words. Release this book together. I figured I could write the male perspective and you could write the female perspective. Our novels already mesh together almost seamlessly. It just needs an ending." He tapped the top of the manuscript.

I looked down at it. *Athena Quinn* with *Hazel Fox. Oh my God.* "You're serious?" This was everything I wanted. "Don't you need to get your publisher on board?"

He shrugged. "I own the publishing house."

Of course he did. "But you want me to write with you? Really?"

"I want to do everything with you."

Kehlani squealed.

I looked over my shoulder and laughed. She'd practically fallen out of her bedroom door.

"I'm so happy for you guys!" she yelled and attacked us with a big bear hug. "Champagne! We need champagne!" She let go of us and ran into the kitchen.

"So how do you think the novel should end?" I asked and smiled up at him.

He reached out and traced the skin above where my towel was knotted.

I shivered at his cold touch. I believed he'd told me all the truths he could. But I couldn't shake the feeling that he was still hiding something. After all . . . he'd written the words himself: something "dark and twisted" lurked inside his estate. And as soon as I'd entered, I was swallowed whole by it. Swallowed whole by him.

He leaned forward, and I thought he was about to kiss me. Instead, his lips fell to my ear.

"I think it should end with me doing sinful things to you, don't you think?" He lightly bit down on my earlobe.

I stifled a moan. He had always been right. I was too far gone. My fate was sealed with his.

He pulled me closer and kissed me like it was the first time. A new beginning.

"You swear I'm not the fool in our story?" I whispered against his lips.

"Fools don't conquer their fears," he said.

It was almost like he was saying that I should fear him. That there was some truth to his fiction. But he wasn't a monster. He had never hurt anything but my heart. And he had apologized for that. He had sworn he'd never do it again.

"But I pushed away my fears for one intoxicating touch," I said, quoting his manuscript.

"No, you dared to love me."

I stared up at him. "You're not a monster, Mr. Remington."

He smiled at me calling him Mr. Remington. "Well, I did warn you that it's the things that are bad for us that feel the best, Miss Fox."

A NOTE FROM IVY

Is Mr. Remington stuck in your head? I don't know how to get him out of mine, but I'm not mad about that. I'll allow him to stay.

I hope your heart raced in more ways than one. And I hope you fell in love with Mr. Remington as much as I did.

Is Mr. Remington still hiding something? Maybe one day we'll get another glimpse!

Thank you to Alison Dasho and the whole Montlake team for taking a chance on this story. Atlas and Hazel completely took over my mind. And it means the world to me that their story was in great hands. It's been such a pleasure working with you all!

And thank you to all the Smoaksters who have been so excited to meet Mr. Remington. The Smoaksters Facebook group is one big family, and I'm so grateful that you're on this journey with me.

Ivy Smoak
Wilmington, DE
www.IvySmoak.com

Thank you for reading *Bad Things Feel Best*! Want to know what Mr. Remington was thinking when Hazel showed up at his estate? Well, now you can! Go to https://www.ivysmoak.com/btfb-amz to get your **free** copy of Mr. Remington's point of view in "Mr. Remington."

An excerpt from

"Mr. Remington"

I have writer's block. And every page I do manage to write ends up crumpled up in the trash. I need inspiration.

But it's a little hard to write a romance when it feels like a lifetime since I've kissed someone. Let alone been in love.

I need to see it firsthand. To experience it again. To remember what it feels like for a woman to moan my name . . .

Scratch that.

A distraction is the last thing I need when I'm already distracted. I just need to observe someone else falling in love.

What could possibly go wrong with that plan?

Go to https://www.ivysmoak.com/btfb-amz to get your free copy!

For more steamy forbidden romance, check out *Temptation*, book 1 of my most popular series. You can meet James Hunter, your new book boyfriend, on Amazon now.

An excerpt from

Temptation

Shy student Penny Taylor always follows the rules. At least, that's how it appears to her classmates. But she has one illicit secret—she's fallen hard for her professor. And she's pretty sure he's fallen for her too.

Everyone loves Professor Hunter. He's tall, dark, and handsome. And completely unobtainable. But it's the secrets hiding behind his deep brown eyes that lure Penny. Secrets darker than she could ever imagine.

James Hunter gave up his billionaire lifestyle in New York City last year to become a professor. The easiest new rule to follow: don't fraternize with the students. It's simple because he's become quite the recluse in his new town—the only way he knows how to keep his secrets buried.

But he never expected to be teaching such a beautiful student. He has to resist her. He needs to walk away. Penny deserves better than a man with his demons. But she's daring him to cross the line. And he's never been one to resist temptation.

Start reading now: https://www.amazon.com/dp/B00VVG6LMI/.

ABOUT THE AUTHOR

Ivy Smoak is the *Wall Street Journal* and *USA Today* bestselling author of the Hunted Series. Her books have sold more than three million copies worldwide. When she's not writing, you can find Ivy binge-watching too many TV shows, taking long walks, playing outside, and generally refusing to act like an adult. She lives with her husband in Delaware. For more information visit www.ivysmoak.com.

Before you go, please consider leaving an honest review.